# ANOTHER DEAD INTERN

## Magic, Murder, and Internship Survival

### Joel Spriggs

# CONTENTS

# Acknowledgments

I'd like to thank my wife Sarah and our children. They put up with my laptop keys clacking on for my restless nights and didn't complain. Kids, you'd better not read this book until you are much older. College age, maybe later.

I'd like to also thank my brother, Seth. Between Seth and Sarah, I can usually kick an idea off one of them and know when I've gone too far.

Finally, I'd like to thank other authors I've read, longer in the past and more recently discovered. Stephen King, Neil Gaiman, Terry Pratchett and Douglas Adams to name some of the older ones I've read as far back as I can remember. Chuck Wendig, V.E. Schwab, Stephen Blackmoore, and Christopher Moore to name some more recent ones. Writing a good book, a bad book, a fun book, hell any book has a long road of reading a ton of other books for inspiration and guidance on what a good story will look and feel like.

# DEATH OF AN INTERN

**A** crisp wind blew through the city off Boston Harbor. The gentle breeze made the chill evening a pleasant reprieve from the heat that followed into the early fall days. A dark figure lurched through the shadows, stumbling in a zigzag before slumping against an old tree, not far from 26 Braddock Street.

He squinted to condense his gradually doubling vision. Number 26 sat in the middle of a block of similar looking red brick walk-ups. Thirteen steps led up to the front door and stoop, where the mysterious voyeur could see the old tarnished plate next to the front door, "H. Connal, P.I."

A window sat open above the little roof over the stoop. Two figures hopped lightly through the window. The first was a tall, slender man in dark clothes, with long silver hair, he sat down with his back against the brick of the building. The other figure was a shorter spritely woman, with a pixie cut in jeans and a gray t-shirt. She leaned back through the window and pulled a bottle and pair of tumbler glasses through it with her before sitting down on the roof.

"So this is customary, Hemlock? To sit and drink in the night when a job is done?"

Hemlock poured the tall man a glass of whiskey. "Yeah," she purred in a raspy tone, "case closed, report off to the client, only thing left is the accounting. So, come out on the stoop roof, have a nice drink, and enjoy the night air."

"Could we not enjoy this inside or on the actual steps below us?"

She poured herself a glass, "we could. And you could cut your hair, stop wearing black on black suits, and not wear so much goddamn gold, you look like a walking dragon's horde. So why do you still dress like that?"

Dave stared into his glass and took a sip. "Tradition," he said meekly.

"Tradition," she growled and clinked her glass to his. "Exactly right, you pointy-eared son of a bitch."

While she drank from her glass, Dave nodded back at her, "one day, you will have your pointy-ears again too, Hemlock."

"Not for a few more years, Dave, not for a few more years." She took another sip and poured them both another glass. "Enjoy your first riveting case with me?"

"To be honest," he pushed a lock of his long white hair back from his face. "It was very boring. We sat there for hours to only take pictures of two people making love?"

"Yep."

"Why?"

Hemlock sighed, sloshing the whiskey gently in the glass. "You spent your whole life among the Sidhe, right Dave?"

"Yes, my Queen wanted me to do all my training with the courts, but never here."

She nodded. "Human relationships are tricky, Dave."

"Davinpor."

"Dave's easier, and sounds less like a sofa."

Dave shook his head and took another drink.

Hemlock continued, "Thing is, when humans bond in a relationship, they want exclusivity in certain things. They consider sex to be one of those activities that a man or woman can expect their partner to be monogamous."

The figure hit the tree he was standing against. A man's inebriated voice rang through the darkness, slightly nasal and partially broken by his own slurred pitch, "you're damned right.

At least some of us expect monoganogamy," the figure paused to belch. "But hell, it's not like we can guarantee it."

Hemlock craned her thin neck to peer over the small roof line, "who's out there?"

The man stepped into the clearing, "just lil ol' me, you remember me? Or should I take my pants off again?"

"Oh, Mr. Gr..."

"Don't." He stumbled forward yanking a hand free from his black duster, brandishing a large revolver. "Don't go around using my name. I know what power names has uh have when used properly. You may not have all mine," he waived the gun between himself and Hemlock, "but I don't want you using any part of my name. You try any of your little fairy magic, and you can feel the business end of a .44 magnum slug."

Hemlock nodded, "OK, how about I just use Mr. G then? Can we agree on that?"

Mr. G shrugged and leaned back on his tree again.

"Mr. G, I don't think we've been formally introduced. I'm Hemlock Connal, and this is my associate, Davinpor."

"I know who you are," he waived the gun sideways, pointing it back and forth between the pair on the roof. "You and your couch boy are the assholes who ruined my marriage, you dirty sons of bitches."

"But Mr. G," Dave leaned forward, holding up a finger, "your current situation is entirely your own fault. Did you not pledge yourself to this monogamy and marriage?"

"So?" He pointed the revolver unsteadily at the tall fairy figure on the roof. "What's your point, Davenport?"

Davinpor winced. Hemlock yelled over, "call him Dave. He hates being called a couch."

"Nah, I'll call him Sofa." He pulled the hammer back on the revolver, the chamber clicking around to the next bullet. "Sofa what's your pointy ass getting at?"

"You entered into this binding with your wife, but broke your pledges. The fact that Hemlock and I were the instruments of your exposure, makes us no more guilty than your cell phone if you forgot to delete messages from your mistress or lipstick on your collar. You wouldn't shoot your cellphone or your shirt though, would you."

Mr. G lowered the pistol. "Nah, Sofa, I probably wouldn't have. I don't use cell phones, because my magic from being a mother fucking wizard kills them," he started yelling. "And I wouldn't have been caught, but you assholes found a way to photograph through my warding." He looked squarely and wide-eyed at Davinpor, "So yeah," he said calmly, "I would shoot you."

He raised the revolver quickly and squeezed the trigger, firing blindly at the roof. The bullet ricocheted off the brickwork between the pair on the roof with a sharp ping.

"Mr. G," Hemlock called down gruffly, "please stop shooting my house. We know you're a quote unquote mother fucking wizard and you must know we're both from the Sidhe, so the bullets won't cause us any real harm."

"Maybe," Mr. G yelled, squeezing off three more random shots and hitting the roof line, "but hells bells, I'll feel better."

He wavered back and forth, then fell back on the grassy verge. Legs spread out in front of himself, he began to sob.

"Why? Why'd you have to take this job?"

"Because, Mr. G.," Hemlock called through her strangled chords, "they are the kind of cases I land that pay."

She nudged Davinpor and handed him the bottle. "Do me a favor and levitate the whiskey down to him."

Davinpor raised a hand, and fingers danced daintily as he made the bottle of whiskey float on down to land neatly next to their assailant.

"What's this for?"

"Well, Mr. G., you may have already had enough, but it seems like you might need it more than us."

"I don't need your pity or your charity," he yelled up but was pulling the top off anyway.

He took a long drink from the bottle, "why not other cases? Help cops with murders or drugs and all? I do that, why can't you?"

"We do, Mr. G. But those cases are few and far between. Most of the covens keep out of the local organized crime, and they generally don't get all murdery in Boston. So, Boston PD doesn't really need us as often. What pays the bills are the cases any private investigators can take on and the cops won't. Those are always insurance fraud, money laundering, and cheating spouses. We specialize in white collar crime for the magical community. You're a wizard, so we got hired to find out if you were having an affair. If you weren't, we either wouldn't have been hired or would've told our client that there was no affair."

He took another drink. "And you ruined my marriage in the process, you dicks!" He yelled.

Davinpor stood at the edge, black eyes glaring down at the drunk. "No, Mr. G, you ruined your marriage. You can't hold us responsible for your reckless behavior, which hasn't gotten any better. Especially considering you are shooting at us in a severely inebriated state."

Mr. G drained the last bit of whiskey from the bottle. "Inebriate this, Loveseat, you son of a bitch."

He threw the bottle hard as he said it. Davinpor was incensed over having been demoted to Loveseat, he was trying to say, "what," when the empty bottle struck him straight on the forehead. Davinpor staggered a few steps on the little roof before falling off into the bushes.

"Now Mr. G," Hemlock kicked her dangling legs over the roof, "there's no need for violence. Hell, you keep it up, you might kill Dave."

Mr. G got to his feet wobbly. He muttered aloud mockingly at

Hemlock, "meh meh meh meh meh, fuck you Hemlock. You've got no professional courtesy burning another detective like that."

The bushes rustled, and a gasping, bubbling noise broke above Mr. G's cursing and rambling.

"Hey Hemlock, I think something's wrong with your buddy." He tried to stagger to the bushes.

"Nah, I'm sure Dave's fine." Hemlock leaned over the edge of the roof, "C'mon Dave, walk it off, it's just a tumble from a roof."

She peered over. Davinpor lay across the edge of the shrubs, seeming to hover in them. His black eyes wide with fear and his long silver hair glittered in the streetlights. His mouth was wet with black and red fluid.

"Oh yeah," Hemlock looked up at the sky and sighed loudly. "The little wrought iron fence is hidden by the bushes."

Davinpor tried to sit up once more, to pull himself free from the fence, but succumbed to his injuries. The last words he sputtered in his dying breath were, "fucking wizards."

"Are you happy now, Mr. G," Hemlock pointed to Davinpor. "Now you can add murder to your list of shit you've pulled."

"Nah," his gun arm hung limply at his side, and he pointed a shaking finger from his left hand at Davinpor's corpse. "He's faking!" He approached the body and screamed, "you're faking! This is another frame job."

Hemlock dropped from the roof, landing on the middle step of the walk-up stoop. She leaned over and checked the body.

"Nope, I'm afraid he's stone dead."

"More lies!" Mr. G yelled.

Hemlock tilted Davinpor's head, so the dead eyes glared back at the panicking drunk. She began moving his chin with his head and tried to mimic Davinpor's serious tone in her raspy voice. "Do I look like I'm joking Mr. G? I assure you, I'm quite dead now."

He pointed the .44 at her, trying to steady his hand. "What

kind of sicko are you? Wasn't he one of yours?"

Hemlock shrugged. "Kind of, he was assigned to me by the courts."

"What?"

"Yeah, I'm still on my banishment term." She tilted her head to show her ears. "See no points, and a cursed voice like I'd been drinking bourbon on fire with wasp stingers. I've got a few more years before the thirteen are finally served out, so the Shadow Court assigns me a consort to help keep me out of trouble."

"What," he pointed the gun at Davinpor, "he was like your parole officer?"

Hemlock nodded, "yep, third one they had assigned me since Dad died. Something about fairy royalty, they can't stay alive around me so easily. That's why I keep calling them my dumb ass interns."

Mr. G suddenly puked. "He was a royal?"

Hemlock rolled her eyes and sat on the short wall in front of the shrubs with the body. "No shit, Sherlock. They seemed to think a Sidhe Lady should be assigned a consort from somewhere in one of the royal families. At least this one wasn't a prince, but he was still something high up to Mab."

"You're the Lady of the Shadow Court? So your mom is..."

"Yep," Hemlock nodded, "Queen Fand."

"I killed a Winter Royal? Oh, crap." He pointed the gun back at Hemlock's heart, pulling the hammer back on the revolver.

"What are you doing Mr. G?" Hemlock leaned back lazily on the wall.

"You got banished, that means you don't have most of your magic. I can actually kill you with this."

She cocked her head to the side and studied him. "Interesting, you shoot me, and it looks like some random hit. You walk away."

He nodded, "yeah, you got it."

7

"A fun theory." Hemlock took a deep breath. "But, how many bullets are there, Mr. G? Your revolver holds five, I'm pretty sure I counted five shots fired. I think you're out."

"I counted four."

"Wonder which of us is luckier tonight, Mr. G."

"I'm bound for a change, and I'm game to try the odds."

Hemlock lifted an arm and held a hand, pointing the finger at him like a gun. "Counterpoint, I do still have some, not much, but some fae magic in me." She cocked her thumb back like the hammer of the gun. "I use just a little trickle of it and have a reflective enchantment on myself. You shoot me, and you'll only be killing yourself."

He smiled wryly. "You're bluffing."

"Either way, I guess this ends for one of us tonight." She squinted her eyes, "So tell me punk, do you feel lucky?"

Mr. G groaned at the bad impersonation. He squeezed the trigger, Hemlock said, "bang," and Mr. G sank to his knees. A hole bore through his chest, a bloom of scarlet spreading across his shirt and spilling to the pavement. After a moment, he fell over completely. He looked to Hemlock and said coldly, "call my coven."

"I'm sure Mr. G, they are nowhere near Boston tonight," Hemlock growled softly, her voice reaching him like smoke on the cold night air. His jaw went slack as he nodded.

Hemlock sighed, shaking her head and looking back and forth between the two bodies, "dumb asses. Now I've got to deal with cleaning up two bodies. I'd better not get a letter from the HOA about this one."

# THE INTERVIEW

It was a quarter past one when Morgan Burns walked the tree-lined street of Braddock Park in Boston. His phone chirped as he walked down the row of identical red brick Victorian town homes. The little voice spoke in his ear, "You have arrived." He took the headset off his ear and stowed it in his laptop bag.

He climbed the thirteen steps to the front door. Other homes on the block mostly had dark, varnished doors. The one in front of him was painted a dark teal shade instead. The old plaque next to the door was black with copper lettering that had turned green from time read, "H. Connal, P.I."

"I guess this is the place", Morgan said to himself.

Morgan knocked on the door and waited. Nothing happened. He glanced around for a doorbell and found no buttons or buzzers. Up above Morgan's right shoulder, He saw a rope. Morgan pulled the cord and instantly heard a loud whooping bark and roar. The cacophony shocked him so much he stumbled on the stoop and almost fell back down the steps.

A window opened from the house to his left. An old woman in a peach blouse with her grayed hair tied back in a tight bun leaned out through the window. She gave Morgan a pleasant smile, and he smiled back giving a nervous little wave.

As the door in front of Morgan opened, the old lady to his left shouted, "Connal, get rid of that damned monkey! That thing is a menace! Why can't you get a normal knocker like everyone else on the block?"

A short woman with a blonde pixie cut poked her head out

the door and stared daggers past Morgan at the old lady. When she spoke, the voice was a gravel-seasoned growl that took him by surprise.

"Myrtle, you old bat! You're the last one that needs to give advice about knockers," she yelled in a raspy roar and gave the old woman a wink.

Myrtle gasped and closed the cardigan around her blue floral dress. "Well, I never!"

"That's not what dad told me, he said 'you hadn't lived in this neighborhood until you experienced ol' Myrtle's knockers!'"

The old woman huffed loudly and slammed her window.

Morgan hazarded asking, "Are you H. Connal, Private Investigator?"

She opened the door, and Morgan saw she wore an azure blue button up shirt with the top couple of buttons undone and untucked from a pair of worn-in jeans.

"You are partially right," she said gruffly. Pointing to the plaque by the door, "it's actually Hemlock Connal, Preternatural Investigator." A slight smile curled her lips.

"I'm sorry, but do you have a cold or some sort of throat infection?'

Hemlock's smile dropped, "Why is everyone always asking that?"

"Well, your voice sounds kind of ... bad."

"Oh, you mean like I've been drinking a bottle of bourbon in a smokehouse for a few weeks."

He nodded and shrank back down the top step. "I'm sorry, I didn't mean to offend you."

She leaned against the door with her arm stretched over her head. She took a deep breath, "Are you a process server? If you are, you can tell the folks in 32 Braddock I had every right to cook those damn pigeons, they weren't marked as pets."

"What? No, I'm not a process server."

"Jehovah's Witness? Mormon?" She croaked out rapidly pointing and looking at him, "I thought you guys dressed better and rode bikes?"

"No, I'm not a Jehovah's Witness or a Mormon."

"I'm not in the mood to donate to anything today."

"I'm not asking for a donation to anything today," Morgan replied trying to hurry out a response.

"OK, fine, you aren't here for anything, I've run out of ideas, why are you on my stoop, looking for me but don't know who I am or what I do." She leaned forward and stared Morgan square in the eyes, almost touching his nose to hers. "Who the hell are you?"

Burns fumbled with the messenger bag over his shoulder. Shoving aside the small laptop and notebooks, he grabbed a piece of paper, unfolding it and handed it to Hemlock.

She read the paper Morgan handed her aloud, "Wanted: Intern. Must be morally flexible, able to handle complex problem-solving. Room, board, and stipend provided. Inquire at H. Connal, P.I., 26 Braddock."

Hemlock folded the paper in half, then tore it in two and dropped it at Morgan's feet. "Kid, I don't know who put you up to this, but I'm not looking for an intern, and I didn't post the ad."

At that exact moment, a seagull flew down past his right ear and landed on Hemlock's head. She rolled her eyes up as though to stare at the bird perched on her head surreptitiously. She scrunched up her face and huffed. "I see," she croaked with displeasure. "I suppose I am probably looking for some help in exchange for room and board, but I think the stipend may be out of the question."

The gull squawked and pooped on her shoulder in a long spray that splattered across to the front door. She turned her head to look at her shoulder. "A modest stipend may be agreeable if you don't mind seagull being on the menu for dinner now and then." She gave an eerie smile and the bird flew off. "Why don't you come inside, and we'll discuss the matter further while I get cleaned up."

She left the door open. Morgan followed her into the building. She stepped lightly over the hardwood floors, the heels of his boots clanked loudly behind her. He followed her through a dark entryway into a small sitting room. The room would have been beautiful with all the wood accents, cast iron firebox, and intricate inlays on the fireplace mantle. That beauty was marred by the random notes and drawings of strange beasts on one wall.

"Don't mind the wall," Hemlock said pointing, "Just some notes and scribbling of brainstorming from my last case. You caught me between cases, good timing. Why don't you have a seat, and you can tell me why you would want to be my quote-unquote intern."

Morgan sat down on an old sofa with faded floral print upholstery across from the fireplace. Hemlock had walked over to a tall black cabinet in the corner with a locked black door. She unlocked the door and left it open. She sat down in a large, gray wing backed chair between the sofa and the fireplace.

"Well, uh, where should we begin?"

"How about a name? What do I call you? Mr. Plaidshirt?"

"Morgan, Morgan Burns," he replied.

"OK, Morgan, what's your background, why do you want to assist an investigator?"

"Funny story, I didn't. I graduated a few months ago with a degree in Journalism. I had a job to start soon in Indiana to write staff pieces for a small business journal."

"Why'd you leave a job before it even started?" As she croaked out the question, Morgan saw something hop from the cabinet. A small figure, roughly nine inches in height, skipped across the sofa and onto Hemlock's chair. The grubby looking little man had a paunchy belly and a mop of light blonde hair shooting out from under a spool of thread it wore like a hat. It had a pair of green pants and a shirt with two buttons.

"I, uh, wasn't, uh, too excited about the position." The little being took out a cloth from the green pants and started cleaning the bird poop from Hemlock's shirt. "I'm sorry, but, um, would it be rude to ask?" Morgan pointed in confusion at the little man that seemed to be erasing the stain from her shoulder.

"Oh him, we'll get to that part later. He'll be done in a bit. Don't let him distract you. Please, you were telling me about a boring job. Why did you take it?"

Morgan shook off staring at the small man and tried looking back to Hemlock. "Well, I went to a small college, and they try to help everyone secure jobs right out of school. They like to brag about some high percent of placement immediately after graduation. An alumnus is an editor on the paper, they hired me on to do profile pieces. Stuff about new companies in central Indiana or ones expanding. My dad told me a job was a job and I needed to take what I could get in this economy."

"Ah, so you took the job?" She tilted her head away from the little creature, it wiped away a small splattering that had plopped on her neck.

He tried not to be disgusted at the fact that the tiny person was licking some neck spatter. "Yeah, I took the job."

Hemlock sat forward, she snapped her fingers and pointed back to the cabinet. The being hopped back over to the cabinet, the door shut and locked behind it. "So what made you leave a secure first job and the Crossroads of America behind to come to Beantown?"

"My dad died." Morgan looked back over at the locked cabinet in the corner, the door was still shut.

"My condolences," rasped Hemlock. "How does that explain how you ended up here?"

Morgan crossed his leg and drummed his fingers on his knee-cap. "I wanted to go into journalism to take on something exciting and dangerous. My father was an accountant. The most dangerous thing he would consider doing was filing an exemption without knowing the exact cent that should be written down."

Hemlock waved a finger at Morgan. "Now, don't go discounting accounting as devoid of danger. It was accountants and bean counters that put away Al Capone."

Hemlock continued, "And I'm guessing you decided you didn't want to spend a boring life like your father and die alone in a warehouse, clutching at a clipboard."

Morgan nodded.

"Why apply for this," she made air quotes dramatically, "internship that is oddly available in September?"

"It took me a few months to get my dad's estate settled. Mom died when I was younger. Nothing was holding me back in Indiana, so I came out here. One thing led to another, I found the advertisement for this internship and thought it sounded, well, exciting."

"Uh huh, one thing led to another?" She gave Morgan an accusing glare. "Why apply for this position? Why don't you apply for any number of reporting jobs out in Boston or anywhere?"

Morgan crossed his legs and felt on his guard. "I'm not sure how familiar you are with the market in journalism, Ms. Connal."

She waved her right hand to cut him off. "No, no, don't call me Ms. Connal, just call me Hemlock. You got that Burns? I hope you don't mind me calling you Burns, it fits you more than a Morgan."

Burns raised his eyebrows, "No, it's fine. Anyway, just leaving college, any entry-level job I'd get would be calling in confirmations, working classifieds or writing up simple puff pieces and obituaries. Not exciting, investigative kind of reporting. And the pay is complete crap. I'd be lucky to afford a room anywhere, not even an apartment. So, when I saw the ad, I figured that at least I wouldn't worry about where to live. I could add a year of investigative training under my belt for the next time I go job hunting."

"That is curiously well-thought-out." She got up and walked

around Morgan, looking him over. "Well, I think you would do, you pass the initial verbal interview, there's the practical interview as well. That comes in a few parts, one we'll do now, the rest will be while we work a case together."

"That sounds great, what are the terms then around payment, room, and board?"

Hemlock walked back to the black cabinet and unlocked it again. She turned to face Morgan, "Terms, yes. You will have a room, upstairs next to the office and other study. Please don't mind the noise, I tend to work late and odd hours, you may be needed for those hours as well. You have free-range of the kitchen, it is kept stocked. The wine cellar has been stocked well for quite a long time as I don't like wine much and neither did my father before me. My room is the suite on the third floor. If you find it missing something, leave a note and it will be retrieved. The stipend, I think we can discuss. I would be open to a flat rate of two thousand five hundred a month, or we could agree on ten percent of the fees I collect on cases we work together. Which would you prefer?"

She turned back to the cabinet, Morgan tried to run some quick math in his head. "What's the average rate you charge clients?"

"Depends on the client, but the average is about one fifty an hour plus expenses with a two thousand dollar deposit."

He tried to figure out how much that was in his head, but ended up blurting out, "I'll go for the ten percent then."

"Alright, time for the other part of the practical interview, c'mon over here." She waved him over and opened the black cabinet.

Morgan approached and something crawled up on Hemlock's shoulder. He expected another little person like the one that had cleaned her shirt earlier. It was, but this creature was also very different. Instead of a tiny person, a small stuffed monkey on a leash had settled on Hemlock's shoulders and studied him.

"Is that Curious George?" Burns came closer to examine a very ornate collar that had been placed on the stuffed animal's neck. He barely noticed some ink-stained characters on its belly when it bared a set of white fangs stained brown at the roots. He backed off quickly, almost tripping over a small trunk.

"Yeah, it *was* a Curious George doll." Hemlock reached up and scratched its neck absentmindedly. "It *was* my Curious George doll before dad needed something in a pinch to bind a yokai that had followed some poor monk over from Japan. Now he's my little buddy, you can call him Yo, but don't get close to him. He's bound to my family line and would likely do something terrible to you if he could."

She pulled a pocket knife and a tattered napkin out of the cabinet and handed them to me. "This is going to sound a bit weird Burns."

"You have had your shirt cleaned by one of the Borrowers and now you've got a menacing Curious George looking to rip my throat out," Morgan said meekly. "I don't know that anything you say will get much weirder than that."

She turned her head to look at Yo, "See? I'm starting to like him already." She looked back at Burns and rasped, "What you're going to do is just give yourself a small nick on your finger, or wherever you don't mind bleeding a bit. Dab some of that blood on the end of the napkin and hand it over to Yo."

Morgan nodded. He pondered over the knife and fabric held in his hands and wondered about this being the weirdest job interview he'd ever had. Burns cupped his left hand to his mouth and breathed on it for a few heavy breaths to warm up the skin. He jabbed the knife tip in the side of his middle fingertip, soaked up a bit of blood on the fabric, and handed it to Yo.

"This has been the strangest drug test I've ever been given, but at least you didn't watch me pee in a cup."

Hemlock watched as the stuffed monkey grabbed the tattered fabric. He turned it around in his hands and sniffed at it for a moment. Yo settled on the area with the blood and bit the corner of the napkin clean away from the rest of the fabric. He chewed on it thoughtfully and swallowed with a loud gulp. Yo leveled a malevolent stare at Morgan and gave pronouncement of the blood in a deep voice that spoke in perfect and articulate Japanese.

Hemlock nodded her head. "Ah, I see. Thank you Yo, I'll let you know if I need you again later." She opened the cabinet again and led the doll back inside.

A bit shocked Burns asked, "You speak Japanese?"

"That's one way to put it," Hemlock croaked and gave Morgan a level stare. "Do you?"

"No, I took some French in college, but Japanese sounded too difficult with everything else I had going on. What did Yo have to say?"

"Why did you stab the side of your finger?"

"When she was still alive, my mom was a diabetic. Heating up the hands lessens the pain, and stabbing the side is less painful with better blood flow." Morgan looked at the still-bleeding finger and sucked the wet blood off it.

She nodded again. "Yo said your blood was sweet, clean, and that the last lie you told was over a month ago."

"He got all that from a few drops of blood?"

"Yep, so you passed this round."

"Great." Morgan felt a little anxious. "Can you tell me about why you have a curio cabinet with a little elf and a yokai, or is that in the employee handbook?"

"Jenkins is a brownie, not an elf. I'll explain a lot of it as we go along on the first case. I believe in," Hemlock turned back to the cabinet and paused considering her words. "I believe in learning on the job, getting some hands-on experience." She pulled a light green plaid jacket and a tweed driver's cap out of the cabinet instead of any creature this time. "I assume you're of legal age for a drinking establishment?"

"Yes," Morgan squinted at the cabinet trying to see inside but couldn't make anything out. "Where are we going?"

Hemlock led him down the hall towards the door, "I've got an intern, we might as well go find a case to work so you can learn. For that, we go get a drink at the Fifth Horseman."

They stepped out to the stoop of Hemlock's building, she closed the door behind Burns and pulled the rope. The howler monkey bellowed and she flashed a wicked grin. When Myrtle appeared at her window again, Hemlock blew a short raspberry at the old woman and skipped lithely down the steps. She beckoned Burns to follow with a slender finger.

# THE CASE

**M**organ followed Hemlock, they turned on Columbus Avenue and walked down a few blocks. She led him past a Chinese restaurant on the corner of Claremont. Along the side of the building was a black wrought iron fence. A battered wood sign hung above a gate that groaned as Hemlock opened it. The sign had a painting of a winged blue horse and old script that read "The Fifth Horseman, est. 1591".

Morgan paused at the top steps while Hemlock started to descend the old stone. "Hey, how is that possible? I thought Boston was founded in the seventeen hundreds?" Hemlock turned to see him pointing up at the sign.

"Oh, Boston was originally founded in 1630."

"So this place predates the actual town by forty years?"

"We could sit down and go through the whole history of this place, but it wouldn't really matter. Try not to overthink it. You're here, it's here. If you sit around trying to make sense of it all the time, Burns, you'll frustrate yourself and not get anywhere."

Morgan shrugged, "fair enough," and followed her down the steps. At the bottom, the wall was solid stone with a small iron goblet on the ground. "OK, what's the use of the sign if there's no way to get in?"

"Yamata did that when he took over the place back in the fifties. He liked the sign, so he kept that, but the entrance requires a cover charge." Hemlock pulled out the same pocket knife from before. She jabbed a finger lightly and squeezed a few drops of blood into the goblet.

She offered Morgan the knife again, but he politely waved her off. He bit the small scab that recently had formed from the side of his fingertip and put a few drops of his own blood into the goblet. "I hope blood isn't required for every transaction with you."

Hemlock let a hoarse chuckle out and smiled at him maliciously. The goblet drained empty, and the stone wall in front of him reconfigured to show an old heavy wooden door set with many wrought iron door nails. Hemlock opened it and motioned Morgan ahead of her. He walked in and felt like he had stepped back a few centuries. The walls were the same large stone they had seen on the exterior, grays and browns mortared together like a medieval castle.

No light from the outside flooded in as they stepped over the threshold. Instead, it seemed to come from heavy wrought iron wall sconces, though Morgan couldn't see any sort of flame or light bulb being used to create the light. The same was true for seven hanging black iron chandeliers, held from the vaulted ceilings by heavy chains. The light sources Morgan could make out came from tall taper candles on the tables scattered throughout the general area.

Burns followed as Hemlock headed to the bar. Her steps fell silently on the thick, knotted hardwood floors, as his boots clunked loudly with each footfall. When they reached the bar, she turned to Morgan and spoke in a soft growl. "I think your first assignment for this internship will be to either learn how to walk in those boots without clunking around or go buy lighter shoes."

"I like the boots, they give me a good solid feel to the world. My dad used to wear boots like these, and relished the fear it would bring people to know when he was coming."

Hemlock hopped up on a bar stool. "Yeah, I can understand needing to strike fear and have a solid feeling. Be that as it may, you are going to be in some situations as my intern where being silent will keep us from getting shot or worse."

Morgan sat down next to her, "There are worse things that can happen to us than getting shot? That seems high up on the bad list for me."

"There are a few things you should probably find out ahead of our first case. The big one is that I don't know what our case will have us chasing and there will be things that I haven't seen before. So you should get a handle on the fact that the only thing we know we will be dealing with on a regular basis is the unknown. Make sense?"

"No," he said flatly. Morgan glanced around. "Why are we the only ones here?"

"Well, it is only three thirty on a Tuesday afternoon. Yamata opened not too long ago, so we're the first patrons of the day. What kind of skeezy joints do you frequent anyway? Should I be concerned about you? Do you have a drinking problem?"

Burns looked around the bar. They had taken seats at a long bar on one side of the extended basement area, the serving area was beautiful smooth mahogany. The stocked shelving behind the bar looked like an old wooden Japanese shrine with a few sinks and some draught taps. There were thirteen tables in the room, some in the middle and some along the walls, with no people sitting at them. Along the wall farthest from Morgan and Hemlock was a stone shelf lined with what appeared to be tiny houses.

"It's not the lack of customers, Hemlock." Morgan turned back to her and nodded to the bar, "We don't even have a bartender."

Hemlock nodded. "Yamata will come out when we actually need something. I'm sure he's taking care of something here, but when you need a drink, Yamata will be here."

"But, couldn't somebody rob the place then?"

She chuckled gruffly. "You don't rob Yamata. You paid a blood price to get in here!" She closed her eyes briefly, and it appeared like her brain reset. "OK, here's a good lesson in dealing with the preternatural world. If you paid a blood price as part of an agreement, you are both bound by that agreement. The blood price paid to enter The Fifth Horseman guarantees the Rules of Congress. They are posted over there," Hemlock pointed to a framed scroll hung above the stone shelf. "If either party violates those rules, the consequences are quite dire. They can include death for the violator and curses on their family lines."

Morgan stared across at the rules, and when he turned back, a man was standing in front of him behind the bar. The man had a short trimmed beard, wore a white chef jacket, and had long black hair tied into a ponytail. Also, there was a pint glass of beer. Morgan glanced back and forth between the beer and the bartender. Picking up the glass, Burns nodded, "Yamata?"

"Hai," he said and bowed to Morgan.

Burns turned back to Hemlock, "I'm going to need this, aren't I?"

She had a short glass of what was either bourbon or scotch in front of her. "I don't normally condone drinking on the job," she rasped, Yamata narrowed his dark eyes at her. "But, from time to time, you will need some... brain lubricant."

Burns blinked at her and nodded. "Brain lubricant," he muttered and took a long drink of beer. "Crisp, but not hoppy, that's good."

"Yamata usually knows what you want before you can ask for it."

"So, now that I'm lubricating my brain, can you tell me what exactly a Preternatural Investigator investigates?"

Yamata laughed heartily at Burns and nodded at Hemlock, "You have a shoshinsha?"

Hemlock rolled her eyes and leaned over her drink. "Cut him some slack about it Yamata, the kid's so green the ivy's got envy."

Yamata chuckled some more and nodded.

"A normal private investigator doesn't get glamorous exciting gigs," Hemlock swirled her drink in her hand and sipped. "Did you know that? The bulk of the job is domestic cases dealing with cheating partners, kidnapped pets, and people scamming workman's comp."

Burns took another drink of his beer. "No murder investigations? Chasing serial killers through alleys? Bringing down drug dealers and kingpins from outside the law?"

Hemlock scoffed. She rasped, "If you think a private investigator can operate outside the law, then you've never been on the receiving end of a civil lawsuit. If anything, a PI would have more rules to follow than cops, especially since we don't have a union protecting us. On top of that, do you think we really get called in to assist in investigations like Hollywood would have you believe? If a PI is called in, at least here, it's a cold case, and they don't expect anything to come of it. Nah, the steady money is in workman's comp cases, the easy money is in the cheating partner business."

"That doesn't explain what a Preternatural Investigator is for me."

"I'm similar to a private investigator, but I deal with a different kind of clientele. What do you think of that word? Preternatural?"

Yamata started rinsing some glasses to keep busy but kept glancing back at them.

"It's an interesting word, means beyond what is normal or natural. So is it just another way to say supernatural?"

"Kind of," she rolled her eyes and knocked on the bar. Yamata took her empty glass away. "Thing is, you can't say Supernatural or Paranormal Investigator because people think you're a bit of a nut job. Preternatural can encompass all that, and a fair amount more, without giving a bad smell to the title."

"So, your line of investigations involves what? Vampires? Werewolves? Ghosts?"

"All that and a lot more, which is why I warned you. Whatever our first case together turns out to be, I can't guarantee what it will be or what kind of being it will involve."

Burns took another sip of beer. "But you can guarantee it will be a cheating spouse or a workman's comp kind of issue? But it will be a cheating vampire spouse? An abducted were-pup? Workman's comp claim from the Ministry of Magic?"

Hemlock smiled and nodded at Morgan, "Now you're getting it, good to know you're a quick learner."

Morgan hung his head over his glass and wondered what the hell had he gotten himself into.

"Hemlock, why are we in a bar?"

"The Fifth Horseman is the best spot to meet and see the widest variety of the preternatural community of the Boston area. I get more business from sitting on this stool than advertising in any publication, including Tobin's Spirit Guide. Spouses that think they're being cheated on, generally end up here. You stay at a stool at this bar long enough, you'll meet a witch from every coven in Boston, vampires and werewolves from every clan. Hell, you'll even meet any number of the Sidhe, including ranks in their royal courts." Yamata set a fresh drink in front of Hemlock and gave her a stern glare at the mention of the Sidhe.

"So we hang out here and wait for a case, then we go do a lot of surveillance and waiting, so we can make some money."

"Basically."

"How long do we have to wait?"

Hemlock grunted. "Hard knowing, but given fate is a fickle thing, I'd lay odds you just jinxed us."

As Morgan set his glass down on the bar, the stones parted, and the door opened again. A man walked in with a head the shape and color of a duck egg turned upside down. Short dark hair haloed around his skull leaving most of the deeply tanned scalp bald. He wore a black uniform with a neon yellow vest and a badge on his sleeve with a heart rate line that read 'Paramedic City of Boston'.

He approached the bar and leaned in a space between Hemlock and Morgan. Yamata set a plain glass of soda in front of him.

Hemlock eyed the glass, "Getting ready to go on duty tonight Jorge?"

Jorge spoke in a low dulcet tone as he stared straight ahead, "Yeah, I've got an order I'm waiting on from House of Saigon upstairs, then I head on shift in about an hour."

Morgan shifted his gaze to see Hemlock and Jorge in the mirror behind the bar, Hemlock was staring ahead too.

"Seems like a strange place to wait on Chinese food if you're not going to have a drink."

"Believe it or not, I was hoping to catch you here. Alone." His eyes met Morgan's in the mirror, and his gaze was piercing.

"Don't be so goddamn dramatic Jorge, the kid's with me," she croaked.

He spun to look at her with disgust, "Isn't this one a little young, Hemlock?"

Hemlock sighed. "What the hell is that supposed to mean? I'm not any older than him. Also, it's not like that," she nodded to me, "Morgan Burns meet Jorge Andario, Jorge meet Morgan, my intern. Shake hands, sniff butts, whatever the hell it is you male egotistical types do to feel better."

Jorge sized him up and down, Morgan waved nervously and tried to grin. He turned back to Hemlock as she was taking a drink. "Can he be trusted?"

"How the hell should I know? It's his first day," she shook her wrist from her jacket and checked a watch, "Heck, it's still his first hour officially."

Yamata stepped forward giggling like a school girl, "Hemlock hired a shoshinsha."

Jorge groaned, "You know how many of the covens and guilds would have gladly provided you an intern? One that wasn't completely green and you could fully use on a day to day basis?"

"I don't want someone from one of the covens. They'd have their coven's agenda ahead of my own and reporting all kinds of other shit back about me. Even if he doesn't lift a finger, Burns will probably be a useful sounding board."

He grimaced and nodded his head, "The covens are too political these days, and at least it's easier to deal with you talking it through with a person. That enchanted rubber duck you carted around was just plain creepy."

"What? Ducksworth was the model of perfection!" She scoffed at him and took another sip of scotch. "Out with it then, the boy won't tell anyone, he's on my payroll. What's got you hunting lil' ol' me down?"

Jorge let out a deep sigh. "I've been seeing something weird the last few months on my shifts. It's been a bit sporadic for me, but I chatted with some guys that work other buses across town, and they've seen the same thing too. We get a call from someone to do a wellness check on so-and-so because they've missed a couple days of work without calling in. Typically, we find one of three things." He counted them out on his right hand, "Dead body, the person took a little staycation with their partner or they just wanted to quit and never bothered calling in."

"So what's the new reason?"

"Semi-vegetative states."

"Come again?"

"We show up, and we find the person, nine times out of ten we have to have a super let us in or a uni come with us to break down a door. The person is in their home, but they are in a semi-vegetative state though. They're just sitting there. They breathe and everything on their own, but they don't know anything, even how to speak. If you set food in front of them, they'll eat, but they won't figure it on their own, we can barely get them to walk. The most we can get out of them is a creepy little laugh."

"How creepy?"

"On a one to ten, around an eight, right around pervy clown."

Hemlock pointed down to Burns. "Kid, you got anything?"

He glanced between the two of them. "Well, uh, how many people are we talking?"

"The ones I know of, maybe about a dozen. Between the other EMTs I've talked to, about four or five a week for the last month."

"Can the police do anything about it?"

Jorge chuckled, "About what? We find them locked in their homes by themselves. No signs of forced entry, tox screens come back mostly clean."

"Mostly clean?" Morgan asked.

"Yeah," Jorge turned back to him. "But nothing too odd on that front, some folks came back with alcohol, some drugs, normal stuff though. Nothing that would cause this kind of thing to happen. As near as anyone can tell, no crime has been committed. Their memories are just, poof, gone, like everything. Besides, now they've got the beat cops running around looking for some copycat of an old serial killer."

Burns raised both eyebrows in surprise, "A copycat serial killer?"

"Yeah, gruesome shit," Jorge sighed. "They found some poor jogger out over in Franklin Park. He'd been strung up, cut, and killed the same way as a whole series of killings back in the eighties and nineties. Always targeted people out on their own, random different parks and trails. They called him the Huntsman because of how he'd catch them and tie them up."

Hemlock thought it over. She sighed, "This sounds like a strange occurrence, yeah, but I've got a problem. Who's the client? If those people don't have anything on the brain anymore, who's going to foot the bill?"

Jorge rolled his eyes. "Yeah, that's why I didn't try to hunt you down about this before now. For a while, the people were mostly ordinary folks, and no one saw any connections outside of the amnesia."

"What's changed?" Hemlock took another drink of the scotch.

"The people that have started turning up with the amnesia have been becoming higher profile. A ballerina in the Boston Ballet Company, a former conductor from the Boston Philharmonic, a forward for the Celtics. Oh, and uh, one of the lieutenants for Bobbi Cotter."

Hemlock half dribbled half spit the scotch on the bar. "Fuck you, Jorge, I'm not taking any jobs from Bobbi Cotter. The last thing I need to do is get in bed with them."

Morgan picked up a napkin and handed it over to Hemlock, "Get in bed with who? Wait, is it who or whom? Never mind, who are we talking about?"

Jorge looked at Morgan with a cocked eyebrow. "Bobbi Cotter? Boston's Butcher of the Irish Mob Bobbi Cotter? Were you born yesterday?"

Hemlock slapped him on the arm, "Lay off, he's from Indiana. The only organized crime they got there is the government."

Jorge settled back, "I gotta go pick up my food soon and head to shift, but no, not Cotter." He opened a pocket on his pants leg, pulled out a small flip pad, and tore out a page to hand to Hemlock. "Here are the names and contact info for the last half-dozen victims aside from the mobster. Take your pick or see if they want to go class action on your rates to investigate. I just want to stop feeling helpless and get back to a time when reviving overdoses was my average night."

Hemlock smiled over at Morgan, "You hear that Burns? Sounds like we got a case."

"Great," replied Morgan. "What's next?"

Hemlock held up the sheet, "We spend the evening calling around to see how many paying clients we can get."

# THE CLIENT

A deep throaty bark broke the night. Morgan's bedroom light popped on as the howler monkey continued to bellow. He slung a leg out of the side of the bed, got caught on a sheet, swung the other leg to over-correct his b a lance but landed his left foot square in a take-out container of cold lo mein. He slipped back on the noodles going tail over teakettle to roll over the bed and fall between the other side of the bed and the wall. The raucous barking laughter of Hemlock at his door began drowning out the howler monkey calls.

Morgan managed to stand up and took stock of the surrounding room. His clothes were folded on the chair nearby, and his laptop bag was on a cleared desktop.

"Burns get some clothes on, we've got company."

Morgan glanced back at his clothes folded on the chair again, felt the cold on his skin, and had the sudden realization that he was in his boxers. Morgan grabbed a pillow quickly and covered himself, staring down Hemlock like her eyes were headlights.

"What, wait, what time is it?"

Hemlock stood at the doorway, in a long button-down shirt and a pair of sweatpants. She shook a thick banded wristwatch free from her sleeve. "It's after four in the morning. You don't have to molest the pillow either Burns, it's not like I haven't seen that kind of thing before."

Morgan blinked the sleep from his eyes, still staring at her but holding the pillow firmly. The monkey continued to howl from the hallway. "We have visitors at four in the morning? Do you normally get visitors at four in the morning?"

"Only the most desperate ones." Hemlock chuckled looking down the hall. "Get dressed, and come down, you never know, maybe our desperate visitor hasn't seen that sort of thing before." Hemlock wove a hand in the air circling the direction of Morgan before she walked off down the hall.

Morgan pulled on his clothes and headed downstairs. By the time he reached the bottom of the steps, the whooping of the howler monkey had ceased. Hemlock led a pair of guests, a man and a woman, from the entry hall into the living room. Hemlock scowled as she flung herself into her large gray wing backed chair. The woman was older and heavy set, with close-cropped red hair. She wore black clothes and a heavy coat with a fur lining. She took the coat off and draped it over the back of the couch before taking a seat. Her companion was a middle-aged man, tall and lanky in black pants, a green plaid shirt, and a leather jacket. He stayed standing at the doorway and eyed Morgan as he came down the stairs.

The woman turned to see Morgan, "Connal! You finally got yourself a man in the house! Why don't you give us a proper introduction then?"

Hemlock rolled her eyes, "Bobbi, this is my new intern, Morgan Burns. Burns, this is Bobbi Cotter and her associate, Joey the Reaper."

Morgan blinked at the pair. "Oh! The butcher?"

Hemlock's head snapped upright and her eyes went wide staring at Morgan.

"Tsk Tsk, Hemlock, what have you been telling the poor boy?" Bobbi stood and approached Burns on the steps. She cupped calloused long-fingered hands around his face. "Oh you are a youngin aren't ya now? And not from these parts, are we?"

Her hands squeezed tightly onto his cheeks. "I'm fwom Indiana, just came yestewday."

"Oh, so fresh." She stopped smiling and frowned. "I don't think you'll need be told again not to use that name for me?"

Morgan searched at the corner of his eye for Hemlock and squeaked out, "No."

Bobbi smiled once more and let go of Burns' face. She went back to sit on the couch, "And I'll thank you not to call Joseph 'the Reaper,' such nasty nicknames you get about with that imagination of yours, Hemlock."

"Bobbi, I'm not for hire. Burns tell Bobbi we're not for hire. How many other clients did we get last night?"

Morgan looked frantically at Bobbi and Hemlock, noticing that Joseph now stared at him as well. "Well, I called all the names on that list, of the six, I talked to three and left voicemails for the other three."

Hemlock sat forward in her chair and spread her hands. "See, Morgan just said we have three, maybe six clients! I can't possibly take on anymore right now."

"No," interrupted Morgan, "The three I talked to didn't believe me and weren't willing to pay our retainer. The other three may not be easy sells either, one was a priest."

Bobbi beamed.

"Burns, you're a horrible liar." Hemlock breathed deeply and sighed. "Bobbi, I don't want to work for you, you're a horrible client. I don't want to do it. Every time you've convinced me to work for you in the past, it's nearly killed me. Why on Earth and the Netherworld would I want to get involved with you again?"

"Because Hemlock," she flashed a wicked grin with a twinkle in her green eyes, "I've always paid my bill, overpaid on many occasions mind you."

Hemlock jabbed a finger at the air, "You know the estimates can always be low and you never come in for a simple case. It's always something that requires overtime and, well, some hazy morality."

"Give us ten minutes to convince you to take this on, and we'll pay you for a full hour at your normal rate."

Hemlock ran a hand through her short hair and stared directly at Morgan. "Look, Bobbi, I don't think it will matter, we know."

Bobbi Cotter mocked her surprise and glanced back and forth between Hemlock and Burns, "Oh, do ya now? Mr. Burns, what is it that you know today?" She glared at Burns.

"Well, we know one of your people, along with over a half dozen other prominent Bostononians, and a few dozen others have lost all their memories. So far, none have shown any signs of recovery."

"How many of them were in the wetworks trade?"

Hemlock coughed, "Well the ballerina's calendar was pretty thin, so she may have been moonlighting."

Morgan stepped toward the couch, Joseph stepped closer to Burns. "Excuse me, but what do you mean wetworks? Your man was an actual hitman?"

Bobbi nodded.

"Just, so I'm clear," Morgan pressed, "We're talking about an actual hitman? Like, 'Luca Brazzi sleeps with the fishes,' kind of hitman?"

Bobbi turned back to Hemlock and hooked a finger at Morgan, "Is he bugged or just thick?"

Hemlock waved a hand in her direction, "He's Midwestern. Don't worry, he's solid."

Joseph stood close enough to Morgan that it spooked him when Joseph suddenly spoke, "He better be."

Hemlock slouched back over the arm of the chair. "As touching a problem it is to have one of your hitters down out of the blue because he thinks he's a plank of wood, I fail to see how it's my problem. You have a guy that lost his memory, go get a doctor to find it. You've got plenty of money to throw at this."

"You've got one thing wrong there Hemlock, I don't need a doctor to find his memory, someone's already found it."

That made Hemlock sit up straight. "What do you mean someone found it?" Hemlock's gaze narrowed at Bobbi, "Why are you here so early? What happened?"

Bobbi sighed and nodded at Joseph. The slender man spoke, "Jackie went funny about four weeks ago. We had a meet set up to lean on some new pups running a neighborhood, but when I went to pick him up, *he* wasn't there. The man seemed fine, but it was like watching a baby learn to pick up a spoon again."

"We got Jackie into some doctors, he's in a hospice outside town, for now. Joseph took care of the meeting without him. What he means by new pups, was a small crew of Colombians had started selling out at Dorchester. The plan was originally to make an example of one of them, that's Jackie's department."

Hemlock winced, "But the plan changed, right?"

Joseph nodded, "I put the fear of God Almighty into them, they agreed to a fifteen percent bump back to cover the corners. It was a decent enough deal."

"Jackie didn't know that part though, did he?"

Bobbi shook her head. "Jackie's still in hospice, I checked myself before we came over, he never left Woburn. Someone else went down to Dorchester, found one of the dealers, slit his throat, cut his tongue out and left him in a pool of blood."

"And you know who took Jackie's job? Don't you?"

Bobbi looked gravely back at Morgan, then to Hemlock. "That's why we need you on this. It makes no sense, and we can't have any of our hands in this cake. Some fifteen-year-old kid got a ride over there a few hours ago, killed a dealer, then tried to take the same Uber back home to Jamaica Plain. Cops have her now."

Morgan blinked in shock, "Her? A fifteen-year-old girl killed, executed and mutilated a drug dealer in the night like a professional assassin."

Hemlock groaned. "Ah, fuck it. OK, fine Bobbi, but shit better not go sideways on me for this. Burns, meet our 'paying client'.

Get a shower, we have to go see Deedee."

"Deedee?"

"Yeah Burns, Deedee's over at the morgue. We need to go see what she knows. We can find out about the victims and maybe get some word-of-mouth of the suspect from her. Police won't want to let us talk to a minor."

# THE MORGUE

**H**emlock stepped silently and swiftly down the thirteen steps of her townhouse. Morgan plodded loudly behind her. She stopped at the last stair of the stoop. Hemlock closed her eyes and breathed deeply, slightly tilting her head with the directions of the wind. Morgan stepped around her and peered up and down Braddock Park.

Morgan forced a break in her concentration, "So, where do we go?"

Hemlock pursed her lips. She sneered at him, "Burns some aspects of this job require a bit of grace and thought."

"You don't know, do you?"

"No, I do know, we have to go see the Medical Examiner at the city morgue. That's not what I was trying to determine when you rudely interrupted me."

"You don't know how to get there then? Here I can Google it." Morgan pulled a smartphone from his jacket pocket and started typing.

"Don't be thick Burns," Hemlock growled at him. "Of course I know where the city morgue is, I'm just trying to find our transit."

Morgan tilted his head back up and cocked an eyebrow at her. "If you've lost your car, I can get us directions for walking there or call for an Uber."

"Dammit Burns, I know where my car is, I barely ever drive the stupid thing. Have you ever been to a morgue before?"

"Only to identify my father, why?"

She crossed her arms, "Well, when you went to that morgue,

you probably had to sign in, right? Let them know who you were and why you were there right?"

"Oh, yeah, the annoying guy at the front desk made me sign in. I remember because he used this strange hair gel and his pen was all greasy from it."

Hemlock pinched the bridge of her nose and crossed her arms again, "Right, well, we need to go check out a body and talk to the examiner. They let you in for your dad because you were the next of kin and required to provide identification. We are not related to the deceased in this instance, and we are not part of the official investigation. So, do you think we will get past that clerk at the front desk?"

"No, I don't suppose we would get past." He stared back down at the phone, "So what do we do?"

"We hitch a ride with someone that can get us in." Hemlock smiled and pointed down the block, "That way."

Hemlock led Morgan while he was still staring down at his phone screen. "Hemlock, this is the wrong way, the map says the morgue is the other way, it also shows the Office of the Medical Examiner only has a two and a half star rating. Why would people rate the morgue?"

"I dunno Burns, maybe they were so unhappy with their autopsy they rose from the dead to leave a bad Yelp review. Our ride is going to be down here."

They turned into a parking lot between buildings. Hemlock approached a rusted green dumpster against another building. "Here we are now, let's see."

She flipped open one side of the dumpster, Morgan peered in next to her. Inside the dumpster sat a small creature. Light flitted and reflected off a doubled pair of slender wings protruding from its back. It wore rags, dead leaves and twigs protruded from a mane of hair. It perched over a dead rat, digging through the ribs with a pair of clawed hands. The pixie pulled the heart from the rat and bit through the middle of the organ, causing a spray of blood to spatter its wings. It fluttered the wings on its back rapidly, shaking the blood loose and drying the wings.

"Hallo Alice," Hemlock rasped down at the being smiling. "I've got a job for you if you can tear yourself from this for a minute. We'll give you a second to finish up." Hemlock stood back from the dumpster.

Morgan leaned close towards Hemlock and whispered "Alice? That thing is female?"

Hemlock frowned and grimaced. "She may not look like Tinkerbell, but Alice is an actual pixie, which will help us much more here than any cute, little, sexualized pocket fantasy."

A beating of wings on the soft morning breeze preceded Alice popping out of the dumpster and sitting on the edge. She spoke in a deep baritone, "Alright, I got breakfast, what do you need Lockley?"

Hemlock pulled her face into a forced tight lipped smile. "My associate and I need you to help us get into the city morgue. Could we get a ride along?"

Morgan turned a shocked gaze to her, "A what?"

"Just a ride along Burns, she'll pop us in her satchel, fly on through the morgue and plop us in with who we need to see."

Morgan looked back at the pixie and noticed a small leather pouch slung under one arm. "In that?"

"Oh hush, it's bigger on the inside. What do you say, Alice? Can you help out a friend."

Alice narrowed her gaze at Hemlock, "One condition, you have to go see your mother, tonight!"

Hemlock flared her nostrils and sighed, "She's got the whole court overseeing me now?"

"Aye, you expected less? It's worth a spot to anyone that can get you to report back now and again, Lockley."

She rolled her eyes at the little pixie. "Fucking shit, fine. Get my intern and me into the morgue, we are looking for a body with the tongue hanging out. Should be a Latino."

The pixie pivoted stares between the two, "Intern? I thought you were ordered to get a consort?"

"Not right now, Alice, can you get us into the morgue or not?"

"Yeah, hop on in, it'll be a bumpy ride though, rat always gives me gas."

"OK Burns, going out on a limb here, but I'm betting you've never traveled via a magic pixie before, right?"

Morgan cocked an eye, "I thought I made that abundantly clear when I asked, 'in that?'"

"Well, didn't know if maybe you were one of those uptight snobby types that only hops a ride with pixies they don't find in a dumpster devouring rat hearts," replied Hemlock

In a blur, the pixie darted at Morgan's face, dried blood flaking brown at the tips of her razor-sharp claws, "Bitch, I will cut you!"

Hemlock swatted the air and plucked Alice from in front of Morgan's face, "Just a joke Alice, you're the only pixie the kid's ever seen."

Alice fluttered and spit a sinewy glob of blood at Hemlock's feet. "Meet your mom tonight then, Lockley, promise it."

"Fine, on my father's grave, now can we go?"

Alice flitted in a loose circle around Morgan and Hemlock. Morgan craned his head to track the pixie but was only able to catch blurs as she wound around them faster. The sky went white in front of Morgan, there was a pop then a noise like "Schluuppp." Darkness enveloped them both. Old worn leather rubbed and chafed against Morgan. The odor of old spoiled milk filled his nose, reminding him of a half-eaten cup of yogurt he'd left in his dad's car once on a hot day. Unable to see, Morgan fidgeted in his pocket and pulled out his phone. The screen illuminated and shone dimly on Morgan and Hemlock lying on either side of giant safety pin surrounded by brown leathery walls.

"Where are we?"

"Inside Alice's satchel, I told you we were going to go for a ride along."

"We've shrunk?"

"No, Alice is massive and destroying the city of Boston to fly us to the morgue. Of course, we've shrunk, don't be obtuse. How else do you expect she's going to get us past the desk at the morgue to see the body?"

"How long will we be in here?"

"As long as it takes something the size of a dragonfly to fly about a mile from my place to the morgue."

They sat in silence for a long while. "Um, why does Alice call you Lockley?"

Hemlock's jaw dropped. "We've been shrunk to the size of a shelled peanut. We are being carried about Boston in the satchel of a ratchet pixie that you just met after literally never having seen a pixie ever. But your question is about my name?"

"Well," Morgan sighed, "I'd like to think I'm coping with change pretty well. I can't do much about the fact that I'm smaller than a key chain. I'm hoping it works out, but I don't know why the dirty pixie called you Lockley."

Hemlock pulled her fingers through her short blond hair. "Don't want to talk about it."

"What about the thing about visiting your mom?"

She rubbed her temples, "Burns, drop it, you can meet her tonight."

"Am I an intern or a consort? What does a consort do anyway? Would it pay better?"

"Sweet fucking toadstools, Burns, let it go. Get your mind back in the game here. We've got a dead drug dealer to look at, killed by some rich cheerleader because of a brain wiped hitman of our only paying client. A client, which, may I remind you, runs the Irish mob!"

The sky lit above them, the gigantic head of Alice peered down, "We're here."

Hemlock cupped her hands around her mouth, "Is anyone out there Alice?"

Alice leaned down to the satchel, Morgan stared up into Alice's open mouth hovering cavernously overhead. The teeth were craggy and yellowed with a small hole that bore straight through at a diagonal in one of the canine teeth was clear as day from Morgan's microscopic perspective. A warm wind hit him, filled with a sulfurous odor of decaying flesh.

Alice whispered down, "There's only one living person out here, Lockley. She's got a white coat, a bunch of tattoos and some fancy glasses."

"That's our ticket," Hemlock yelled, "Punch us out Alice!"

Alice glided against the currents of the ventilation system to a point high in the room. She unceremoniously upended the satchel and shook out her pair of guests. Hemlock closed her eyes and fell purposefully with her shoes pointed to the ground. Morgan forgot the first rule of hitchhiking and promptly panicked. Which was why when Alice's spell reversed itself, Hemlock landed feet flat on the floor and standing straight up. Morgan fell flat on his back flailing his arms around, giving a shrill shriek and pulled a small table of instruments over on himself.

Morgan stopped flailing when a scalpel fell dangerously close to his ear and stuck in the tile with a twang. He opened his eyes and, reluctantly, stretched out from his curled fetal position, gradually standing up again. The woman Alice had described to them prior to the great dumping was staring at Morgan. He felt her intense gaze like the hot sun beating down at him on a cloudless late summer day.

"Um, sorry about the mess," squeaked Morgan, "First time traveling by pixie, they didn't really warn me."

Alice chuckled overhead. She darted around the room and settled to sit in the tray of a large old hanging scale near an exam table. Her weight did not register on the scale.

Dark green eyes rolled behind thick black-rimmed spectacles, "Who's your new buddy, Hemlock?"

"Morgan Burns, this is Boston's Chief Medical Examiner, Dierdre Volsung. Dierdre, this is my new intern, Morgan Burns. Dierdre, you may now proceed to lightly haze my intern. Not too harsh though."

Dierdre nodded at Morgan. "Charmed. Call me Deedee, I hate the way people over-pronounce Dierdre. It always sounds like dear drah or dear draw, just annoying, don't you think?"

Morgan swung his head back and forth looking between Hemlock and the medical examiner. He finally choked out, "Yeah, I suppose so, I guess?"

Deedee approached Morgan, making vast strides with swaying grace on her long legs. "Jorge made a drop off earlier, he mentioned your little ward, Hemlock." She looked down the narrow bridge of her nose, letting her glasses slide down for her eyes to be visible above the black frames. "Honestly, I didn't believe him that you'd taken on such a normie. You could almost nickname him Mayo."

Hemlock leaned on a dissection table. "OK Dierdre, as much as I'd like to watch you make my intern here squirm a bit with this sexual tension and derision, we're on the clock."

"Oh, business it is then." She straightened up, "You came without official requests, so whom are you here to talk about?"

"I'm going to guess it's Jorge's delivery," Hemlock said. "Got anything on the menu here in the Latino drug dealer cuisine? Maybe cooked up by what would look like a five star mafia hitman kind of chef?"

Deedee rolled her eyes again, "Hemlock, have some moderate respect for the dead that come through my doors. You know I hate your food analogies."

"You got him or not?"

She sighed and crossed her arms. "Yeah, that is the guy Jorge brought in early this morning. He's over here on exam table four. I was going to get started with him after wrapping up some more initial paperwork."

Deedee strolled back, more casually, past a few bare exam tables to one that sat with a lumpy black body bag stretched out. She began to tug the zipper down and spread out the open body bag flaps. "So, who's the client? The family of the victim or got hired by the family of the kid to prove her innocence?"

The bag opened laid flat now with the victim still dressed in blood-soaked clothing. His eyes were closed, but his mouth was opened and slack jawed. The tongue laid out in a flap from a full cut across his throat. Hemlock picked up a pair of thin forceps from a dissection tray. "Neither." She leaned in close, picking and moving the tongue a bit to peer around the wound area.

Morgan peered around Hemlock, "Awfully gruesome way to go, are the eyes always shut when they come in?"

Deedee stared intently at Hemlock's prodding while answering Morgan. "No, not normally. That's actually indicative that when the girl did this she went deep with the blade." Deedee pointed down to the trails of blood around the tongue. "Ignoring the fact that she cut deep enough to pull the tongue out, there is only evidence of one cut. She cut through enough skin, muscle, and everything to sever both carotids and both pairs of jugulars. When she did that, the killer did a real kindness to Santiago here."

Morgan mumbled agreement and looked back up at Deedee, "And why is that exactly?"

"She cut everything that was taking blood into and out of this man's brain. He fainted within seconds due to lack of blood, brain death soon followed. Santiago suffered only briefly, it could have been a lot worse. The killer on this case was a practiced hand and knew what they were doing."

Morgan cocked an eyebrow, Hemlock saw his gobsmacked

expression. "Lean in here and check this out Burns," she growled. "There's a lot of muscle in a neck and a wide area to cut across." Hemlock lifted a flap of skin with the forceps. "See that, the cut is uniform across Santiago's whole throat. Think you'd do that the first time out killing someone?"

Morgan tilted his head. He leaned in and made some motions across Santiago's neck with his hands. "I'd like to think I would, but I'd be more likely to make a jagged cut back and forth."

"So, not working for the victim, not working for the accused." A smile gently curved on Deedee's thin lips. "Who are you working for Hemlock?"

"Client confidentiality, Dierdre. You know I can't talk about that." Hemlock straightened up and dropped the forceps.

Deedee stretched across Burns to zip the body bag back together. "Hemlock, are you coming to Julia and Eduardo's party?"

Hemlock grimaced, "Those two want me to come to a party?"

"Well, you were saying you need to get into better graces with the covens, all of them will be there. You could at least take the time to show you care and gain some ground. Mine will be there."

Morgan gawked open-mouthed at the pair. "I'm sorry, Deedee, you're a witch?"

Deedee gasped smiling, "Goodness, Hemlock. Jorge told me your intern was green, but this could make a spring forest blush!"

Hemlock scowled and jabbed a finger towards Deedee. "That shit right there. Those snide little judgmental comments are why I have problems with the greater magical community in Boston. You all band together in this town that's old as hell and think your shit doesn't stink anymore." She jabbed the finger back towards the body bag, "And that's the kind of thing that happens."

Deedee scoffed, "No, this is not magic, this is a deep throat laceration, and the police already have the girl that did it in custody."

"Deirdre, use that brain you claim is so amazing," Hemlock knocked on her skull to mock her. "If the police had no one in custody, but dumped a Latino drug dealer on your table like this, what would you and the BPD Gang Unit be saying about this body?"

Deedee sighed, "We'd be saying that this was a gang hit, and it's meant to send a message from the other gang."

Hemlock continued to press. "Do you know anything about the suspect BPD has in custody for Santiago's murder?"

"Young girl was all they said."

"Young ain't the half of it, try teenager. Fifteen-year-old cheerleader from Jamaica Plain got arrested for doing this. The girl even took an Uber to get down to Dorchester. If the high-schooler that slit Santiago's throat is as experienced at executions as a mafia hitman, then student loans must be getting way out of hand."

Deedee stared at the body bag and crossed her arms. She tapped a long crimson fingernail on a porcelain white canine. "I see your point, but do you think she was compelled by one of the covens to commit this murder? That would end up warranting a summary execution for anyone connected to it."

"I'm not sure of the details entirely yet, but I think somehow the teenager got the memories of a hitman. Then she ended up running a job he was scheduled to do at some point."

"Not impossible," Deedee considered, "But not something easily done either. I'm not sure how off the top of my head. It does give you another reason to come to Julia and Eduardo's party, mingle with the covens and get a feel for it yourself."

"Yeah, you're right. I really hate those two. Julia's got the personality of an oyster cracker and Eduardo, who used to be normal Eddie, is so pretentious. I think his head is in danger of impacting his own colon." She sighed. "Depends, it's not tonight is it?"

"Why? Dating the intern?"

Hemlock chuckled. Morgan flushed beet red and started sputtering, "No, no no, she's just got to go see her mom tonight."

Deedee's eyebrows shot up in an instant. "Back with Mommy's court?"

Hemlock shot a narrowed stare at Morgan. "Nothing like that, Deedee, just checking in with mom. You do that too right? Or do they not let her out of the sixth pit anymore?"

"And there's your problem Hemlock. You are too damn snarky and cynical. The party is this Friday, it's a gender reveal party. You should both come, the North End coven is throwing it for them, but all the covens are invited."

"Gender reveal party? Eddie knocked her up?"

"Yep, and we're going to cast a spell to see it at the party."

Hemlock rolled her eyes. "Fine, we'll be there."

Morgan's eyes widened. "Hey, one last thing Deedee. Jorge mentioned there was a copycat killer running around. I think he called him the Huntsman. Do you still have the body from that murder here?"

Deedee shook her head, "No, we got the autopsy wrapped up and released him to family. No reason to keep them around if they have a family to collect the body."

"Was there anything strange about it? How many have there been?"

"Five so far, most recent was in Franklin Park. They found him strung up off a trail in a wooded area. The Huntsman usually ties them all up and bleeds them one way or another."

"Was there something in the old murders that was kept out of the papers or never released to reporters?"

Deedee tilted her head at Morgan, "The boy does have some brains Hemlock! I did check into the files on that. The old reports showed that the victims always had their tongue cut out. Not like Santiago here, just pulled from the mouth and cut. Strange thing is, in all the Huntsman's murders, the tongues were never recovered at any scene. They believe he kept them as trophies. It was never released to the public, not even the families knew. We'd get everything sewn back up, including the lips, and the morticians were happy enough to do the makeup."

"Is there anything else strange about those?"

She nodded, "Yeah, the Huntsman was active sporadically from 1967 to 1999. Then nothing for the last twenty years. He'd kill about one a year according to the files, but we've had closer to one a month recently."

"Seems like quite the uptick for someone who's very geriatric if it's the original killer. The five victims though, did they have their tongues still?"

Deedee shivered, "No."

# A KILLER'S LAIR

**H**emlock placed a quick call. A few minutes later, she was thanking Deedee for her time and waving Morgan to follow her back to a scale. Alice's knobbly knees and legs dangled over the side, one foot tapping out a short rhythm.

"Alice," Hemlock knocked on the bottom of the metal tray, "Can we get another quick lift? We need to head down to Roxbury. If you wouldn't mind dropping us off at the corner of Ruthven and Walnut."

She leaned over on the tray, hands and eyes peeking out over the edge, "You already owe me some time with your mother for the ride in. What'll you give me to take you out and over there, Lockley?"

"Why you ungrateful little turd muffin," Hemlock spat back at Alice. "You and I both know that was a big enough favor to cover more than one trip today."

"Yeah," she agreed, "But you didn't specify, Lockley. So, my side on that deal is at an end." Alice raised herself higher, her eyes glowed red and smoldered. "And may you be drawn and quartered by a hundred of my sisters and brethren if you don't honor your commitment!"

Hemlock rolled her eyes. "Settle down you wretched little Tink, I agreed, so I'll meet the old bat." She sighed, "Does mom still have to travel with the Riders or has she given up having to use that whole retinue?"

Alice chuckled, "The Queen must always travel with her riders. Would you expect any monarch to travel without their

guard? The Riders of Danann always herald her into this place."
She leaned down again and raised an eyebrow at Hemlock, "Now
how do you intend to pay for the next leg of your travels?" Alice
nodded at Morgan, "I could do with a small chunk of his leg."

Morgan clambered back in shock, "What? My leg?"

"Nah, she said a chunk of it," Hemlock waved him back. "Hey
Deirdre," Hemlock shot back at the office, "Got anything fresh I
can use as pixie fare?"

Deedee called out from an adjacent office, "Check the mini-
fridge, you'll want the bin next to my sandwich, but not my
sandwich. If you touch my sandwich, I'll practice Egyptian
mummification rituals on you while you are alive."

Hemlock saw the little dorm room sized refrigerator sitting
on a counter, and pointed to Morgan to go to it. Morgan found
the bin mentioned by Deedee. It was a small deli container that
contained a bulbous egg-shaped bit of meat with the coloration
of a kidney bean. He fumbled with the lid to open it and pre-
sented the scrap of meat up to Alice.

Hemlock pointed up to her, "That covers our fare?"

Alice poked her nose into the bin, sniffing deeply. "Oh, fresh
human pituitary gland! I've got to come here for lunch more
often."

The pixie cradled the freshly cut gland in both of her grubby
fingers, they were massaging it gingerly. Drool began to run
down her chin as her mouth began to gape, rows of sharp teeth
grew. As Alice's maw kept expanding she pulled the gland entirely into her once smaller face. Her skin stretched to eventually
envelop around the gland. She gnawed down on the organ, each
grind of her mandible making a squishing wet schlop noise,
like a boot being pulled from the rain-soaked mud. After a few
chews, Alice's eyes rolled back in her head, and she began moan-
ing in ecstasy. The meal was too large for her to keep her mouth
closed around it. With another deep chomp, a little spray of liquid shot out and the few drops splattered like raindrops on

Morgan's boots.

Morgan covered his nose, "Ugh, revolting," he said staring at the splatter on his boots.

He bent down to wipe it off, Hemlock grabbed his arm. "Don't do that, not if you want to live."

Morgan cocked an eyebrow at Hemlock.

"She still considers that part of her meal; if you rob her of those few drops at best we won't get our ride out of here. At worst, she'll slit your throat for stealing before she flies off."

"Why can't we have Deedee walk us out then?"

"There's no record of us coming in. As much of a friend as Deedee can be, I don't want to cause her any trouble. Like having to explain why or how she had visitors in here without security clearance or being checked in. It will cause questions on any case with a corpse she autopsied and cause a lot of pain. We need to avoid that, but we also had to see the body for ourselves."

Morgan felt something tug at his boot. He snapped his gaze down, Alice had finished her meal in the scales tray and had wrapped her arms and legs around the foot of his boot, like a cat holding a toy. A long coarse tongue slid out of her mouth and glided across the surface of the boot, picking up the droplets with a sandpaper scrape. His lips curled down and he looked away.

Alice flew back up to hover eye level with Hemlock. After a few sandpaper licks across her own hands, she asked wearily, "Roxbury, you said?"

"Yep, the sooner the better," replied Hemlock.

Alice flitted around them in flashes, soon Hemlock and Morgan found themselves packed inside Alice's satchel once more.

Morgan tilted his head around, reaffirming his leathery surroundings. Then he shrugged off his sudden changes again. "So, how is it the security guy won't see Alice fly past him?"

Hemlock flashed a smug grin. "The same way you've probably seen dozens of pixies and little fae critters throughout your life but never saw them. He'll ignore it."

"Huh?"

"Yep," rasped Hemlock, settling back against the softened brown surrounding. "You see something blur past like that or hear something strange, and your normal little human brain decides it was a trick of the light, a cicada that flew off. You'll fill in anything that makes sense to you; right up until someone like me introduces you to a pixie like Alice chowing down on a rat in a dumpster."

Morgan nodded, "That actually makes a lot of sense, when I was in college everyone would take cookies from the dining halls and throw them to squirrels. We got some gigantic ones because of all the cookies being tossed. One time, I thought I saw a massive one from the corner of my eye that looked like it was part animal and part child. It scampered off before I got a good look at it, but I figured I wasn't getting enough sleep at midterms."

"Ah," Hemlock grinned, "Miniature faun. They are a bit rare in a miniature form, but I'd heard of a few tribes like that roaming the Midwest."

Alice opened the satchel and called down to them once more, "Last stop folks, Roxbury."

Hemlock stood up. "This time, just stand up, Burns. Try not to embarrass us here."

Alice upended the satchel, shaking it violently from side to side. Hemlock and Burns appeared on a sunny street corner. Hemlock managed to once again stand straight up and appear steadily. Morgan stumbled a step or two, but didn't fall over and flail on the ground.

The pixie didn't bother to stay long, she flitted off in the sky. Morgan lost track of her, his eyes surveying the landscape and trying to adjust to the sudden intensity of daylight. The narrow street on which they had been dumped was crowded with old two and three story duplexes and boarding houses. Some surrounded with chain link fencing.

"Where are we Hemlock?"

"We're down in Roxbury, it's a bit rougher neighborhood. Back at Deedee's I called Roy, a retired detective my dad used to work with from time to time. On a bit of a lark, I asked Roy about that serial killer and lucky us, they had a suspect. They got close to him a few times, but could never find any real evidence, a lot of times this one guy seemed to be in the wrong place at the wrong time. It never sat well with Roy though, and he said a few guys in the department would keep an eye out for this guy, David Stevens. David would be about mid-seventies now, and his last known address is here."

Hemlock stopped walking; they stood outside the rusted chain link fence of a dilapidated duplex. The yard was an overgrowth of crabgrass and waist high goldenrod. The house itself was a strange mix of white vinyl siding on a front porch, and older yellow asphalt siding on the rest of the structure. Once vibrant yellow had mellowed into a blotchy darker yellow, reminiscent of deli mustard.

Hemlock swung the gate open, it groaned with a metallic whine. The chain link shook loosely when Morgan swung it shut when they passed through. Two white mailboxes sat by the front door, Hemlock pointed to the top one labeled "Stevens".

"I think we're in luck, let's see if anyone's home." Hemlock rang the doorbell.

"Just to be perfectly clear," Morgan kept looking ahead, "You want to meet someone suspected of being a serial killer and get invited into his home?"

"I doubt we'll meet any killers today, Burns. Especially if no one is even home." She tried the bell again, and they heard a second ding-dong from inside.

The door knob shuddered for a moment and then the door swung open. A younger man stood in the doorway, tall and gaunt. He wore jeans and a green flannel shirt with a gray wool sock hat, and had a scruffy curly red beard. "Yeah, what?"

Hemlock smiled cheerily, "Hello, we came to have a word with Mr. David Stevens. Is he home today?"

"I'm his grandson, Jesse, he's not 'round right now. What's this about?"

Hemlock produced and handed him an off-white business card from her pants pocket. "Jan Smith, and this is my associate Robert Han, we deal in antiques and estate sales. Some time ago, your grandfather had contacted us about selling a few antiques. Unfortunately, we had a very busy summer and this is the first we'd been able to come around to see what the elder Mr. Stevens wanted to offer. May we wait inside for his return?"

Jesse read the card for a few moments, "Oh, he was finally looking to offload some of this old shit. Gotcha."

"Yes, may we wait for Mr. Stevens? It was quite a trip down here for us."

"Well, grampa's not going to be coming back. We had to put him in a nursing home. I'm starting to box some of this stuff up for sale, you're welcome to come in and look around. Maybe you know what old thing of junk he was trying to sell?"

"He wasn't very specific." Hemlock took a deep breath in, Jesse smelled like smoke, but had a sweet odor. "Say, I imagine there's a lot of stuff, sounds like your granddad was a bit of a pack rat. We'd give you a fair price on a few things if we could go peruse his collection."

"I don't know," Jesse scratched at his chin nervously. "I've got some errands I need to run."

Hemlock nodded back at Morgan, "Shame really, we won't be back this way for a few weeks. If trust is a matter, I could say, leave you with a security deposit. I've got a couple hundred bucks in cash, and could give you a check for anything we may end up buying."

Jesse reached his right arm up his left sleeve to itch it, "Yeah, yeah, I think that could work. You both look like good folks. You got two hundred then?"

Hemlock reached into a pants pocket and pulled out a pair of hundred dollar bills.

"We have the lower floor of the duplex, and grandpa kept some stuff in the basement too. I shouldn't be gone longer than a couple of hours." He snatched the pair of bills from Hemlock's outstretched hand.

Morgan watched from the door, mouth agape as Jesse strode past him, put the hood of his jacket up and walked on down the road. "Hemlock, what just happened?"

Hemlock stood by Morgan to make sure Jesse disappeared from view. "We bought ourselves time, a lot of time. He's got to go get his fix."

"But how did you know he was a drug addict? Did Alice say something?"

Hemlock stepped back from the window, "She didn't have to, did you smell him when he opened the door? That odor of sweet smoke on the air? That's what heroin smells like cooking."

"Oh, I wasn't aware."

Hemlock pushed past him into the main house, entering into a dining room. The hardwood floors had thin layer of dust and cat hair. An old carved wood table sat covered with layers of mail and old newspapers.

"I'd hope you wouldn't know what that odor meant, otherwise I'd have to question my employment of you."

Morgan followed her into the dining room and started rummaging around on the table.

Hemlock strode away from the dining room, heading towards the kitchen. "Notice anything yet Burns?"

Morgan shuffled through the newspapers. "Most of the mail here is addressed to David Stevens, a lot of it unopened. Guessing the grandson has been collecting it for him. There's a lot of spam. The only things opened are from a retirement and long term care facility called Westley Manor. Some empty envelopes from the Social Security Administration."

Hemlock yelled back through the kitchen, "Anything else?"

"There's a ton of old newspapers here, and they continue into the living room, so far though, the dates only go back to about seven months."

"How many empty social security envelopes did you find?"

"I count six. I'm guessing the grandson has been here for about seven months, and he does newspaper delivery? Is that still a thing?"

Hemlock appeared standing in the doorway, leaning on the varnished molding. "Yeah, it's a pretty easy job, only requires a few hours of investment a day and you can get paid in cash, daily. Between that and the fact that you don't have to file any paperwork for employment on it. It's a great option for a lot of folks that want to collect unemployment but still have more cash. Also, a good idea for anyone otherwise unable to pass a background check, drug screen or employment eligibility test. Why do you think Jesse is doing it?"

Morgan looked up, "Do you know or do you just want my opinion?"

"If this is going to be an internship, Burns," Hemlock rasped crossing her arms, "Then you are supposed to be learning. I always enjoyed the Socratic Method myself, so I want to see what you know or can deduce about our findings before I tell you my opinion of it."

Morgan nodded. "Well, since you clued me into Jesse's drug habit, I'm guessing he couldn't pass a drug screen and may have a few arrests in his past for possession. Likely, because of the empty envelopes, he's been cashing his grandfather's social security checks." He flipped open one of the Westley Manor invoices. "My guess is between the bills for this home and the costs of the retirement home, he's barely able to cover everything each month. In fact, this invoice also says past due, so he's behind on his grandfather's retirement home."

"I'll bet he has one or two months before the community forces him to start signing over the social security checks. He's likely hoping we'll buy all the furniture and antiques so he won't have to sort it. Notice anything else?"

Morgan paced the room, staring into the adjacent living room, the walls were all neutral tones of brown and gray. The paint was a bit dimmer shade on an empty spot on the wall with holes in the middle and wires dangling around them. Antique end tables and coffee tables were covered in melted candle wax. Long white metal rectangles ran along the baseboard.

"He's pawned the television that used to hang in the living room. It's cold in here, and there's baseboard heaters. So, I'm going to guess he's let the power bill run past due and the electric company has already shut off the power to this part of the house. Does that match what you found in the kitchen?"

"Come see for yourself."

Morgan's boots clunked on the hardwood floors, entering the kitchen in long strides. He opened the refrigerator, the door stuck a bit then groaned open. Morgan stumbled back from the stench, slamming the door shut again quickly. "Jesus, I've never seen that much mold in my life."

"Yeah, you might be the first to have opened that in a couple of months. What do you think of those?" She pointed at a magnetic bar on the wall above the oven. Six long bladed knives of different widths hung on the bar.

Morgan pulled one free. He ran a finger gently along the thin blade. The edge sliced easily through layers of callous on his finger. He let out a long whistle as a razor-thin scarlet line welled up through the slit. "Those are some mighty sharp knives, and about the only clean thing here." He nodded at the sink full of dirty dishes. "Off limits?"

"I'd guess that too. These knives must hold some meaning to old David. They're meat cutting and boning knives. Looks like he was a meat cutter or a butcher by trade, and gave Jesse enough hell about not touching them. Looks as though he's ignored them even in his grandfather's absence."

An old Coleman propane tabletop camp grill sat on the stove. He put a hand out on the counter and pulled it away shaking it, a slimy coating unwilling to shed away. Morgan paced around to a sink and turned on the water to wash his hands. "Well, he hasn't cleaned the counters in a while, and has been cooking a lot of bacon as greasy as this is. The oven was electric too, so Jesse's had to use that old camp grill. This is strange though, check this out."

Morgan nodded at the sink, Hemlock walked over and put a slender finger under the tap. "Ah, he's still got hot water, good find Burns."

"What's it mean, though?"

"Utility companies have to hit a threshold on the bill before they shut you off. He was probably running television, lights and everything else so much that the power company hit the limit in a few months. My guess is they shut him off around May or June, which is why the fridge is so disgusting. The water heater must be a gas unit, maybe the last gas powered appliance in the home, the gas bill for that would be very low. So, it would take most of the year to get to the point for them to shut it off. He may even have kept it current, with it being so cheap."

Morgan shut off the water and surveyed his surroundings again. He spotted a towel crumpled on the counter. When he picked up the towel, it held its crumpled shape. Morgan dropped it in the sink and wiped his hands on his jeans instead.

Hemlock walked to a shut door on the other side of the kitchen. She swung the door open, revealing a darkened stairway.

Morgan chuckled, "Did you bring a flashlight?"

Hemlock held out her palm. She stared directly up into Morgan's eyes. Her cheeks puffed out, and she began growling deep in her chest. The rattle followed up her throat. She stretched her neck, lifting her head higher. Hemlock snapped her neck down and spat a ball of fire into her cupped hand.

"How's this work for a flashlight?"

"As long as we don't burn the house down, great." Morgan pointed at the ball of fire, "Is this why your voice always sounds so wretched? You're secretly a dragon that can hock loogies of hellfire?"

Hemlock glared at him, the ball of fire curling orange and bright in her hand. "I'm not a dragon, Burns. Though, thank you for not making a joke about being a Mario brother or sister. I'm more used to that one." She turned away and started down the stairs.

Morgan followed closely behind her to be able to see the steps ahead of them. "OK, so if you aren't a dragon, what exactly are you? You must be something more than human. How you talked to the pixie about your mom made it seem like that too, but the way you talked to Deedee makes me believe you aren't really a witch either."

Hemlock bobbed her head around to get a clearer view of the wood steps as they descended into the basement. Morgan's boots clunked loudly on the steps behind her. "Burns, you ever been told you have the subtlety of a sledge hammer?"

"My aunt Bernice said the exact same thing one Christmas when I told her I preferred the can of jelled cranberry sauce to her homemade one. Why?"

They reached the concrete slab at the bottom of the steps. Hemlock took a cautious stride, trotting lightly across the floor as she saw old laundry piles laying like haystacks on the floor. "Burns, what do you think it takes to be a witch? Or a warlock or wizard for that matter?"

Morgan pulled his phone from his pocket and flicked on the flashlight function from his phone. "I dunno, I suppose you have to be born into it somehow. Have some special gene or blood or what not, then get training and all that. Maybe go buy some tomes or make some sort of deal with the devil?"

"Which devil?"

Morgan's boots fell heavily on the concrete floor, echoing across the dark space as he searched another side of the basement. "What do you mean which devil?"

Hemlock popped up in front of his cell phone light, wearing a Cheshire grin. Morgan stumbled back and fell over a mound of clothes. Hemlock chuckled, "I told you Burns, you need to work on making your steps silent. Here, give me your hand."

Morgan grasped her hand and tried to pull himself away from the mound, but fell back into it again.

"What I mean is," Hemlock sighed, "They all actually get their start as a normal person like everyone, even the ones that claim some sort of pure bloodline. Magic is innate at some level in everyone, and they train up with it. Some use magical instruments and devices, like wands and what not to help with focus. There are endless odd amounts of tomes and grimoire to help them work through it and cast spells. At some point or another, they all decide they need more power. At that point they call on some infernal being, a dark lord, a devil, even a powerful fae to grant them more power."

Morgan stared at her in the light of his cell phone as Hemlock wandered off searching again. He pointed to a far corner. "Hemlock, I think the water heater is over there, if that means anything." She turned and began a careful walk around another mound of old clothes.

"So there's more than one devil? It's not just Lucifer, Beelzebub, Satan, whatever the churches all want to call him?"

"Oh, no, there are loads of them, they all get so confusing too. There's some that like to be all goat-like and cloven-hoofed, some look like a weird bat thing, others just like a regular guy. They're all about the same though. They can grant power in exchange for devotion from the witch or wizard to do that dark lord's bidding. Sometimes that bidding is against another dark lord, it really is a funny dance they all do."

Hemlock raised her cupped ball of fire to the water heater. "This is a bit newer, installed in the last five years, and it is a natural gas model." She knelt to the wall, finding a small metal box. "Hey, Burns, you any good with electrical work?"

Morgan tried to stand again and slipped back on something squishy that stuck to his boot. He slumped back on the mound of old clothes and pulled his boot free. "A little, why do you ask?"

"Gas water heaters, they generally don't take power right?"

"No, I helped my dad install one at our house once. They have an electric control module in the newer ones, but those get powered off a small thermocouple from the pilot light. What'd you find?"

"There's an old breaker box mounted next to the water heater, but the wires don't lead anywhere other than being cemented into the wall."

Hemlock held the cupped fire in one hand, she reached out and opened the small breaker box. It began stiffly with the resistance of age and rust. She brought the light closer to the box. "Hey Burns, I don't think Jesse's going to get to do much with the house."

Morgan finally got the boot off his foot, "Why's that?"

"Because ol' granddad was the Huntsman. I just found his trophy case."

Hemlock strode back into view of Morgan's light, holding her fireball in one hand and dangling a necklace in another. She lowered it for Morgan to see better in the fire, that she held a leather strap with many leathery looking chunks attached to it.

"What are those?"

He leaned up for a closer inspection. Each meat-like chunk was only an inch square and shriveled.

"My guess, by the number of them, is they are a piece of the tongue of each victim."

Morgan turned his lip up in disgust and shrank back away from the gruesome necklace. "Where's the rest of the tongues though?"

Hemlock pointed to the edges of one. "There are bite marks around the edges. My guess is he would keep a small part of each as a trophy, and," Hemlock gulped, "eat the rest."

"That's not the only set of trophies," Morgan said, he shined the light down on the sole of his boot. Hemlock hunched over, there, stuck to the tread, was another one inch square of human tongue.

She swept her ball of light over the ground and found three more chunks of tongue, stuck to the floor, chewed and dried in place. She turned her firelight back to Morgan, "I think the police will be interested in talking to Jesse too, this one just went weird."

"Ugh, here take my boot, I'm going to try to get out of this hill of clothes before I'm sick."

Morgan placed a hand deep through the clothes, and his hand closed around a plastic bag. He stopped trying to push himself up and pulled out the bag. He held it in front of his face and brought his light up to the bag. A dozen little circular yellow pills stamped with a brain on them hung in the plastic.

"Hemlock, if Jesse's got a bad drug problem, why didn't he finish off this stash of pills?"

# TACO RUN

Hemlock tread softly in short quiet steps. Morgan clunked loudly behind her. As they approached the corner of Ruthven, Hemlock spun on her heel and stopped. Morgan stumbled, almost walking into her.

"I need to borrow your cell phone for a moment to make a quick call."

Morgan rummaged in a coat pocket; he unlocked the phone and handed it to Hemlock. "You don't have one yourself?"

She started to dial a number, "No, they don't usually last long with me, so I stopped paying for them."

Hemlock stopped typing and held the phone to her ear, "Hey Roy! Hemlock again, thanks for that address. Yes, yes, it did turn out to be a good hunch. Here's what's there." Hemlock continued to recount what she and Morgan had found inside the home and Jesse's expected return.

She clicked the phone off and handed it back to Morgan. He fumbled it between his hands a few times, "Hemlock, why is the phone so hot? This is worse than when my ex would play Candy Crush for hours."

"Part of why I can't keep cell phones," she explained. "I have too much innate magical interference. It causes some issues with complex electronics. I can use computers if I use a cabled keyboard and sit far enough away. Cell phones though, they end up getting too much of a direct hit. If I use that for more than ten minutes, it'll fry. If you start heading down a path of a witch or wizard, you'll have the same issues in time. Might take you a hundred years to get there, but it'll happen."

The phone cooled as Morgan turned it over in his hand. He stared down at it, "So, I can become a wizard and do magic, but I'm going to start wrecking technology? I've meant to disconnect a bit more, but I'm not sure I could survive without my phone."

"Could be worse for me because of my nature."

Morgan frowned. "What's that mean?"

Hemlock chuckled, "Don't worry about it, you'll find out. I'm hungry, you want to grab a bite to eat?"

Morgan yawned, "Yeah, I'm starving. Know anything good around here?"

"I was thinking tacos, sound alright?" Hemlock rummaged in her jacket pocket, pulling out the little baggy of yellow pills.

"Were we supposed to take that out of there?" Morgan poked at the bag, "With that being evidence and all?"

"I left a few behind for them to find, y'know, next to the little pile of gnawed up tongue bits. I doubt our friend Jesse will remember how many pills he had left or admit that to the police. These will be for our own little investigation." She popped the baggy of pills back into her pocket. "So tacos, yeah?"

Morgan unlocked his phone and started tapping the screen. He stared at the map on the screen. "Looks like we're about a mile away from the nearest Mexican place, should I call an Uber or do you want to hitch a ride on the pixie express again?"

"Nah, Alice already took off. I know a place though, we can get some answers and some food."

"Where's that at?"

"Hey, Burns?"

Morgan continued to stare at the screen, "Yeah?"

"Put the phone in your pocket and leave it there."

He glanced up, Hemlock scowled menacingly. "Oh, right."

Morgan shut the phone off and slid it back into his jacket pocket.

"Thank you, Burns." She turned around in place looking in each direction. "Today's Wednesday right?"

"I believe so. I could check on my phone, but it's staying in my pocket."

She ignored the comment, "If it's Wednesday, then she'll have her truck set up out at the wharf plaza."

"Great, who's got a truck at wharf plaza?"

"Taco Yolanda, fantastic tacos, better drugs, but she closes up by three. She'll be set up at Waterfront Park near the long wharf."

Morgan pushed his hand towards his pocket, then stopped himself, resisting the urge. "Hemlock, it's already past two, and we've got to be at least five miles from the waterfront. How do we get there if I don't get my phone out to call a cab or an Uber?"

Hemlock stared at him and blinked. "Magic, Burns, we're just going to hop over there."

She pulled a piece of chalk out of her pocket. Hemlock rolled the stick of chalk over her knuckles and began walking, staring down at the segments of sidewalk. She paced quickly past five cracked sections, stopping abruptly again before an unbroken square of pavement.

Hemlock knelt down, placing a knee firmly on the ground. She stretched over the sidewalk, drawing a series of concentric circles. She leaned carefully over the sketching to add in symbols at various points and intervals in the circles. When the chalk was nearly down to a small nub, she stood up, dusting off her knees as she stepped back to Morgan.

"OK Burns, this will be your first teleportation, so we'll go together. The important thing to remember is to make sure you jump in with enough momentum to be able to hop out, do you get that?"

He nodded his head up and down, "No, that makes no sense."

"When I seal the spell a portal will open up where the chalk drawings are. You need to jump into the portal with enough force that you'll be ejected out the other side correctly."

"I think I get it." Morgan bent his knees and hopped a couple of times. "So I hop in and it will hop me out somewhere else?"

"That's the long and the short of it."

"Why didn't we just do this and avoid paying the pixie before?"

"We can't teleport in or out of Dierdre's office, she's got it protected from using magic inside there. Alice's magic is a bit different, so she could get us in and out. Ready?"

Morgan nodded. Hemlock stepped forward to the chalk lines. She took a deep breath in and spit into the middle of the circles. The lines began to swirl, gray concrete began to shift between shades of black and green. Morgan stared down at the swirl of colors.

"You kick it off by spitting on it?"

"Human magic needs some investment of will, about any bodily fluid works for that. Spit is easiest, could use blood, heck I even knew a guy that would do it with urine, but it's gross and I get a nervous bladder."

Morgan leaned forward and poked a toe nervously at the hole. "I don't know about your spit portal here Hemlock. I mean, could this give me cancer? Is this going to kick me out where you mean or will I end up in the bay."

Hemlock sighed and pinched the bridge of her nose. "The portal is not going to give you cancer Burns, but if you don't hop in the damn thing, I'll be giving you a beating before long."

"Hop or jump?"

"Oh for fuck's sake Burns, hop in!"

He looked down at the portal and back to Hemlock again. He jumped up high and landed in the middle of the vortex of color. The world went dark around him. Morgan could only hear a rushing of wind. A second later he felt himself thrown and flying at a small mound of grass. He landed roughly and heard a light padding on the grass nearby. Morgan turned over and saw Hemlock standing next to him.

"See?" She waved a hand up and down her body. "Neither of us are dead, and no cancer. Next time though, don't leap so hard. You'll break your neck doing that."

"I'll remember that," Morgan muttered getting to his feet. "Where are we?" He turned around gawking at the area he just landed. Morgan found himself in a large grassy patch. Nearby was a long, red brick building. The sides opened out with vendors and restaurants. Farther across the small park was the harbor. It was close enough to be bothered by the noisy gulls but far enough to mute the waves crashing by the sounds nearby traffic.

Morgan turned to the busy roadways behind him. Parked close by were a pair of food trucks. The one on the right gave off an enticing aroma of grilled burgers. It was black with bold white lettering to announce "Best Burgers in Boston." Polished chrome accents gleamed in the afternoon sunlight.

The other truck was older and dirt splattered at its wheel hubs. Bright yellow and red colors painted on the side of the vehicle had faded to a strange shade of pink and a tone like an old banana peel. The front half of the truck had no openings. It bore the only fresh paint having a bright red box painted on the panel with canary yellow text that read "Taco Yolanda's."

A Hispanic woman was at the window inside the back of Taco Yolanda's food truck. The slender woman was leaning down to lay across the counter, her head hanging out of the window over the edge. Her dark hair was pulled tight back in a bun, her eyes, rimmed with dark circles and crows feet, drooped sullenly. A cigarette balanced at the edge of her lips, smoldering with little wisps of white smoke.

Morgan's eyes widened and his upper lip curled. "Hemlock, how about we hit the burger place instead? I know you wanted tacos, but I think this one's about ready to be shut down for health code violations."

Hemlock's lips curled into a Cheshire grin at the revulsion on Morgan's face. "Your burger guy will make you sick. He's been using old meat because he can't afford fresh with the overhead of everything else you see. Yolanda there may look like a cruising pit of salmonella, but the ingredients are fresh, and they are literally the best tacos in the city."

"You're joking." Morgan's brow furrowed deeper.

"Nope, plus we've got a side reason. Yolanda has more on her menu than just tasty Mexican food. She slings on the side for one of the gangs. We need to see if she can help us figure out who's selling these pills."

Morgan rubbed at the stubble starting to show on his chin. "Really? She risks her business selling drugs out of that?"

"Tacos make money, selling drugs to rich businessmen and lawyers near the financial district makes more. It's an ingenious cover for her too, she can move around place to place, really vary her clientele."

Morgan's brows shot up in surprise. "Businessmen and lawyers buy drugs from her?"

"How is anyone surprised by this? Rush Limbaugh had an oxy habit, yuppies and suburbanites are the biggest growing population of drug addicts in the country."

Hemlock started strolling over the lawns to the taco truck. "By the way Burns, I want to see how you do with something like this, so you take first shot at getting info."

Morgan nodded, staring directly ahead.

As they approached the window to order, the smoking woman stood. She was tall and gaunt. "What'll it be?"

Hemlock gave the menu a quick look. "I'll go with two pork tacos, sour cream, with chips and salsa."

She scribbled down the order. "And you?"

Burns stared at the menu mouth agape. "Uh, I'll go with the

same, no lettuce."

She finished scribbling, "Twenty-two seventy. Cash or card?"

Hemlock nudged him in the ribs while she put some cash on the counter.

"Oh, and we need some drugs too. Please."

The woman behind the counter scoffed, her eyes went wide. She took a long draw off the cigarette and threw it at Morgan, it burst into a puff of sparks as it hit his chest. "Fuck off narc!"

Hemlock bowed her head and rubbed her temple with one hand. "Yolanda, it's Hemlock, this is Burns, he's with me, we're not working for the police."

"Yeah? Exactly what a fuckin' narc would say!"

"Oh for the love of, thanks Burns." She took a deep breath and leaned on the counter. "I got the case from Cotter, it doesn't even involve you, but I need some info and my intern here has the social graces of a cinder block."

Yolanda crossed her arms. "I don't owe Cotter anything. The people I bump kick the bump up to the Irish for my territory."

Hemlock reached into her pocket and dug the little baggy of pills out. She slid it onto the counter on top of the cash.

"It's not about territory, it's about some killings and one of her hitters suddenly losing all his memory. It's coming back on her bad and I think it may have something to do with these pills. Seen anything like this before?"

Yolanda rolled her eyes, but picked up the baggy and the cash. She pocketed the fifty dollar bill. "It's not oxy, and the stamp isn't used by anyone in town for ex. I heard about some gangs down Dorchester trying to move something new. Word was it was like ex, but they were saying immersive or something like that. It wouldn't move up here, and they were starting to cross territory. I stayed away from it."

Morgan turned back to the counter, almost tripping over his own boots, "Are you sure they were out of Dorchester?"

She palmed the bag and held it up to closer to her eyes. "Yeah, yeah, some Colombian crew down Dorchester. Pills like ex but not ex, had a brain stamped on 'em. What's Cotter got in this game anyway? Not liking the competition?"

"People are ending up dead," Hemlock deadpanned.

Yolanda scoffed, "Yeah, what else is new?"

Hemlock reached up to get the baggy of pills, "What's new is the people taking those are doing the killing."

"No shit?"

"No shit, Yolanda. Now how about the tacos?"

# THE DRUGGIST

**H**emlock and Morgan sat in the Christopher Columbus Waterfront Park, looking out over the bay and ate their tacos in silence.

Connal finally broke the awkward silence, "So no lettuce?" She nodded at the mostly devoured tacos.

"Nah, don't like it. Never have, it just has a flavor to it, ends up taking over all the other flavors. I don't mind some salads, but tacos, burgers, sandwiches, you name it."

"A flavor?"

"Yeah, like a green flavor is the only way I know to explain it."

"Green flavor, hmm."

The awkward silence sat in, broken by the occasional crunch of chips. Morgan made an attempt to finally break it. "Mind if I ask you something boss?"

"Boss?"

"You are my boss here, and I'm working for you, right?"

"Sure, ask away."

"What did you mean about your 'nature' earlier?"

Hemlock stared with lowered brow at Morgan, chewing a chip menacingly at him.

Morgan swallowed hard, "I mean, I need to start to get a better jump on things that might be coming our way, right? If I'm going to find out later when we meet your mom, shouldn't I get any shock out of the way now?"

She sighed and lay back on the grass. "Yeah, you're probably right. Ugh, let me see." She covered her eyes from the sun,

"Where to begin, where to begin?"

Morgan crumpled the paper wrapping and the remaining chips loudly. "Why don't we start at the beginning. Why is visiting your mom such a big deal that Alice made you promise? Couldn't you give her a call?"

Hemlock uncovered her face and closed her eyes. "Can't, phones don't reach the Sidhe from here."

"She? No, just your mom." He drank from a bottle of water.

"No, Sidhe, spelled S-I-D-H-E, pronounced like she with like a sort of inflection though. It's a different realm where the various fae come from. Elves, Brownies, etc. My mother is Queen Fand of the Shadow Court."

Morgan choked and blew water through his nose. "You didn't say you were royalty!"

Hemlock sighed, "And this is why I didn't start off with that when we met. The short story is mom is Queen of the Shadow Court, dad was a human. They had a bit of an affair, and I was born. I split time between dad and mom until an unfortunate incident when I was thirteen. Then I ended up being raised with dad full time. He died last year and I took over the detective agency from him."

Morgan kept trying to wipe the water off his jacket and pants. "How old are you?"

"A gentleman never asks and a lady never tells." Hemlock sat up on her elbows and winked at him. "Twenty-three Burns, only a year or so older than you."

"Ah." Morgan nodded, "Then why do you sound like you've had a smoking habit for about five decades?"

"Cursed, also when I was thirteen."

Morgan cocked an eyebrow. "What happened when you were thirteen?"

"Well, children coming from affairs with humans are pretty common in the Sidhe, so they aren't regarded as bastards like in human nobility. So, when I was spending time with mom, Queen Fand, I was being trained in matters of court. When I was with dad for visits, he'd take me along on cases he was working. He also tried to break out some of those stiffer attitudes the court creates and was a bit of a joker."

Hemlock chuckled, staring off at the clouds for a moment. "I made a bad decision to play a prank on someone at court. Tricksters aren't uncommon in the Sidhe, so I thought it would be laughed off. I mean, some stuff Pan got up to was way worse. Apparently I played it on the wrong person, it had some lasting effects. He wanted me executed by the Shadow Court. Restitution was reached, but part of it was I'd be cursed with the voice and banished from the Sidhe for thirteen years."

"That seems a bit much for a prank."

"Well, I tricked a noble from the Summer Court into falling in love with a pine tree."

Morgan's brows shot up. "You did what?"

"So there are a number of courts in Sidhe. Summer and Winter are the big ones, they reign over the seasons and are usually at odds, the Shadow Court is kind of like Switzerland. They're neutral and help barter treaties, hear disputes, deal with relations with humans and what not. Anyway, there's this guy in Summer, he never said much at court, so I enchanted a persimmon he was eating. He fell in love with a tree. I didn't know that love enchantments on fruits for Summer were a bit stronger."

"Oh?"

"Yeah, he supposedly still bears the scars from the pine cones. You see, he made quite a strong and physical display of his love for the particular tree, while a party was being held in a courtyard. It was very graphic."

Morgan nodded. "Anything else I should know?"

Hemlock stood up and gathered the trash from her tacos. "Your internship is kind of, um, court ordered."

Morgan followed her to a trash can, "What do you mean?"

She began to walk and waited for him to follow. "Part of my banishment also meant I needed a consort at all times. Not a spouse, but someone to be responsible with me, not for me. My dad generally filled that role, until he died. The court tried to assign one to me, but it typically didn't work out well."

"How so?"

"They kept getting killed. They assigned three separate consorts from the Sidhe. Three!" She turned and held up three fingers. "Three fae that were raised in the courts, so they figured it would be good for me. Maybe help my manners or something. Whatever it was, they'd not listen to me about something on a case or how to act on this side of reality. Next thing I know, they'd end up dead."

"So, why me?"

Hemlock shrugged and started walking again. She found a section of unbroken sidewalk, reached into her pocket and withdrew another stick of chalk. "Honestly, I don't know. I told mom once that I seemed to help dad just because I gave him someone to talk through the tough stuff. Maybe she figured if I had a regular person to do that with, it would be helpful and I'd have an easier time keeping you alive."

"So the bird?"

"The bird was a messenger from Queen Fand that you had been chosen."

Hemlock caught Morgan smirking, "It doesn't mean I have to keep you alive, Burns. Just that I have to start the whole process over again if you die."

He slumped a bit, "Oh. So, where are we off to now boss?"

"We have some time before we need to visit my mom."

"The queen."

"Yes the queen, don't interrupt."

"Sorry."

She finished sketching circles and symbols on the pavement

and stood . "We still have questions and I know a guy that might have some answers. We've got to go visit the Druggist."

Hemlock spat on the circle; the portal opened up and began swirling. "Go on, Burns."

Morgan shuffled to the edge and looked down. Hemlock gave him a shove; he fell through the hole and flew out another side landing painfully on another square of pavement. Hemlock hopped through landing one foot between his legs.

She bent down to help him to his feet. "Seriously Burns, you've got to start getting through the portal without falling every time. It's cheaper than taxis, but we'll have to stop using it if you're going to become a liability."

Morgan peered up and saw a painted wood sign with a winged blue horse. "What are we doing back at the Fifth Horseman?"

Hemlock glanced back at the sign. "We're not here for Yamata or a beer this time. I told you, we need to see the Druggist."

"Druggist?"

Hemlock nodded across the street, Morgan stood. Across the narrow side street, more brick buildings stood, storefronts on the first floor, bay windowed apartments lining block for three stories above the shops. The brick had been painted white, but the side facing the side street had begun to chip and flake with age. Windows jutted out from the face and side of the building and sat encased in decorative trim work painted tan to accent the white brick. The little shop in the first floor had a pair of large plate glass windows etched with logos of pizza peels and the name, "Ma's Pizza".

Morgan grimaced, "So, we meet this druggist at Ma's Pizza?"

"No, he lives above the pizzeria."

"Ah."

Hemlock rolled her eyes at him, "C'mon, let's go see him."

Hemlock strolled swiftly across the road, passing the pizzeria. She skipped up the steps of the stoop next to Ma's Pizza. At the door, she pressed a buzzer on a small box with a speaker. The box clicked, over static a nasal voice spoke, "Yeah?"

"Hey Lenny, it's Hemlock."

The box crackled and the voice repeated, "Yeah, and?"

"Lenny, I got something I need you to look at, can you let us up?"

The speaker was silent for a moment then crackled with static again. "You payin' this time?"

"Yeah, yeah, now can you let me up?"

A buzzer rang out and Hemlock opened the door, holding it for Morgan after she had passed into the entryway. She went up a tiled stairway to Apartment 2B. She knocked. The door opened, but clattered to a stop at a few inches, held from moving further by a security chain. A bulbous eye peered out from under the chain.

The same nasal voice from the speaker downstairs, "I'm serious about the money this time, Hemlock! Cash. Up. Front."

Hemlock leaned back on the wall, peering into the apartment through the gap. "I've got cash on hand for you, Lenny. Besides, you know me, I always pay."

"Not always on time though," the voice whined in a whisper through the door.

"I'll pay upfront this time Lenny. Four hundred work?"

"I'll have to see what you need."

"Then you'll have to let us in. Bartering through closed doors isn't how friends operate, Lenny."

After a few seconds of silence, the door slammed shut and the chain scraped out of the slide. The door kicked open with a man standing in the frame. Time wasn't kind to Lenny, he appeared withered, shrunken in the clothes he wore, a pair of black jeans and a black long-sleeved shirt. A halo of long wiry hair encircled his bald head, book ended at both sides by furry elephantine ears.

He sneered at them from the doorway, then stepped aside. "Come on in, your highness," he said in a mocking tone.

Hemlock padded into the apartment with Morgan's boots clomping heavily behind her. Morgan marveled as he walked in. The apartment opened into a single room with a door on the opposing wall and a window on the adjacent wall to his left. The vibrant green on three of the walls reminded Morgan of fresh spring meadows. The blue on the wall with the window made it feel like he was staring out at the sky. With each step into the room, he felt he was sinking deep in a thick orange shag carpet. Lenny shut and locked the door. He walked to the middle of the room and fell back into the only piece of furniture in the room, a furry purple overstuffed bean bag chair.

"Who's your friend, your highness?"

Hemlock rolled her eyes so fast she worried they'd reach a terminal velocity and be lost to her skull. "Lenny, this is Morgan Burns, my new intern." She nodded back and forth at them both, "Morgan, this is Lenny Dolarhyde, the Druggist.

"Great to meet you Lenny." Morgan reached out to shake his hand, Lenny stared at it vacantly. Morgan slowly pulled his hand back, "Nice place you got here, did you have to kill the muppet yourself or do they export directly from Sesame Street?"

"Easy there, Burns. Lenny needs the comfortable environment and the colors to work his magic."

"What sort of magic is that?"

"It's not really magic, Mr. Burns, I take drugs, professionally." Lenny lay further back into his pile.

"Don't be so modest, Lenny." She strolled over and clapped him on the shoulder. "Tell the kid a bit more about what you can do."

Lenny sighed. "There are a number of substances that interact chemically with the human brain in a variety of ways. Most common drugs like opiates and derivatives cause a serotonin reuptake in the brain, which makes you feel happy and high. Others, like certain doses of DMT, will cause psychedelic hallucinations. Depending on the doses and the current chemistry of your brain"

"I don't get it." Morgan's eyes narrowed at Lenny. "People pay you to take drugs? What do they get out of it?"

Lenny turned up a lip and shrugged his shoulders. "It's different from one person to another and one drug to another. For instance, last time Hemlock turned up, she needed an analysis of what was distilled in some wizard pepper dust. It turned out to be an extreme sleep aid, and she tried to make off without paying me the three fifty she agreed on." Lenny glared over at Hemlock. "This time, we're going to go money up front, all of it, plus what's owed from your last time, before a report."

"Horseshit," Hemlock spat back. "We always have the same arrangement, half up front, half on report."

"No, that's horseshit, Hemlock! Last time you put the half up front, but wanted to watch the results. I let that happen, and woke up with nothing." He stood from the bean bag chair, jabbing a bony finger at Hemlock. "From now on, there's no trust arrangements with you. You pay up front, the full amount, and I'll get the report to you. Which means you'll need to pony up at least fifteen hundred for me to take anything new on from you."

"Fifteen hundred? C'mon Lenny, the bill I skipped on was only six."

Hemlock winced, Lenny sat back into his bean bag chair, it squeaked releasing air. Lenny smiled broadly.

Morgan clunked closer to the pair, "Wait, Hemlock it is true then? You screwed Lenny?"

Hemlock closed her eyes tightly and nodded. "I wasn't proud of doing it, but I needed some extra cash to deal with another part of the case. Can we just go a grand and call it even, Lenny? Six for what I owe and four on this case?"

Lenny crossed his arms and looked at Morgan. "Fifteen is my

offer. The other five is interest, fees, and asshole tax."

Morgan shrugged and grimaced at Hemlock.

Hemlock picked the little baggy of pills from her pocket. She held the half dozen round pills in front of Lenny's face. "Alright, fifteen. Seen these before Lenny?"

Lenny reached out and plucked the bag of pills from Hemlock's hand. He picked one pill out, looking it over close to his bespectacled eyes. "I've heard about them a bit. Friend of a friend that buys. They said some gangs down in Dorchester started pushing it earlier this year. On the street, it's called stolen memories. It's supposed to be a completely immersive hallucination that puts you into a memory you've never had. I haven't had the opportunity or necessity to try it myself yet."

Morgan wagged a finger at the drugs. "Why would someone want to do that though? Wouldn't it be enough to play a video game or watch a movie?"

Lenny chuckled, Hemlock laughed. "I like this one Hemlock, you got a real noob this time around. Kid, how many drug addicts have you known?"

"Well, none really."

"Ever tried anything yourself? Took a hit when someone passed a joint?"

"Well, yeah, couple of times in college."

"Oh," Hemlock put her hands on her hips, "That's a ding on your employability, didn't know you were a stoner Burns."

Lenny rolled his eyes, "Fuck off, your highness, you and I both know you've done some shit way worse than a bit of pot."

"Meh, maybe."

"Kid, the people taking this can't afford a high end gaming console, and they want a better escape than that. It's people with a shitty enough life that they want some escape for it. That or they hate themselves and their situation enough that they need something else."

"Why this though? Why not just some weed or cocaine?"

Lenny shrugged again. "Not sure there. Could be a number of things. Hell, people will take a lot of different things to get high. Coke, opiates, those are only the tip of the iceberg. Think about how meth is made for a minute. Cooks have been known to use antifreeze, anhydrous ammonia, lithium, and a host of other nasty shit in their recipes. Krokodil is another nasty one, it's based on a synthetic opiate. The homemade stuff the Russians came up with can cause the flesh to rot off your body. And jenkem? That shit is just plain disgusting."

"Is this stuff cheap? The stolen memories?"

"Last I'd heard, this stuff sold low, if a couple of guys I talked to were right, then this baggy here would run about two hundred. Makes it about twenty a hit. How much did you pay for this?"

"Fat load of nothing," Hemlock replied.

"Where'd it come from then?"

"Murder scene," Morgan answered before Hemlock could cut in. "We pulled it from a home of a man that may be a serial killer."

"Well, isn't that special," Lenny said wide-eyed. "Hemlock, who's your client on this one?"

"You know I can't talk about that Lenny. No more than I'd expect you to be telling people our business together."

"Shit, you're in bed with the mob again, aren't you?"

Hemlock pointed down at Lenny, "This isn't like last time, I'm being careful and it's no concern of yours, thank you very much."

Lenny held up a hand to waive her down. "Fine, my fifteen up front, and your business is your business. I'll get a report to you later tonight if this is a rush job. Two things though, don't use my name in anything you give back to your client. I don't need Bobbi Cotter's gang knocking down my door."

"Sure, and the other thing?"

"Tell me about this murder scene. I want to be sure of what I am dealing with here."

Hemlock recounted what they had found at Jesse and David Steven's house, why they were there and the difference in trophies.

"So, you think that these pills may actually be someone's distilled and reproduced memories? And they drove Jesse to go kill someone in the same manner as his geriatric father? Cool."

Morgan raised an eyebrow. "You aren't concerned about that? Potentially seeing a murder? Possibly being driven to do it yourself from the borrowed memory?"

"Kid, I've seen some fucked up shit on drugs. I have clients that need me to deliver messages to various inter dimensional beings. The only way to contact them is via a drug or cocktail to stimulate the neural cortex just right. And some of those beings are way worse than anything I've ever seen on this plane of existence. I've taken drugs to drag testimony back from the heart of a demon. But at least now I know to use a muscle relaxer with this to make sure I don't go sleepwalking with it."

Hemlock pulled a bundle of cash from a hidden pocket in her jacket. She counted out fifteen bills and handed them down to Lenny. "Any chance we can get a report tonight? Oral account while it's all fresh and I'll get your paper copy dropped off at the house later?"

Lenny stood and walked Hemlock and Morgan to the door. "Probably. Not sure how long I'll be down, but how about we meet over at the Fifth Horseman around say, two in the morning? That gives me a good 8 hours to get through it all."

Hemlock and Morgan made it to the hallway. She turned around but before she could mutter her thanks, Lenny had slammed the door, the deadbolt snapping like a gunshot.

# OH, HI MOM

**M**organ followed Hemlock out of the building, his boots clunking behind her soft footfalls. She led him past Ma's Pizza and around the corner on the side street across from the Fifth Horseman. Hemlock found the same spot they'd ended up when teleporting from the park and taco truck. She began to draw another portal spell.

"So where are we off to now?"

Hemlock didn't look up, continuing to sketch out the circles and symbols, glancing out to check her directions. "Well, it's almost dusk. So, it's time to pay the piper and go visit my Mom."

"You act like chatting with your mom is such a horrible thing to do, at least you still have one parent to visit."

Hemlock stood and punched Morgan in the arm.

"Ow! What was that for?"

"Just because I have a mother and bitch about her doesn't mean I'm taking her for granted. There's a difference here, Burns."

"What's that supposed to mean?" Morgan rubbed his arm absentmindedly.

Hemlock closed her eyes and sighed. "You were raised by human parents, right? You weren't putting me on about anything? Plain old mom and dad?"

"Like I said, Hemlock. Dad was an accountant, and my mom was a diabetic that died of cancer when I was younger. As far as I know, nothing special about them other than their innate abilities to die young."

"Right." She went back to the chalk circles and symbols,

studying to see if she had put them down correctly. "Look, I'm not trying to negate the fact that having parents is a great thing. My dad was loving and one of the best people I'd ever known. I mean he may have trapped the vengeful spirit of a yokai into my Curious George doll, but we were in a tight spot, and he had no other choice. But my father was human."

Morgan sat on the curb nearby, leaning forward on his knees. "And your mom wasn't human? What's different about that? You said she was the Queen of the Shadow Court or something of the Sidhe, but what does that mean? Pointy ears?"

"Goddamn it Burns, do I have pointy ears?"

"No."

"Shit, actually mom does have pointy ears."

Morgan turned his head laying on his arms, so she could see him smiling.

"Don't be a dick, Burns."

Morgan chuckled and turned away.

"The Sidhe are different. Not quite human in the way they love their children, but still similar. They're more like a middle ground between humans and animals. There are very strong ties, but also a sense of raising you to be an incredibly independent person. Being raised in court and the royal families makes it an even worse experience. It's intense."

Hemlock stood and nudged Morgan with a foot. She nodded her head to the circle. Morgan got up and turned as Hemlock spit into the center of the chalk spellbinding. The outlines swirled around to the spinning portal that Morgan was starting to get used to gazing into.

"How long does it take to get used to this?"

"Hopping in and out of the portals? Few times and you should be a pro." Hemlock flashed him a Cheshire grin.

Morgan thrust his chin forward staring down into the churning hole. "I mean, at what point will I be able to go through it and still be standing like you do? Not falling over or rolling into a shrub?"

"Depends on the person." She hopped forward and dropped through the portal ahead of Morgan.

He looked down at it, lip curled up in a queasy expression, his color draining from his face. "Ugh, maybe if I lean down."

Morgan bent his knees. He shut his eyes and put his hands together, arching his arms outward. He made a couple of practice diving motions. When he was about to make his move and dive into the portal, Hemlock's arms reached back through the portal. Her hands grasped firmly on his wrists and yanked him from his stance, pulling Morgan through the portal.

When he stopped screaming, Morgan realized he was laying down, curled in a ball on something soft. He unclenched his fists and felt around, his hands were greeted with soft grass and loose soil. He stood, brushing off his pants. Hemlock leaned against a tree nearby, laughing at him. Morgan heard more chuckling and turned to a small group of children on a nearby sidewalk laughing from their bikes.

Morgan tightened his lips and glared at Hemlock. "Is this going to happen every time?"

She shrugged, "Eventually, you'll get the hang of it."

Morgan and Hemlock were standing in a small patch of grass. One side surrounded by a semi-circle of trees, the other leading to a narrow lane road with some small houses. The roar of traffic began to drown out the laughing as the kids rode off.

"Where are we?"

"On a verge near Fellsway. Somerville area of Boston, kind of northwest of where we were by some miles. On the other side of the trees is a highway and a bridge over the Mystic River. This is one of the few access points Sidhe nobility are safe enough to crossover from their realm to this one."

Morgan turned to the north, "Over Mystic River?"

Hemlock nodded.

"Bit on the nose, isn't it? A little too obvious to be worthy of a safe passage."

Hemlock shrugged, "You would expect, but they like that kind of thing. They find it funny. Plus passing over running water does wash away a lot of spells and enchantments. The river is called such for a number of reasons. It was one of the first entry points found and utilized for the Sidhe in America when European settlers came over. The river has been itself subject of heavy enchantment on both sides since to guarantee safe passage along its roads and bridges."

"Why isn't that more common knowledge?"

"It is, if you know how to parse it."

Morgan scratched his head and swatted absently at a mosquito. "What do you mean?"

Hemlock flashed her Cheshire grin. "They were called fairy tales for a reason, though this one was more a nursery rhyme or poem. Ever hear that one, 'over the river and through the woods'?"

Morgan nodded.

"Get the gears to click Burns. Some of it's metaphors, some isn't."

He glanced around, he pointed towards the river to the north of him. "Over the river means over the Mystic River? And through the woods was because that used to be woods over on that side before it was developed?"

"Kind of, but if you pass over the river in to Sidhe, there's still woods there. What else?"

"That's not grandmother's house over there, is it?"

Hemlock shook her head. "Not by a long shot, the house was the metaphor. Grandmother or grandfather's house in this case means the Shadow Court of the Sidhe. You ride over that bridge knowing your way, and you'll pass directly into their kingdom.

The castle that keeps the peace between the other courts and realms of Sidhe."

Morgan pointed a finger out across the lawn to the trees. "So if I go over that bridge, I'll end up in another world?"

Hemlock raised her eyebrows. "You wouldn't. Myself, I used to be able to come and go at will, but not since my banishment."

Morgan dropped his hand to his side. "Who else can then?"

Hemlock shrugged one shoulder. "Loads of folks that know how to summon the path. Lots of witches, wizards and warlocks know how to summon it. Any changeling or half-fae being can do it by nature as well. You probably can't because you're a normal mortal and haven't taken up any magical training yet."

"So I take up some training, learn a few little tricks and I can start adventuring through the lands of the Sidhe?"

Hemlock sat down laughing. "Sure, you can just start roaming the lands of the Sidhe! You must want to die a violent bloody death."

"Explain it to me then, why would I die a violent bloody death?"

Hemlock stopped laughing and sat cross-legged on the grass. She patted the ground in front of her. Morgan sat on the dry grass across from her, unable to easily cross his legs in the stiff jeans and boots. Hemlock scanned the skyline. "Looks like we've got a few minutes, she'll be crossing over with her riders at dusk."

"How do you even know that?"

"It's how the Queen, ugh mom, operates. When Alice said I needed to visit mom, this is generally what happens. She will cross over the Mystic at dusk with her riders and look for me here. Since I can't go back over while I'm in exile, this has become our de facto meeting point. Once she has the word out that I need to visit her, then she'll start looking for me here."

"What if you don't show up?"

"Then her little messengers will start showing up with more intensity and aggravation. This time I kind of lucked out with needing something from Alice. If I didn't, pixies, brownies, all the little critters that come over randomly from the Sidhe would start haunting me to get that promise. They start out with offers to be helpful and it most often degrades to them getting nasty."

"How bad can they get?" Morgan rested on his elbows, leaning back.

"I have a car, it used to run fine."

Morgan cocked an eyebrow and turned his head to her.

"They ate the pistons."

"Just the pistons? Not the whole engine block?"

Hemlock sighed and looked to the sky. "They thought it was a subtle hint."

"Hmm." Morgan nodded and furrowed his brow. "Subtle, I guess."

"I only wish I wasn't driving it when they did that."

"Maybe a little less subtle."

"Anyway, if you aren't at least part Sidhe yourself then you have to be welcomed to the realm by at least one being. Without a guide or sponsor in, you're fair game for anyone to hunt or enslave. They don't exactly honor your American citizenship there."

"You say beings, what all is over there?"

"You think about it from any old myth or legend, Shakespeare, fairy tales, whatever, it has some root of truth with the Sidhe."

"So orcs, goblins, dwarves, elves?"

"Yep, all your old school Tolkien oddities."

"Giant eagles and tree ents?"

"Giant all kinds of things, and they all love to have some fresh human to eat or enslave."

"OK, not the place to be a mall rat."

"Nope, if I ever get past this exile, I'll have to take you over. It is fantastic when you have a good guide. There's this place outside of the castle, it's not a pub but not someone's house. They have the best brown meat stew."

Morgan narrowed his gaze at Hemlock, "What kind of meat is in brown meat stew?"

"It's best not to think about it. Just eat it and enjoy the flavors."

Hemlock turned her head westward to the shrinking sun.

"Is it some kind of magic? That Fand crosses over at dusk? Like she's tethered over to the Sidhe until night descends on our world?"

"No," Hemlock chuckled. "She's pretentious and likes to show off. Hell, for all I know she could've been that bird that pooped on my shoulder the other day when we first met."

With the closing daylight came decibel rending roars of motorcycle engines. Hemlock rolled her eyes, Morgan turned suddenly to the road, plugging his ears and searching for the source of the echoing cacophony.

Three motorcycles pulled around the bend from the bridge, engines revving as they all jumped the curb to land in the grass near Hemlock and Morgan. Two riders stayed mounted, they both rode matte black bikes and wore all black leathers with black helmets and visors. The middle rider wore tighter gray leathers and a green helmet. She sat on a motorcycle that matched the style of the other two, but the paint was a luminescent dark green to match her helmet. She cut the engine and made a fist with her right hand, apparently signaling the other riders to cut their engines too.

The woman pulled off her helmet, revealing a face that looked similar to Hemlock's and a similar pixie cut with a left side shaved down close to the scalp. Her rosy cheeks swept down to a sharp chin, met by an equally dagger-like nose. Her ears came to actual points behind the short crops of hair, each arrayed with a series of piercings and finely woven chains. Morgan ogled her, "Hemlock, if I didn't know any better, I'd think she was your sister."

"Yeah," Hemlock croaked, "Like looking at my twin isn't it?"

"Not as much a twin," Morgan continued staring as the female rider dismounted the motorcycle. "She's a bit taller and a bit more, um, developed. More like your hotter older sister?"

Hemlock punched him in the arm. "Stop getting horned up, Burns. That is my mother. Imagine if that were your mom."

The pair of riders in black dismounted and followed behind their Queen.

"Hemlock, how lovely to see you tonight," she spoke in a honeyed tone that sang across the evening breeze and warmed the soul like a raging fire.

"Yeah, hi Mom," rasped Hemlock in a gravel-laden voice that could drag the brain through sand-paper. It was a voice that could leave a soul feeling frozen and choked like a harsh winter wind. Queen Fand flinched at the sound of Hemlock's voice.

"Oh sweetie, I can't wait for your beautiful voice to return. It is still just so out of place for you to sound like an ogre with a three pack a day habit every time you open your mouth."

Hemlock sneered. "It's not like I had much choice in my punishments, and you didn't defend me much at the trials."

Fand swayed a hip and slung her hand on it. "Little Lockley, you enchanted an Earl of the Seelie Court to fall in love with a pine tree."

Hemlock chuckled. She leaned an arm onto her mom, "That was funny wasn't it?"

"For the first five minutes when the Earl was trying to dance and court the tree."

"Seelie Court?" asked Morgan.

"That's what the Sidhe call the Summer Court," Hemlock

barked back at Morgan. "Try to keep up here, Burns. Don't embarrass us."

Fand gently removed her daughter's hand from her shoulder. Hemlock crossed her arms, "I remember you still laughing with the courts as he stripped naked."

The Queen scowled. "I'm sure you recall how nobody was smiling when the Earl began cramming pine cones up his rectum."

Hemlock turned back to Morgan. His brows steepled with concern and eyes bulged in wonder. "Yeah, I remember. He managed to pop seven up there while the guards chased him to make him stop."

Morgan spoke weakly. "Were they able to remove them? Painlessly?"

Queen Fand turned her head sideways, a gesture reminiscent of a snowy owl. "What a curious question. Hemlock, who is your curious little friend?"

"Mom, this is Morgan Burns," Hemlock gestured between Morgan and Fand. "Burns, this is my mother. Queen Fand, ruler and leader of the Shadow Court of the Sidhe, Broker of Peace between the Dozen Beings, I think I'm missing some titles. Wasn't Destroyer of Nachos in there?"

Fand smiled broadly, a Cheshire grin that matched Hemlock's. "No sweetie, Destroyer of Nachos was never one of my titles, that was yours."

Hemlock nodded. "Yeah, right. Anyway, Burnsy over here is my new intern or consort I guess."

Fand's smile went flat, and she cocked a pencil thin ginger eyebrow. "Oh, is he now? You're sure you don't want another of the Sidhe? I'm sure we can find someone from Summer or Winter that you haven't scared off yet."

Hemlock turned her head and squinted at Fand. "Funny, Burns turned up on my doorstep answering an ad for an internship I never posted. I figured that was maybe some of your doing."

Morgan ignored Hemlock and Fand, but took an interest in the riders in black still on their motorcycles behind their Queen.

"I don't know what you're talking about, Hemlock. Would it seem like I honestly have the time? When these sound like such extreme measures to go meddling in something that you're supposed to take care of on your own?"

Hemlock crossed her arms and sighed. "Then there was the bird."

Queen Fand scowled at her daughter. "Bird? What bird?"

Hemlock shifted her weight to her hip. "Right when I was trying to turn away Burns here, a damned seagull came swooping down and landed on my shoulder."

"Oh, there you go," Fand countered wagging a finger. "I haven't shifted to a gull in decades. That would be a bit too obvious. Why would you even have suspected me?"

"Because the bird shit on my shoulder before it took off."

Fand began chuckling, then doubled over in laughter. "Your proof is that the bird pooped on you?"

Hemlock shut her eyes and took a deep breath while her mother continued laughing. When she opened them, she caught sight of Morgan slowly approaching the riders.

"Something got your goat, Burns?"

Morgan stood next to one of the bikes with its rider. "Hemlock, do you see what they're riding?"

Hemlock rolled her eyes, "Knowing my mom, she's probably got her riders on some sort of high end weird ass bike."

Morgan nodded at the bike and called back, "These are classic mid 40s Indians! I didn't even think you could get parts for these anymore."

Morgan turned away from the mother and daughter and faced the rider. "These are stunning bikes, I always wondered, are the suspensions very rough?"

"They won't answer you, Burns," Hemlock shouted back at him. "They aren't really alive."

Morgan had turned back to hear Hemlock. "That's silly, Boss. How could they be dead and sitting here on these beautiful bikes?"

As soon as the words had left his mouth, Morgan turned back to the rider. His visor flipped up suddenly, revealing a bleached skull, two fiery dots of opalescent green flame lit deep in the eye sockets. Morgan stumbled back and tripped backwards over a tuft of weeds.

"What?" Morgan turned his head back and forth between Hemlock and the pair of riders. "Why?"

Fand leaned close to Hemlock, "You didn't tell him about the Riders?"

"A bit, but not much really," Hemlock whispered back. "Sometimes half the fun is watching him freak out." They both giggled like schoolgirls.

"What's so funny?"

Fand waived to her riders, and they gave a single-fisted salute. "Master Burns, please meet a pair of my personal guard that shepherd me wherever I go. These fine men, and some finer women, belong to the Riders of Danann."

Hemlock helped Morgan to his feet. He joked as she pulled him up, "What's the interview process like for that job?"

"Remember that little thing I said about mortals trading a lot of things with dark ones and powerful beings? So they can acquire more potency and abilities?"

Morgan nodded silently.

"Mom over there is one of those."

Morgan looked over Hemlock's shoulder, Fand gave a broad grin and a dainty long fingered wave to him. "Is she a dark one?"

Fand chuckled again, Hemlock whispered, "Powerful. Mighty enough that desperate witches and wizards would pray to and summon her. If she liked them enough, the price was to serve as a Rider of Danann, protect and serve her majesty, Queen Fand, without question, immediately following their death."

Morgan's eyes popped with surprise. "How long do they serve?"

"Typical term is about a hundred years. Which is pretty reasonable considering practicing witches and wizards can extend their own lifetimes well into four or five centuries. There was even one rider, he lived as a talented sorcerer for centuries. Then traded even more time as a rider for more time alive. When he finally did die, at the hands and pitchforks of a local village, he'd wracked up a term of two hundred and forty-six years in the Riders."

"Holy shitballs, was the guy's name Rasputin?"

Hemlock shook her head, "No, it was Bob"

Morgan chuckled, "Bob? Just ... Bob?"

Hemlock nodded and Fand appeared behind her, rested her head on her daughter's shoulder. "Oh Bob! Now he is a blast, everyone always loves Bob. He knows how to liven up a party!"

Hemlock shifted a hand to her hip, "Yeah, about Bob. Bob gave me the idea for that love spell. That one with the Earl and the pine cones. The one that got me banished for thirteen years!"

Fand smiled sweet as a milkshake and eyes twice as thick, "Like I said, Bob knows how to party, too bad his term is up in a decade."

"I thought you said they couldn't talk?" Morgan called over, studying the skeletal riders more carefully.

"Not so much speak with vocal cords," Fand answered rolling her eyes, "It's more telepathic or possession. They keep a lot of their magical abilities they had in life. Like Bob, he does this great trick, but he has to have a watermelon and a grapefruit. Don't ask why, but a cantaloupe will not work."

Hemlock sighed. "Instead of debating the past, mom, can you

tell us why Alice said I had to meet you tonight?"

"All business and no pleasure with you, Lockley."

Hemlock crossed her arms and fluttered her eyelashes at her mother. "Yes, it's not like I'm doing anything right now. Burns and I are trying to figure out who's stealing people's memories to distill into a narcotic that's being used in a small turf war with the Irish mob in Boston. Multiple people have died so far, a lot of innocents because someone stole and distilled the memories of an uncaught serial killer. But, no, idle chit chat about my banishment and Bob take precedence."

Fand cocked an eyebrow and tilted her head. "How much of the memories are getting stolen?"

"About everything. They're left with mechanical abilities like using the bathroom and walking. They can remember eating but can't remember how to make food." Hemlock narrowed her gaze on her mother's eyes. "Why is that of interest though?"

Fand frowned and shrugged her shoulders, avoiding Hemlock's glare.

"Mother, what aren't you telling me? Or would the better question be, what did you want to tell me? Are they the same thing now?"

Fand crossed her arms and glared at Hemlock, one eyebrow cocked. "Can't a mother just want to spend some time with her only daughter? Must I have a hidden agenda?"

From behind her, the two riders revved their engines, loudly chopping the silence of the night.

Queen Fand rolled her eyes. "They are too good at serving the good of the court over the will of the Queen." She sighed deeply. "Alright, there's been some oddness in the Sidhe. Specifically in the Forest."

Hemlock pinched the bridge of her nose. "Please tell me it was in the forest of rainbows and unicorns,"

"No, everything is fine there, I'm sorry to say it's the other one."

Hemlock sighed. "Dammit Mom, really?"

Burns held up a hand, "Um, excuse me, but what's the other forest? Enchanted bunnies?"

"No, Burns," She croaked. "It's the Forest of Decay and Nightmares."

Morgan threw his hands up, "Well that sounds lovely! I imagine the tourist board there must have an easy time marketing vacations."

Hemlock gave Morgan a slow smile. "Don't be so melodramatic Burns. What's wrong with the Forest of Decay and Nightmares, your highness?" Hemlock bent and gave a mock curtsy.

Fand avoided meeting her daughter's eyes, instead she examined her fingernails. "Well, lately it's been more the Forest of Decay, less of Nightmares."

"How many have gone?"

Fand mocked counting fingers on each hand. "Only about, a couple hundred."

Hemlock's eyes went wide, and she tilted her head. "A couple hundred is most of their population in the forest. Where have they gone, mother?"

"The nightmares are what I wanted to discuss. Someone or something has been luring them out of the forest, out of the Sidhe altogether. I've had the Riders head out to Summer and Winter, along with the Badlands and all the other territories. They aren't around. The only lead we had was one person witnessed something but it doesn't sound right."

"Who was it? What did they see?"

Fand sighed. "A dryad of the forest, Sarcomon."

"Sarcomon? The Sarcomon?"

Morgan cut in, "Who's Sarcomon?"

"He's not just any dryad. Sarcomon is their high priest and king. What did he see?"

Fand sighed. "He saw a child."

# HE'S KILLED
# OVER LESS...

Close to midnight, down the block from the Fifth Horseman, the full moon shone down. Broken light filtered onto the street around trees and the brick buildings. A thin figure loped on four paws through the night. The wane outline of a hound paused briefly at each tree and hydrant to sniff the other dogs that had marked their territory in the day prior. He was a large dog, similar to a shepherd, but taller. He stopped at a hydrant close to the entrance of the Fifth Horseman. After a long sniffing, decided this was the one he'd been waiting for and lifted a leg. He let loose a long and full-bladdered stream.

Coincidentally, it was at that moment the pavement next to the dog shifted in color and a swirling portal silently formed. The dog sniffed the air, noting a change, but still letting loose a torrential stream. The form of Morgan Burns suddenly flew out of the portal. His legs were moving, trying to catch a landing he was entirely unsure would exist. The unfortunate result of which being when Morgan's Boot clipped the top of the fire hydrant. He tumbled onto the great brindled hound, who hadn't stopped urinating.

Hemlock hopped lightly out of the portal. She turned swiftly to the yelping of the scared dog. He ran off, leaving a long, wet trail of urine in his wake. Morgan sprang up panting from his crumpled heap on the pavement, he darted his head left and right. "What the hell happened?"

The portal closed between them with a soft pop. Hemlock

walked closer to Morgan, she glanced up and down from his face to the darkened splotches on his pants. "I think you hopped out of the portal, straight onto a pissing dog."

Morgan continued panting. "Yes, I figured that out. Why?" He pointed staggering at the dog running off and back to his pants. "That can really happen? Just hop out of a portal? Right into the path of flying urine?"

"Look Morgan, it's magic. It's not safe. Just because you appear suddenly somewhere doesn't mean that everything ceases happening. I've popped out of portals into the path of a bike messenger once, bastard nearly killed me. You learn how to stick the landing and you'll be less likely to get pissed on."

Morgan tried to brush off his clothes. He gawked at Hemlock, slack jawed. "So this sort of thing will continue to happen to me?"

Hemlock curled a lip in a half sneer and shrugged.

"Can't we take a cab or an Uber?"

"You got money and time to be taking taxis everywhere? With the case we're on, we could be dealing with more deaths every day, hell, every hour that we spend wandering about. Do you want that on your conscience?"

Morgan shook his head, eyes wide. "No, not really, but I'd rather not end up maimed or covered in dog piss either, Hemlock!"

Hemlock shook her head. "Jeez, whine whine whine." She poked a slender finger into Morgan's chest, "If you'd stop whining for a few minutes, you might actually learn about what we're doing."

"I've learned a great deal so far." Morgan started counting on his fingers. "I've learned you have a cabinet of creepy things in your house. You're apparently fairy royalty. You hop in and out of magic portals all about. Pixies are really nasty critters. Oh and let's not forget the new bombshell," his voice raised in pitch and volume, "There's a Forest of Nightmares and Decay! I didn't even know there were things like real nightmares, but they're being brought here en masse by some bratty kid!"

She frowned at him and put her hands to her hips, elbows akimbo. "Burns, you've got to chill out a bit. Stress will be the real killer in this kind of situation."

"Easy for you to say, you've lived with all this! I'm playing catch up here."

They stood on the sidewalk, glaring at each other in the crisp night with the sounds of traffic and patrons of the Fifth Horseman filling the quiet.

"If events are so dire and pressing, what are we doing back at the Horseman, Hemlock?"

"We're going to go get a drink, and figure out our next steps while we wait on Lenny."

"There's literally nothing else we can do, with nightmares running around wild, but go have a drink?" Morgan pointed to his wet pant leg. "Couldn't we have taken a cab then and avoided the dog pissing on me?"

Hemlock shut her eyes and sighed. She waved her hands at Morgan, "It's the nature of the job, investigation is all hurry up and wait. We hurried up to get back here, now we wait. If we took a cab, I'd have been out probably forty bucks, and we couldn't get a drink while we wait for Lenny to finish his trip. Is it unfortunate that you got pissed on? Sure, but we'll go get a drink, chat about what we learned, and Yamata's got a small library in there. You can grab a reference on nightmares and familiarize yourself. Sound good?"

Morgan took a deep breath. "This will get easier?"

"Eventually." Hemlock nodded to the bar. "Baby steps, c'mon, let's go see Yamata."

Hemlock led Morgan down the steps to the stone wall blocking in the Fifth Horseman. They took turns paying the cover charge, each depositing a token few drops of blood in the iron goblet.

The wall parted when the cover was paid. Hemlock and Morgan walked into a raucous room with a sea of people crowding around tables and the bar. All around the bar, they were talking loudly and laughing at stories. A man with dreadlocks and a scraggly beard sat on a stool at the far corner next to the back wall with the shelf of tiny houses. He wore a knit parka and beanie; he was playing a set of pan-pipes with horned beings the size of Alice dancing around him. A guitar and mic sat nearby him, but they weren't plugged into any outlets.

"Ah, shit, Jayne's here tonight." Hemlock sighed. "I hate that guy, he's such an ass."

Morgan squinted across at the corner. "The guy with the pan-pipes? What's so bad about him?"

Hemlock turned to face Morgan, bug-eyed and smile so forced it was dangerously close to pulling muscles.

Morgan quirked an eyebrow at her, "Please don't smile like that, it scares me."

Hemlock nodded. "Which is what it feels like. You'll start a normal conversation with him, then you'll realize what he's saying is so inane and self-absorbed you'll be making that face to try to get away. There's a reason he's playing those pipes with the dancing demons on his own. They are the only damned things in this whole bar that want anything to do with him anymore."

"Does Yamata hire him to play live music or something? It looks like he's got a mic and a guitar with a pickup."

Hemlock sighed and shook her head. "No, he brings that shit with him and has it enchanted, it doesn't need power. Yamata kind of tolerates him and the singing out of pity. It's pretty crappy music. Like he tried to play a cover of Brown-Eyed Girl, but he forgot the lyrics. So he ended up mumbling through it. If he's playing the pan-pipes for the demons though, then he's wrapping up his little 'set'." Hemlock raised her hands to gesture air quotes for the set. "Thank the gods we missed it."

Morgan craned his neck, gawking awkwardly around the

crowd. "Yeah, I'd be leery of a guy who spends his time in a corner making tiny demons dance around. Any reason he's so strange?"

Hemlock leaned close to Morgan. "Half-breed, like me," she whispered.

"Guessing not with someone from the Sidhe?"

She shook her head. "Nah, there was a kerfuffle around him and his mother. She was a witch with one of the covens, out in Waltham. His mother didn't just make any deal with some rando dark lord to gain power. She supposedly fell in love and made him with a nasty one from one of the demon dimensions."

Morgan's eyebrows rose a notch. "One of the demon dimensions? Multiple? Is that how you have multiple devils and whatnot?"

"Oh yeah, loads of them. Why do you think there are so many demonic names and horror stories around. Lucifer, Beelzebub, Crowley, Azazel, I could keep going, but yeah, at least eight distinct demon dimensions, maybe more. Anyway, his mom got in and cozy with one of the big boys there, got knocked up, had Jayne over there."

"So halflings from the Sidhe is common, but not demon-spawn?"

"No, it's mostly," Hemlock slapped her hands together strangely with limp wrists, "Incompatible parts, if you catch my drift."

Morgan nodded with pursed lips. "Love can find a way, I suppose."

"Rumors are the other covens bound together and had her killed when he was about eleven. He used to have a tail, but word on the street is Jayne lobbed it off himself when he was about eight or nine to stop getting bullied at school."

Morgan raised an eyebrow, still staring across at the dancing demons. "I imagine that makes it easier to sit around playing pan-pipes, not having a tail." Morgan looked back to Hemlock, as she nodded.

"Drinks?" She asked.

"Same as last time?"

"Sure, I'll go hunt up a table. Don't forget to ask Yamata about a reference text for nightmares while you are putting an order in."

"We can't order from the table?"

Hemlock grimaced and sucked in her breath. "Kind of. When the Horseman gets busy like this, then Yamata has a troop of spriggans that work for him. They'll get the liquid for your glass, but they can't carry glasses themselves. You've got to go get glasses and mugs from Yamata, and they do the rest."

Morgan leaned close with a scowl. "Dumb question, but what is a spriggan?"

"It's like a sprite, little winged folk that will flit around. Look closely."

Hemlock pointed to a nearby table. A grizzled man in a Cincinnati Reds cap had an empty glass in front of him. The man raised his hand. Within a few seconds a blur of light flashed up and a small winged figure with gray-green skin appeared. It sniffed the glass; with a wave of its hands the glass began to fill from the bottom up with beer.

"That's quite a trick," Morgan said. He'd turned back to Hemlock, but she had already started crossing the crowded room to find a table. She waved a finger to the bar, and Morgan headed that way.

The actual bar itself was crowded with patrons as well. Most of the people sitting on stools around the taps seemed normal enough. In any other tavern, Morgan would have guessed them to be accountants, construction workers or programmers. Morgan noticed a space between a curly-haired man in a tan sportcoat and a silver maned man in black pants and jacket. He wedged himself in between the two men to try to get Yamata's attention.

Down the bar, Yamata had his hair pulled tight into a long ponytail once more. He lost the chef's jacket, instead wore a black t-shirt and an apron over loose jeans. Morgan caught Yamata's attention with a raised hand, receiving a sharp nod in return.

Morgan looked at the man close to him in black, and started chuckling.

The priest was still wearing his collar, and nursing a drink. He turned to Morgan's chuckling. "Something funny, son?" The air was heavy with the smell of evergreen trees and alcohol when he spoke.

"Sorry, Father." Morgan stopped laughing. "Seems like a bad joke I'd heard. You know, like a wizard, a priest, and an accountant walk into a bar."

The priest leaned back over his drink. "I don't think you'll want to finish that joke in here, boy."

The curly haired man to Morgan's left nodded agreement and took a pull of his beer.

At that fortuitous moment, Yamata walked up. "Same as earlier for Hemlock and you?"

The priest's eyes went agape. He turned his head slowly to Morgan. "You're with Hemlock Connal?"

Morgan turned to look at the priest, wrinkling is forehead. "Is that a problem, Padre?"

Yamata leaned forward on his arms on the bar. "Mr. Burns is Hemlock's new intern."

Both the priest and the man on the other side of Morgan stood from their bar stools. The priest picked up his drink and said, "Norm, I think we can find somewhere else for me to enjoy my gin and tonic." Then they walked off into the crowd, muttering and glaring at Morgan as they went looking for other company.

"What's their problem, Yamata?"

"In time, Hemlock causes a bit of trouble for everyone. You should steer clear of the clergy." Morgan nodded.

"Drinks though?"

"Yeah, same as before," Morgan said and Yamata was getting glasses from behind the bar. "Oh, and Hemlock said you had some reference books. Do you have any guides or books on nightmares?"

Yamata gave a sharp nod and held up a finger. He walked out of sight to a back room and came back a short moment later.

"That was quick," quipped Morgan.

Next to the glasses, Yamata set down a half-inch thick paperback volume. It was small, about as big as a postcard and depicted a black and white sketch of a crazed horse with red eyes. Morgan read the title aloud, "Nightmares in a Nutshell, part of the O'Mally Press Menagerie." He squinted back at Yamata. "Are you serious?"

"Hai!"

"Do they have many of these?"

"Hai!"

"Should I be only slightly scared or completely terrified?"

"Hai!"

"Good talking to you Yamata, it's been illuminating," Morgan said.

He tucked the book under his arm and picked up the glasses. He wove his way through the crowded bar to find Hemlock seated at a small table with four chairs near the back of the bar. Jayne had spun a chair around backwards and straddled it. Hemlock was resting her hand on her fist, staring at a point on the wall above Jayne.

"Excuse me," Morgan said as he sat the glasses down. "I believe you're in my seat."

Jayne pointed to the empty chairs opposite him. "Plenty of room, friend."

"You don't seem to understand me. I'd heard you lost a tail once. I don't think you'll pick up any new tail from my employer if that's blunt enough for you." Morgan leaned against the table staring down at Jayne.

Hemlock stifled a laugh, Jayne chuckled sarcastically. "You must be the intern I heard about. I was just telling Hemlock that if she needed an assistant she should've called me up. No one with more experience in the greater Boston metro."

Morgan scoffed, "Experience with what? Twiddling your little bone flute for your demons?"

Hemlock laughed heartily, laying her head on the table.

Jayne stood, poking a finger into Morgan's chest. "Real mature, noob." He turned to Hemlock again. "I'll see you at Julia and Eduardo's party Friday. Maybe by then, you'll have dropped the clown."

Morgan turned the chair back around while Jayne walked away. "Very alpha male of you Morgan," said Hemlock

He shrugged as he sat. "It looked like you had probably already told him to buzz off, but it didn't take."

Hemlock raised a hand. A ball of light floated gently above the table a second later. A small spriggan with skin the color of an artichoke fluttered above the empty glasses. It blinked two sets of lids over its black eyes.

"Whiskey for me, Lager for him," Hemlock said to the spriggan. It filled the glasses and vanished.

"Still," Hemlock continued lifting her glass, "You pissed him off, he'll be looking to repay that to us sometime."

Morgan lifted his own glass. "Some bridges are worth burning so you don't have to cross them."

"You should get pissed on more often, Burns. It's brought out some spirit in you."

Morgan didn't respond, he took a long pull of the lager. He sat back and picked up the book. He began thumbing through the chapters.

"Nightmares in history, nightmares as people, nightmares as animals, nightmares as transcendental enlightenment. I'm noticing a theme."

Hemlock sipped her whiskey and nodded.

"Relative Interconnectivity and Absolute Interconnectivity across normalized nightmare cluster patterns." He set the book down and sat back. "This damn thing reads like a programming manual. What the hell does all this even mean?"

Hemlock swirled the brown liquor in her glass. "Humanity has had a complicated relationship with nightmares over the centuries. They can have a kind of symbiotic link with people. They're also more of a colony with a hive mind, but no ruling queen or king. The cluster in the Forest was one of the last known big groups. They'd been hunted to near extinction."

"So they're a protected species?"

"Yep, a highly dangerous endangered species."

Morgan nodded and sucked in a breath. "Your family are like fairy zookeepers to an endangered mythical species"

Hemlock scrunched her nose. "We try to keep them in the Forest, but I wouldn't say we're zookeepers per se. Zoo keeping supposes you are trying to display them. That area of woodlands was set aside specifically for... containment."

"So they aren't supposed to get out?"

Hemlock took a sip, and shook her head.

Morgan picked up his glass to take another drink, but stopped. "Hey, did anybody in your family or the royal court ever study them?" Morgan tapped the cover of Nightmares in a Nutshell.

She rolled her eyes and grimaced. "There was the Grand Duke of Knutley. He took an interest in them when he was younger and would take at least weekly excursions into the forest. He seemed to understand them at a level on which the rest of us couldn't comprehend."

"Is he still around?"

"No, he ended up taking his own life. At least we think he did."

"Mysterious death?"

"In a sense, he died of cheese."

"Cheese?"

"Yeah, he had an allergy to most dairy products. One of his servants found him dead next to a massive wheel of extra sharp cheddar. It appeared that he ate a few pounds off it."

Morgan took a sip from his beer. "How old was the Grand Duke?"

"That was why we wondered of a suicide, he was in his late two sixties."

Morgan stared into his beer. "That would be suspicious indeed."

An empty chair squeaked against the floor. Morgan looked up, Lenny sat down, one leg shaking against the table and beady eyed.

Hemlock checked a non-existent watch on her wrist, staring at the bare skin she grimaced. "Lenny! It's only midnight, we didn't expect you til two. What's up?"

Lenny stared at the table unblinking, leg twitching. He reached over and grabbed Hemlock's glass from her hand, throwing back the half glass of whiskey in one swallow. He raised a shaky hand.

In a puff of smoke a spriggan waiter appeared. He hovered near the glass and sniffed. It waved a grayish hand and started to pour whiskey back into the glass.

When he slowed pouring, Lenny said without looking up to the little sprite, "Make it a double." It kept pouring to a full glass, then puffed out of local existence.

Lenny drank the full glass without stopping. He slammed

the glass down and took a deep breath. "That was some fucked up shit you gave me, Lockley. I have seen hobbits come down from spacecraft asking me to join them in the twelfth dimension to repopulate the planet Corlonia. I have had conversations with demons from more than just the eight demonic dimensions. But I never want to see *that* crap fest again."

Morgan frowned, "There's more than eight demon dimensions?"

Hemlock whistled to get their attention, "Focus up here, wrong detail sport. What's got you so spooked Lenny?"

Lenny's leg kept trembling, and he shifted his gaze from the glass to stare Hemlock directly in the eyes. "It wasn't an out-of-body kind of experience, Hemlock. It was a complete fucking in body experience. I felt everything, the way the guy wanted to do it all, the motivation and the love for it."

"Can you start us from the beginning? What all happened?"

"I took a pair of the pills and a tranquilizer. After I knocked out, I had the most vivid dream and trip I'd ever experienced. Even on the tranquilizer, there was no haziness or blur to the feeling. Everything felt crisp and real, like I was actually in Franklin Park myself."

Hemlock nodded, "OK, so you started out in Franklin Park?"

"Yeah, I was hiding in a dark area off a trail, and it was night. It was weird, I knew the park better than I know it myself. There were memories and checklists running through my head of places in the park where I had a hoist set up and the guy coming soon. Then the guy ran in from the clearing and I knew him. Owen Jackson, 1919 Chesapeake Lane. Husband to a plump little wife, father to 2 daughters. Overweight himself, he had started jogging at night to try to get fit. The spot I was at was where he stopped every time to catch his breath, his third goal point in the run."

Lenny rubbed his temple. "The guy ran right up to the tree I was standing behind, he was panting and bent over. He didn't even hear me step around the tree. I swung once with some kind of blackjack or sap heavily down on the back of his head. He was laying there, bleeding a bit where I cracked him on the skull."

"I didn't stop though, I grabbed his legs and dragged him to a nearby area off the trails. I've never had any training with knots or rope, but I was tying this guys arms with some kind of nylon cord. I got him tied with his arms and legs bound in one length of rope. There was a hoist on a tripod, I think it's used for deer hunting. I hooked Owen up to the tripod by the knots on his ankles and cranked the hoist to hang him."

Lenny stopped and took some deep breaths. "What happened next Lenny?" Hemlock asked.

"I waited. I stopped and sat next to the guy waiting for him to wake up. When Owen woke up, he was scared and I liked it. I felt such a rush when he woke up, it wasn't like anything I'd ever felt just having him there and knowing that it was pure fear of me. It was surreal. Owen tried to beg, but I told him what was going to happen. That I needed his tongue. If he resisted or screamed I would go to his house and kill his entire family. I listed off everything about this guy's life like he was my brother. I even told him he could survive and go back to his family. He seemed to believe that, but I knew it was a complete lie."

Morgan interrupted him, "How did you know that?"

Lenny shrugged. "I have no idea, but I just knew. I failed biology in high school because I refused to dissect the damn fetal pig. But I knew with complete certainty. At his weight, and as long as Owen was hanging upside down, no matter how careful I was going to be, severing the tongue would cut straight through the lingual artery. He could bleed to death in a few minutes. I took out a boning knife, the thing was razor sharp. I cut a quick slash across his throat. He thrashed around for a second while I dug around in the wound. He kept gasping and gagging on the blood. And then I cut the tongue out, like it was just another piece of meat."

Hemlock put a hand on Lenny's arm. "Just another piece of meat?"

Lenny looked down at her hand, shock still written on his expression. "Yeah, I was like a butcher or something. And I held this tongue, it was bigger than I expected, but not bigger than he expected, if that makes any sense. I sat down on the grass and I ate part of it. Raw. I ate this damn thing raw and enjoyed the warm coppery blood flavor while I watched the life drain out of the innocent man on my hoist. And it was like when I ate the tongue and saw him die, at that moment I found peace. I'd been at torment the whole time, enjoying myself but incredibly annoyed and at that single point in time the annoyance melted away."

Morgan finished the last bit of his beer. "What's a serial killer that murders so ruthlessly got to be tormented by?"

Lenny's leg stopped trembling. "From the start to that point, it was like I had this conversation running through my head. Some argument between me and the devil and it kept going through my head, the same few sentences back and forth between me and a demon. Something about a missing woman and the devil had eaten her. I kept arguing about wanting the woman and some beer. It's hard to know why. I've never known any demon from any of the various dimensions to appear and eat a person for no reason. Or allow another human to argue with them afterwards"

"That is extremely odd," agreed Hemlock.

Morgan squinted at Lenny, "Wait, was the woman's name Chrissy?"

Lenny's gaze snapped straight to Morgan. "How the fuck did you know?"

"Did he say to the devil, 'I want my Chrissy and I want my beer.'"

Lenny nodded, breathing deeply. Hemlock raised an eyebrow, "What gives Burns?"

Morgan rummaged in his pocket and pulled out his phone. "Those are the lyrics to a song called Titties and Beer by Frank Zappa." He clicked a few buttons on his phone and it started playing the song softly.

Lenny continued to nod, "Yeah. He kept running through the same three or so lines of that song and it was annoying the hell out of me until Owen died and I was eating the tongue."

Hemlock sighed. "So, the guy kills because he gets a song stuck in his head? Who the fuck does that?"

Morgan rubbed his eyes. "Bit messed up to me. What do we do next?"

Hemlock stood, "Pay our tab, get a few hours sleep, head to the BPD station that took our tip about our killer and find out a few things."

She turned to Lenny and put a hand on his shoulder, "You'll be alright?"

Lenny shrugged her off and got up. "It's not like I have any other choice," he muttered as he slumped away.

# GOOD COP, BAD COP

In an alley, a man lit a cigarette. He leaned against the wall of a police station next to a fire exit. He hovered a bit away from the brick work with his shoulder, as not to get his tan suit jacket dirty.

The man barely blinked when a circle formed in the alley-way within ten feet of him and began swirling colors. He took another drag from the cigarette as the form of Hemlock Connal hopped lightly through the portal. A young man flung himself out of the portal, entangling himself in Hemlock's legs causing them both to fall to the asphalt. The smoking man laughed out a puff of long white smoke.

Hemlock looked up at him through the heap of her and Morgan. "Morning Griff," she said hoarsely staring up at his dark skinned face with salt and pepper goatee.

The man flicked the half-smoked cigarette on the ground and stamped it out. "I wondered when I'd see you, little lady." He reached down to help her up, "And this time you brought a new friend."

She brushed off her jacket while Morgan gained his bearings and stood. "Griff," Hemlock rasped, "This is Morgan Burns, my new intern. Burns, this stately gentleman is Desmond Griffith."

Morgan tried to pat some dust and dirt from his jeans as he turned to Griff. He checked the pockets on his pants to make sure the keys and wallet were still there. Then a quick tap on the pockets of his lightweight trucker jacket, finding his phone intact and the small book still there as well.

"Detective Sergeant Griffith," he corrected her.

Morgan stopped trying to sweep dirt and gravel off his jeans and reached out to shake hands. "Good to meet you Sergeant."

The two men clasped hands firmly, looking each other in the eye. "Finally, you managed to get a decent assistant, Connie. He can shake a person's hand and be socially conscious with humans."

Hemlock sighed. Morgan released his grip. "I'm quite human last I checked, Sergeant Griffith."

Hemlock said gruffly. "Burns here recently graduated from college with a journalism degree and wants to pad his resume with some investigative experience."

"Uh huh," Griff flashed a smile. "You did tell him most of your cases are trolling cheating spouses and insurance fraud, right? Course that didn't stop your last assistant from getting himself killed."

Hemlock chuckled, "Yeah, about that. The first case we picked up wasn't exactly a 'Watch the asshole' kind of situation."

"That so? Whatcha got, Connie?"

Morgan sucked in a deep breath and blew it out with puffed cheeks.

"Let's see," replied Hemlock, "We seem to be looking for a drug supplier for a new narcotic that keeps making people kill."

Griff's smile vanished. "You called in the Jesse Stevens thing?"

Hemlock and Morgan both nodded.

He squinted briefly, "How did you two find that guy? There was evidence in that house to link over a dozen murders that spanned multiple decades."

"I called one of Dad's retired buddies at another precinct about an old suspect. He gave me the name and last known address for Jesse's grandfather David. You still have him in custody?"

Griff scoffed, "Yeah, kid's due for arraignment this afternoon. Magistrate denied bail given the horror show of the murder he committed. Plus the evidence either links him to the other murders or links him to the person that committed them. It's not like he could really afford bail anyway, he's already requested a public defender."

Morgan spoke up, "Let me guess, he thought the murder was a bad dream and knows nothing about all the rest of the murders?"

The detective nodded and turned back to Hemlock. "With a head like that, this one might actually live longer than one case." He pulled out a key chain and opened the door he had been smoking near. "I can't legally let you question him in an interrogation room, Connie. But I can let you talk to him in lockup, it's not very full today."

Griff walked inside, Hemlock and Burns followed closely down the back hallway of the station.

Morgan leaned to Hemlock and whispered, "Connie?"

"That's what he always called my Dad, you know, short for Connal," she whispered back. "I kind of prefer it over what he used to call me."

"Which was?"

"Hemmy."

They were led through a heavy barred door to the lockup area. Griff waited by the door. Lockup turned out to be two massive cells on either side of them as they walked in. A barred wall and doors holding a few prisoners on either side in the large brick area. Jesse was curled up on a bench in a cell with a couple of drunks, still in the same flannel shirt and jeans from when he answered the door the day before.

Hemlock leaned on the cell doors and croaked, "Hiya Jesse."

Jesse squinted up at them, his voice was shaky and haggard. "You, you're that junk buyer."

Hemlock grimaced. "We weren't entirely honest with you

there, Jesse. My real name is Hemlock Connal, and this is my intern Morgan Burns. I'm kind of a private investigator. I wanted to ask you a couple of questions."

Jesse shuddered, the bench stained with sweat where his forehead lay.

Hemlock leaned her arms through the bars and waved a hand. "I think about now it's been almost, what? Eighteen hours without a fix? Starting to feel some pain?" She flicked her wrist and the empty hand suddenly had a little baggy with a single pill in it. "Maybe you want to push that off a bit longer, eh?"

Jesse's face lit up when he saw the pill, instant recognition hitting and threw himself towards the bars. Hemlock jerked back pulling away before he could grab it.

"Easy fella, questions first, pill second."

"Hemlock," whispered Morgan, "Are you sure this is a good idea? Giving drugs to a guy due in court today?"

She shrugged. "What's it matter to us? We've got an investigation, and we can't be slowed to the speed of bureaucracy. Hell, that'll insure more deaths than anything."

Jesse slumped next to the bars, "Ok ok," he pulled at his hair, bringing a fistful away. "I'll say anything."

"Jesse," Hemlock said softly, "I've only got a few questions. First off, do you remember anything about killing anyone?"

His breathing became rougher and Jesse sobbed. "I don't. I thought it was a dream, every time I took those pills. It was so real, the clearest trips I ever had. No rough come downs and it was cheap. Until the night that I killed that guy. I came off the trip, in my grandpa's basement soaked in blood and had like a chunk of some dude's tongue."

Hemlock nodded. "There was only one person? You don't remember killing anyone else?"

Jesse shook his head, sneering at the floor. "No. I uh, I didn't take it again after that. I couldn't."

Morgan held a finger up at Hemlock and leaned down to Jesse. "This might sound a bit strange, but when you were killing him, did you have an annoying song stuck in your head that didn't go away until the guy was dead?"

Jesse slowly gazed up at Morgan, and shuddered. "It, it was 'Hit Me Baby One More Time', Brittany Spears. How did you know?"

Hemlock knelt and handed the pill in the baggy through the bars to Jesse. "Call it a lucky guess."

Jesse grabbed the baggy, He scuttled quickly to a corner of the cell with the toilet. He used the toilet seat to crush the pill in the small bag. He snorted the powder in one long inhalation and fell back onto the floor, convulsing.

Morgan stood gawking at Jesse, like a kid watching a monkey throwing poop at the zoo. Hemlock nudged his shoulder and pointed to the door.

Hemlock called from the barred door, "Hey Griff, we're done here."

A uniformed officer showed up at the door, unlocking it to let Hemlock and Morgan out of the holding cell area. "Griff had to take a call, he said to let you out when you were done and send you over to his desk. You know the way?"

"Certainly officer uh," Hemlock answered in her smokey tone, causing him to turn to look at her in surprise and allowing her to see his name pin. "Smith, yes, thank you Officer Smith, Griff's an old family friend, I know the way."

Hemlock led the way with Morgan trailing behind, staring at the station like a lost puppy. They walked into an open area a dozen or more desks paired up and facing each other in little islands. Uniformed and suited officers were navigating the sea of desks like ancient wayfarers set on familiar tides. They appeared unaware or uncaring of the cacophony of voices and phones. A few desks had freshly arrested suspects handcuffed next to them, awaiting processing.

"Welcome to the bullpen, Burns. Shout if you see Griff, they're always moving around."

She caught sight of him first and nudged Morgan, pointing across the room, "Over there, with Kowalski."

They awkwardly wandered around the maze of desks towards a pair of desks with tall mounds of files. As they parted the sea of police station employees, they found Griff. He was hanging up the phone at a desk covered with mounds of folders and paperwork flanking a keyboard, mouse, and LCD monitor. A stack of papers teetered dangerously close to toppling into an avalanche of bureaucracy.

Opposite Griff's desk sat a similarly shabby desk, though the paperwork towers only stood half as high. A name plate was visible among the chaos, "Detective Leon Bozonovich". The second half of the plate had been painted over in a slightly different shade of black, and the white lettering on Bozonovich was a bit thicker font. Behind the desk, sat a rail thin man in gray slacks and light blue suit. His hands cradled behind his Caesar cut, and he stared at the ceiling chomping gum loud enough to be heard over the din of the station activity. The stiff long bristles of his light brown mustache danced back and forth with the chewing, like a mindless broom being controlled by an invisible sorcerer, sweeping the same mote of dust for eternity.

Griff looked up to see Hemlock and Morgan approaching. "All done with our suspect?" Griff asked.

"Yep. I didn't get much new information out of him though."

"Didn't think you would, the guy's a bit of a burnout. Kept twitching and rocking like a baby when I tried to question him," said Bozonovich.

Morgan turned his head to the side and pointed at the detective, "Your name is Bozonovich?"

"Yeah," he replied. "We related or something?"

"No, not at all." Morgan turned back to Hemlock, "I thought you said his name is Kowalski?" Morgan was scanning the room a bit.

Griff started chuckling, Leon rolled his eyes and leaned far back in his chair and scoffed. Unfortunately, the leaning and scoff combination worked badly for him and Leon started choking on his chewing gum. The choking threw his balance off. He fell from his chair, which luckily dislodged the wayward Wrigley's from his windpipe, to the raucous laughter of anyone near enough to have seen it.

Leon gasped for air as he struggled to right the chair and stand. "Fuck you Hemlock, you know you're not supposed to use that name anymore."

Morgan squinted back to Leon again, "So his name isn't Kowalski?"

Hemlock tried to stop giggling, but was having a hard time with Griff now laughing hard enough that he laid over his desk.

She took a deep breath. "His name is Bozonovich now, it used to be Kowalski."

"Oh," Morgan said, his eyes getting bigger. "Well, I guess it was simpler for you to take your partner's name after it became legal. I mean, Kowalski-Bozonovich would be a lot to fit on a driver's license."

Leon looked around at them shaking his head, while Hemlock and Griff both doubled over in laughter again.

"Hemlock, your friend is more of an asshole than you are!" Leon turned to Morgan, "I'm not gay!"

"I'm not judging alright," said Morgan. "I may be from Indiana, but I didn't vote for Pence, if you catch my drift."

"For fuck's sake," Leon sighed, "I'm not gay!"

"Oh, very proactive of you then, taking her name," said Morgan nodding. "Especially with a name like Bozonovich, lucky these guys don't all call you Bozo."

Hemlock tried to breathe through her tears. Leon pulled a Glock from his holster and held it by the barrel, "I swear Connal,

I'll pistol whip this guy if he says one more damn word."

She got up and finally got the laughing under control. "No, no no. It's fine Leon. Just let me, one sec." Hemlock pointed back to Morgan, "Leon, this is Morgan Burns, my new intern. Morgan, this is Leon. His name was Kowalski, but he had it changed to his mother's maiden name because of a cartoon."

"The Madagascar Penguins?" Morgan asked.

Hemlock nodded.

Morgan turned back to Leon, "And you thought Bozo was better?"

Leon's eyes widened, and he raised the Glock back, "It's Bozonovich, you son of a bitch!"

Griff stood, taking charge of the situation, "Sit down Leon. You don't want another mandatory ten hour sensitivity training, right?"

Leon relaxed and holstered the weapon. Sitting back down Griff turned to Hemlock and Morgan again, "You two got it all out now? Can we move on?"

Hemlock grimaced, realizing they'd pushed Griff a bit too far with Leon.

"Like I was saying though," Leon said, "Perp's a complete burnout, nothing to get from him but a conviction."

"He wasn't burnt out," replied Hemlock. "He was in withdrawal. His habit must have been getting bad, that guy was in a lot of pain."

"He's in for a lot more pain, he's due to be arraigned for murder this afternoon," said Leon.

"How many?" asked Morgan.

"We've got what looks like thirty-nine victims total," said Griff. "Thirty-one of them were killed in the eighties and nineties, eight in the last six months. The evidence in the house ties our guy to all the old murders and one of the new ones."

"That guy wasn't alive in the eighties, and he would have

been at most ten in the late nineties," rasped Hemlock spreading her hands. "You can't be expecting to convict him of them, right?"

Griff hung his head, sighed and nodded. "No, neither us nor the District Attorney think it's a set of charges worth even considering. But we can get a dental match on the one murder that he's linked to from the house, which gives us reason to charge him with the other seven recent murders."

"But you can only link him to the one, right?" Asked Morgan.

Griff nodded, but Leon said, "Just because we can't find any evidence in his house of the other seven, doesn't exonerate him. Jesse seems to be obviously carrying on his grandfather's M.O. We can prove he did the one, the other seven will follow."

Hemlock leaned back, sitting against the edge of Griff's desk. "And what happens," she purred, "When another murder fitting this exact profile happens while your suspect is in jail?"

Leon scoffed. "You think there are multiple copy cats? We looked it up, Jesse is the only relative of David Stevens in five hundred miles. We could get the grandfather on the older charges, but we're not sure he would live long enough to see trial in his condition."

Morgan grimaced, "Hemlock's got a different theory, which will sound crazy, but is more likely."

"Crazy theories won't help us get a conviction, noobie," Leon spat venomously at Morgan.

"Leon," Griff said cautioning. "I dealt with Jack Connal every now and again when he was alive. He helped us solve some strange cases, and the problem usually went away even if the paperwork wasn't pretty. I saw some strange shit with Jack, stranger after Hemlock started working with him. You two think this is falling in," Griff fluttered his fingers in front of him, "That whole world?"

Leon raised an eyebrow at them, Hemlock nodded to Morgan, "Take it away chief, let's see how much you've grokked what's going on."

Morgan stared doe-eyed at the expressions worn by Leon and Griff. He felt better with the trust Griff was extending him.

"You guys had a chance to dig through the mail and other stuff at the Stevens' residence?"

They nodded, Leon sighed with boredom.

"So you picked up on the same thing we did, right? David had a change in his health about seven months ago, the long term care facility bills and social security checks confirm that to us. The older murders, they seemed to stop in the late nineties, when David was approaching sixty. He must have been getting too old to keep up the habit. New murders started six months ago, it doesn't feel like a coincidence, does it? David goes to a nursing home and the killings start again?"

"Sure," Leon replied. "Jesse moved in, found all his grandfather's old crap. He might have found a kill journal somewhere that detailed everything or maybe the old man even told him, serial killers are sickos. He could have been grooming him for the last twenty years to start up again."

Morgan held up his index finger, warning off that thought. "If that were the case, you'd expect to find more evidence in the same place for his involvement in the other recent murders. We also can't confirm what Jesse and David's relationship was like prior to David going to the retirement home. Did you read the line items on the bills? The care described with bathing and feeding schedules doesn't create a picture of someone able to orchestrate copycat killers. It is the image of a man in a near vegetative state."

Griff shrugged, Leon sneered. "So what?" Leon asked. "Old fart had a stroke, kid picks it up."

"We started on this whole case not focusing on the murders, but an issue a paramedic was telling us about. There have been people for the last six to eight months randomly losing all traces of their memories and entering semi-vegetative states.

The paramedics or the police would get a call because someone hadn't heard from a person in a few days. They'd do a well check and find the person there, dehydrated and in their own filth, but alive. David Stevens may have been one of the first of those cases and written off as an old guy that let himself go or had a stroke like you think. There are no tests to support a stroke in any of the memory victims though."

"Memory victims?" Leon rolled his eyes, "You're not buying into this Griff?"

"Shut the fuck up, Kowalski," Griff barked. "I'll tell you what I think when he's connected some more dots."

Morgan turned back to Hemlock, she smiled and nodded for him to continue.

"Along with everything else you found at the Stevens house, you got a little baggy of pills, right?"

Griff sat forward and clicked the mouse on his desktop. He keyed in a few things to the computer. "Yeah, right here in the inventory. Still in testing, but initial field tests didn't have it marked as a commercially manufactured drug. It didn't test positive for any common opioids or narcotics."

Morgan's eyes went wide, and he wagged a finger at him. "Precisely, and I'll bet it doesn't come back with any conclusive results from further analysis. We think that drug is what's linking the memory victims to the murders."

Griff sat back in his chair, staring over steepled fingers. "How?"

"Consider a way to completely steal a person's memories. If someone could manage to take an entire lifetime of joy, happiness, sorrow and love, copy all of those memories and promise it as a vivid trip, how many drug addicts do you think would try it? If it's not a scheduled narcotic, it would be less risky to sell on the streets. And if they can copy the memories across a big batch of pills, the source material would be cheap. No smuggling involved, all the raw ingredients are just walking around in people up here." Morgan tapped the side of his head.

Griff squinted across to Morgan. "So, you think someone turned David Stevens memories and experiences into a usable substance. By popping one of the pills, you get a guaranteed trip for killing a person. But how does that connect out to turning Jesse Stevens into a copycat that murders seven or more people?"

"He didn't!" Morgan scratched his head, holding up a finger trying to contain his excitement connecting it all. "Jesse only killed one person, which is why you found the bag of pills, it scared him off. He took it a few times, and eventually it kind of took over his system. He may not even have known what he was doing. He was just going on autopilot to carry out a repetitive task, which this had become for David after thirty plus murders spanning multiple decades. The other killings were likely the same, each a case of a person taking enough of the same batch to start carrying it out. We all lucked out that Hemlock and I ended up at that house."

Leon's left eyebrow was creeping higher up his vast forehead. "That's a great story kid, but it won't hold water. Besides, what other proof do you have of this cockamamie explanation?"

Hemlock smiled ruefully. "You probably let our other proof out on bond already."

Leon looked dumbstruck. "Careful, Leon," Hemlock warned, "that look comes too easily for you."

"What the hell are you talking about?" Leon asked.

Griff closed his eyes tight and lay his head on the desk, groaning. "The kid?" He mumbled.

Hemlock nodded. Griff sat back up, breathing deeply, "How's she connected to it?"

"You guys think it was a little odd that some fifteen-year-old cheerleader form Jamaica Plain ended up in Dorchester killing a drug dealer at one in the morning?"

Morgan grimaced, "That would strike me as odd any time of the day really."

"You have two connections." Hemlock counted off on her fingers. "One, if you test what drugs you find in that dealer's place, it probably matches the baggy of pills you got at the Stevens place. Two, another one of the memory victims was Bobbi Cotter's hardest hitter. Didn't that murder fit too exactly the exact profile for a territory and drug hit?"

Griff nodded, "It was odd, but we couldn't get much out of her, the parents had her lawyered up before we got her printed. If it weren't for all the blood and the Uber driver's sworn statement, I wouldn't have believed it."

Morgan almost leapt over to Griff's desk. "Do they have a listing of what the girl was carrying when she was arrested? Maybe she still had more of the pills on her too!"

Hemlock's eyes widened, and she sucked in a breath, "Ooh, good idea Morgan."

Griff started pecking at some keys, as they hunched around his monitor.

Leon groaned, "This is a bunch of horse shit, Griff, I can't believe you're even listening to this."

Griff peered over his monitor at Leon, "It's not. Right here in the arrest report."

He turned the monitor on its armature for Leon to see the text listing that included "Small plastic baggy, three pills unlabeled, light green color." Accompanying the item was an image, the pills were the same size, shape and similar markings as the ones found at the Stevens home, only the color varied.

Leon stared up at the creepy grins on Hemlock, Griff and Morgan's faces and muttered, "Well fuck me in the goat ass."

Hemlock and Morgan stared at Leon. Griff threw a pad of post it notes at him, Leon swatted at the flying stationary. "I told you to stop saying that!"

Griff settled back into his seat. "You two do realize I can't get warrants or even really push for the investigation to take this kind of turn?"

Hemlock nodded, eyes shut.

Griff leaned forward, speaking softer, "Do you have any idea what weird, magical shit would be used to steal all of someone's memories?"

Hemlock sighed. "You're not going to like it," she rasped. "Nightmares, a bunch of nightmares."

"I bet they would be a nightmare, as bad as this is," said Griff.

"No," replied Morgan, "Actual creatures called nightmares. They're apparently real and a bunch of them recently went missing from a kind of nature reserve."

Griff waved his hand toward Morgan, "So you intend to...?"

"Hunt some nightmares and whoever is controlling them," said Hemlock.

Leon chuckled, Griff gave a tight-lipped nod. "They give out hunting licenses for that?"

"Nope," replied Hemlock, "We'll have to chum the waters, so to speak."

# RATCHET PIXIE
# INFORMANT

The fire exit swung open hard, Hemlock storming out into the alley way followed by Morgan, his boot heels clicking heavily on the pavement. The door slammed shut behind them. Hemlock began pacing the alley. She pulled a fresh piece of chalk from an inner jacket pocket. Tapping it against her lip, Hemlock kept pacing quietly.

Morgan stood by the fire door, leaning against the precinct's brick wall. He sighed, "So, what's the next move boss? Have you ever actually hunted nightmares?"

Hemlock stopped pacing. She scratched at the shorter side of her pixie cut scalp with the stick of chalk. "Not really, I went on a few jackalope hunts prior to the banishing, but they're a different animal altogether."

She knelt at a clear section of pavement with the least amount of oil staining. "We'll need a bit of research, did you bring that book Yamata lent you last night?"

Morgan reached into an inner breast pocket of his trucker jacket and pulled out the small volume of Nightmares in a Nutshell. The cover image of the crazed horse staring back at him. "Yep, don't leave home without it now."

"Good," said Hemlock. "You take a few minutes to scan through and see if there's anything we can do to lure them out. I need to call someone to us, should've asked her yesterday if she's seen anything strange or not, but we didn't have a good picture yet."

"OK," replied Morgan. He started scanning through the index for topics that might help them figure out how to lure nightmares. The L sections didn't help as it concerned mainly with living with nightmares, livery and a few other unrelated items. The T section had an entry for trapping nightmares, page fifty-four. Flipping to page fifty-four, under a bold section heading that read, "Trapping Nightmares" he found a single word, "Don't".

Flipping back to the front of the index, Morgan found under the A section a listing for attracting nightmares, page thirty-two. He found the section, Morgan read aloud, "A nightmare is a creature of constant hunger. It requires little to no nourishment for its physical form, as it is unreliably corporeal. A nightmare draws its forms as necessary from the ether. As a being of ethereal plights, it's hunger derives from the need to fuel any magical requirements to maintain or change state."

Morgan peeked up from the page. Hemlock was drawing out a circle in the chalk, with a set of runes and symbols. It didn't appear similar to the ones she had used for teleporting them around the city. "Interesting section, keep going," she said.

Morgan stared back down to the page and continued. "While other magical creatures and beings can do this with a connection to latent magical energies in their surrounding world, the nightmare has evolved a way to transform extracted negative emotion into an energy form it can store and feed on for many years between feedings. As the nightmare has evolved this method to derive energy from negative emotions, those that exhibit high or abnormal levels of negative emotion can be easy targets for a nightmare and attract them more easily. Anyone with a major depressive disorder, a history of mental illness or suffering recent tragic losses would be most susceptible to attracting nightmares."

Hemlock stood from the alley pavement, studying her chalk sketching. "Is that the whole of the section?"

"The passages are short, I guess that's what they mean by 'In a Nutshell'," replied Morgan. He stared at the circles and symbols. "This one doesn't look like the others I've seen so far. What's this spell supposed to do, Hemlock?"

"How much of that book have you read so far?"

Morgan shrugged. "It's a short book, I skimmed it a few times, read about half of it well enough to remember it so far."

She pointed the chalk like a finger back at Morgan, "The last section you read aloud discussed the semi-corporeal nature of the nightmare. Do you recall what that means about its ability to be detected?"

Morgan scrunched his eyes shut. "Uh, let's see. Yeah, being of ethereal plights and unreliably corporeal, normal human beings can only see it while it is in the process of feeding. Which means it's sitting right on your chest. So, it's basically undetectable by normal people when in the same room or nearby. Those with a magical affinity can see the nightmare though, as they have practice and have an eye for the ethereal. Though humans with affinity still need minor assistance. So, I think that means the Sidhe, like yourself can see them. Witches and wizards though may need some sort of potion, spell or something you rub on, I guess?" Morgan opened his eyes and shrugged.

"Yep," Hemlock said nodding. "That's about the basics I remember from one of my tutors when I was younger too, and why we had a relative that could go into the forest and study them. Hell, he could be the source for most of that little manual you got from Yamata."

Morgan agreed, checking the references in the back pages out of curiosity. "So are you trying to call someone that we can ask about nightmares then? Like your relative, the Grand Duke of Knutley, wasn't it? I thought he was dead though? Cheese or something?"

"Yeah," Hemlock said, "Poisoned or suicide, whichever. No, we need to talk to someone alive, in Boston, able to see nightmares, and, most importantly, likely to have been stalking around as much at night as our perpetrator."

Morgan shut his eyes and sighed deeply. "Alice?" He asked.

"Yep, you guessed it." She rifled through the right pocket of her jacket, pulling out a thin sheathed dagger.

Putting his book back in his own jacket, Morgan cocked an eyebrow and walked towards her. "How did you manage that? I'd swear that knife is bigger than your pocket."

"Dagger, Burns," she rasped unsheathing the dagger. "It's a dagger, there's a difference between a knife and a dagger."

Morgan tilted his head. "Yeah, what's that?"

"What's what?" She asked.

"What's the difference?"

"Oh," Hemlock held the dagger up and turned it over a few times. "Daggers always have symmetrical blades, knives don't."

"How'd you fit it in your pocket though? That coat's a bit small isn't it?"

The jacket Hemlock was wearing was a waist length trim black leather number. It had a diagonal zipper leading from the left side of her collar bone to her waist. She patted at the pockets, "There's more room in them than you'd expect." She winked and grinned a broad smile.

"You enchanted the pockets," Morgan nodded at her.

"For fuck's sake Burns, yes, I enchanted the damn pockets. What else am I going to do?"

"Would it be at all practical to," Morgan shrugged, "I don't know, buy clothes with actual pockets."

Hemlock narrowed her gaze on him and pointed the dagger at him, jabbing the air. "Burns," she growled, "have you ever tried shopping for women's clothing?"

He shook his head, eyes widening at the dagger flicking closer to him.

"Let me clue you in to one of the biggest lies ever pushed

on women's fashion. Pockets. You get pockets that are useful all over your pants and coats right? Jeans have four and even one for a special little pocket watch, but are they all useful, yeah?"

Morgan nodded, edging away from the reach of the dagger.

"Ever looked at a pair of women's jeans or leggings? If there is a pocket, it's either too small or tight to be useful. Or it's only a piece of fabric sewn to mimic a pocket and the cheeky fuckers didn't put anything at all there. Jackets don't get much better, the pockets on this one were real, but small enough to barely put a hand in, not big enough to even hold a decent set of gloves."

Morgan, eyes still wide, nodded, "That sounds like a tremendous pain in the ass."

Hemlock flicked the dagger point up sharply. "Yes, it is. But, I love this jacket and a few others. So, I've made some minor modifications. Chiefly, that the pockets link up with a small set of cabinets in my room back home. If the item is something in those cabinets and I can see it in my mind clearly, I can summon it to my hand and pull it in and out via my pockets."

Morgan breathed a sigh of relief. "That definitely sounds advantageous and easier to carry with you then remembering a purse."

"You couldn't begin to imagine," she said turning back to the chalk circles and symbols. "Now, before me I have drawn a circle and inscribed it with runes to direct the summoning of a small pixie of my calling in the nearby area. If she's in this realm and not the Sidhe when I complete the spell and call her name, she'll come directly into this circle."

"What if she was over in the Sidhe?"

Hemlock chuckled in a rolling gravel tone. "The spell would fail and fizzle," she shrugged. "Not likely though. Alice doesn't like to go back too often. She has easier hunting over on this side and enjoys the little things here, like animal overpopulation."

Morgan pointed down at the circle. "And this spell I'm guessing with the dagger, that means you have to bind it and fuse it with something stronger than saliva?"

She nodded. "Yep, calling and putting a compulsion on another being requires a bit extra juice. Nothing but the high octane output will do in this case."

Hemlock ran the dagger down the pad of her thumb. The blade was sharp though, and the blood took a moment and the coercion of her pressing the base of the thumb for a flowing line of scarlet to form. Three times, she called out, "I call Alice Bitter, Sidhe pixie and friend." With each calling, Hemlock swung her arm down across the circle walking around it to create a triangle of her own blood spatter. When the third spray flew down with her words, the circle and symbols began to pulsate a soft purple color. The blood began to flicker in its triangulation.

A moment later, the circle was gone, and in its place sat Alice. The greasy pixie still in rags, sat over a dead goose. Sitting opposite her, and also picking at the carcass was a large crow, blood caked in its feathers and wings. Alice looked up briefly to see the grinning face of Hemlock. The pixie turned back to the goose again, then flew up quickly, flitting her wings in agitation. The crow perked its head out of the goose's chest cavity, blood dripping from its black beak. It turned its head to the side and cawed loudly, then went back to eating on the goose's internal organs.

"What the hell is this Hemlock?" She spat the question, wiping gore from her face with the back of a filthy hand.

"I'd ask you the same thing." Hemlock nodded at the goose rending, "I don't normally catch tag-alongs when I do a summoning. Tell me, Alice Bitter, what were you up to?"

"That?" She nodded back to the crow and the dead goose. "It's just Ted, we do some work together, don't we?"

Morgan approached next to Hemlock and pointed to the birds, "Is Ted the crow or the goose?"

Alice laughed and slapped a knee. "You've got to keep this one, Lockley! He's a proper tit."

Morgan coughed lightly and tried to smile through gritted

teeth.

"Nah, Ted's the crow!" She reached down to the goose, pulling free a long white feather and used it as a napkin for more of the blood. "Ted trained up better than the other crows, and he runs some jobs with me. Sometimes a bit of work, sometimes we scrap up a bit of food. In this case, we teased and drove this nice juicy meal right in the path of a bike messenger. The bike broke his neck nicely, scared the living shit out of that messenger though." She laughed again, "You'll like this one Lockley, the wheel hits the goose, it lets out this horrible choke honk, sounds like someone strangled a clown. Messenger freaks out and falls off his bike going real fast. Anyway, this guy's not wearing a helmet and his skull meets a fire hydrant like a mallet meeting a watermelon."

Alice made fists on the side of her head, blowing them away with fingers flaring, "Didn't think we'd get a twofer like that. Then you go and pull us away when we only really got started on this girl here." Alice slapped the side of the goose. She looked up at the head, then reached over and pulled the eyeball from the socket. She began chewing on it like a grapefruit. "So, what's up?" Alice asked, spitting chunks of gristle while talking and chewing.

Morgan stared down, eyes raised in abject horror. Hemlock nodded with tight lips for a moment, eyes darting back and forth between Alice and Ted. Alice took another gushing bite of the eyeball.

"So," Hemlock said, finally breaking the silence, "I need to know if you'd seen something odd over the last few months. Any nightmares?"

Alice screwed up her eyes thinking. "I keep having this one I'm wrapped up in a taco shell, but then realize it's a giant version of myself about to eat the Alice taco."

Hemlock shut her eyes for a second, wagging a finger, she continued. "No, not bad dreams. Have you seen any actual nightmares? The creatures? Nasty looking things, sometimes shift into a horse form? Possibly with a little kid roaming the night?"

"Oh, Little Sally Hellscreamer!" Alice turned to the crow, "Hey Ted, these guys want to know about Sally Hellscreamer!"

The bird popped his head back out of the goose corpse and gave a chuckling caw. Ted promptly dug his head back into the splayed belly.

Morgan and Hemlock glanced back to one another, and turned again to Alice. Alice popped the rest of the eyeball in her mouth and wiped her hands clean.

"I think that might be it. Did this 'Sally Hellscreamer' ride a nightmare or have some with her?" Hemlock asked.

"Oh yeah," replied Alice. "Seen her around town across the rooftops lots of times with different nightmares. She keeps about the same circuit around town. You haven't heard her?"

"No, can't say I have," rasped Hemlock inquisitively. "Since my banishment, I have to concentrate more to use any of my Sidhe abilities."

"That explains it then," said Alice. "Start keeping an eye and ear out, and you'll catch wind of her."

"Hang on,"Morgan cut in, "This kid rides them?" He waved his hands up at the sky above the alley. "She just hops on their backs and rides them through the Boston night sky.?"

"Nooo," Alice said, exasperated, "She doesn't just ride them across the sky. She has to sing to them while she's riding them."

Hemlock and Morgan both looked at Alice and said, "Huh?"

"Yeah," Alice flitted her wings and began flying circles around their heads. As she picked up a bit of speed, she pulled up her knees and held invisible reigns in front of her, riding an imaginary horse. "You can't just ride a nightmare, you'd be crazy, they would rend your mind easier than Ted over there shredding goose liver with his beak!"

Ted pulled his head out once again, tilted it back and forth, and cawed menacingly. Alice fought the imaginary horse, losing the battle to an invisible mouth chomping through her brain, making her a zombie. Morgan and Hemlock nodded in unison, drawn into Alice's strange lecture.

"Assuming that the nightmare is in a form to ride."

"Yeah," said Morgan. "That's what the book meant!" He smacked Hemlock on the arm, "I didn't get it at first, it said that nightmares were semi-corporeal. They don't have a single solid form, do they?"

Alice snorted. "Of course they don't. Duh." She flew down closer to them. "In order to pull the nightmare into a form you can handle you have to sing to it. When you hit certain notes and sing to it in its native sound, the creature will pull itself together in a form you can ride and control. But it's very tricky."

"Tricky how?" Asked Hemlock. "Like knowing all the words to a Fall Out Boy song?"

"You can't sing pop hits from the radio to it," Alice said rolling her eyes. She hovered slowly in place, pulling in closer to Hemlock. "You have to sing in the sound of the nightmare. It's a cruel sounding wail, it can break the night like a mirror and shatter the calm of the most sober person."

With Hemlock and Morgan's attention fully on Alice, she hung in the air, wings a flutter, a few inches between them. Alice took in a deep breath and let loose a soul-grinding shriek that started in a low octave and undulated up and down in pitch in long waves, slapping their ears like axes chipping at grinding stones. They both grasped their ears, trying to block out the wretched noise.

When Alice stopped the whining squall, they waited a few extra seconds to be sure she wouldn't start again before relaxing the grip on their heads.

"There's the sound I've been missing every night as she lopes the rooftops in search of brains to burgle?" Hemlock asked.

Alice nodded.

Morgan shifted his hips to lean forward in closer to Alice. "You mentioned something about a nightmare rending your brain if you disturbed it without the, uh, shrieking. What do they do with your brain at that point? When I was reading the book on them it said they feed on strong negative emotions, but didn't detail anything about being overly destructive."

Alice laughed, shrugging. "They are dangerous creatures stirred from the nether and older than the emerald ages of man. What would you expect them to be? Harmless?"

"Alice," Hemlock interrupted, "When you say rending a brain, what else can they do? Can a nightmare consume all meaningful memories a person has accumulated through a lifetime."

"Yep, just like that," she snapped her fingers. "If they don't feel like browsing for a particular memory to feed on your latent emotions of the memory, they can rip the whole set free of your soul."

"Is it consumed and gone or do they pull it free to store like a camel with water?"

"What's a camel?" Asked Alice, genuinely confused.

Hemlock sneered, "Um, you maybe saw one at the zoo, looks like a ratty brown, tall horse with one or two humps on its back."

Alice's eyes widened, "Ooohhh, bump mules. Those are called camels?"

Morgan nodded. "Yeah, they store extra water and fat with the humps, so they can make long journeys across deserts where they may not see more water for a long time. Can a nightmare do that with memories?"

"Probably," Alice replied.

Hemlock crossed her arms, "If they can do that, could they regurgitate the memories or segments of them in a form someone could view and maybe even copy?"

Alice shrugged, "No idea, I've heard of them doing it, but I've never watched the process. If they ingested the memories, then I'd guess there would be some way to extract them."

Morgan groaned and sighed.

"What?" Hemlock asked.

"I get it now, this is like magical meth or crack, isn't it?"

Alice fluttered closer to Morgan's face, her wee beady eyes squinting into each of his eyes. "You look like you're serious, and I don't see any signs of concussion.

Morgan tried to swat her away from his face. "Ha ha, real funny Alice," he said. "Really though, think about it." He started counting points on his fingers. "We have this drug in pill form, confirmed at a few different scenes now. We have people wandering around that have lost all of their memories. Those memories are cropping up in the hallucinations. We have nightmares being ridden and commanded across the rooftops of Boston by night. Put it all together and you have the source materials, a means of extraction, and the end product. We're missing just the middle now."

Hemlock's eyes widened. "You think the kid's working for somebody!"

"Precisely, Hemlock. If we think about it, yeah, it's strange this kid is doing these things, but it's running errands for someone. We're not likely going to find some kid looking to create a drug empire or have knowledge of refining complex thoughts and emotions into a drug like this."

"So, we need to find the cook and their lab, but it doesn't change what we need to do right now," she said turning to the pixie. "Alice, can you draw out a map of the rooftops you've seen the kid riding nightmares?"

"Sure, you got a piece of paper?" Alice flitted back down to the pavement where Ted was still snacking enthusiastically on entrails. "Dammit Ted, leave me some, you gluttonous slug!"

Hemlock rummaged through her pockets, shutting her eyes in concentration. A moment later, she produced a clean piece of white printer paper, slightly folded to fit through the smaller pocket opening. She handed it down to Alice.

The pixie gripped a feather on the dead goose, ripping it free with a grunt. She stabbed the sharp end of the feather into the gaping wound on the bird, then proceeded to start sketching with the makeshift quill and bloody ink.

Hemlock and Morgan watched in wonder as Alice zipped back and forth around the paper and the goose. When she was done, a detailed map of a path lay before them. A loping path was sketched around notable monuments around the greater Boston area.

"That work for you guys?"

Morgan and Hemlock looked to one another and then back to Alice, nodding appreciatively. "Do they hit this route every night?"

Alice grimaced, "I'm not sure, probably going to be a crap shoot. It's been a few nights though, so perhaps you'll luck out."

She zipped back to the corpse and started digging through the open abdominal cavity. Alice searched around reaching in deeper. She pulled her arms out and huffed a deep breath, "Ted, did you eat all the liver *and* the kidneys?"

The raven popped its head back out of the guts. A bit of gore spattered off his beak as he cawed three times.

"Ted, you miserable asshole," Alice yelled standing up from the mangled and bloody goose. "You know those are my favorites, you should have shared!" She jumped over the body running after Ted.

For his part, the crow hopped away unfolding and flapping his wings, cawing in a laughing and taunting tone as Alice chased him around the alley.

Hemlock examined the map in her hands trying to ignore the murderous pixie chasing her partner in crime. Morgan had been watching them and laughing, but finally turned back to the map and Hemlock.

"So," Morgan said awkwardly, "What's the plan now chief, camp out somewhere on the map?"

Hemlock didn't look up from the map. "The trail they seem to follow doesn't make a lot of sense right off, but they hit some pretty diverse ground across the greater Boston area. But she does stay south of the Mystic."

Morgan tilted his head to get a better glimpse of Alice's bloody masterpiece. "If she swings close enough to Braddock that we might catch her off your own rooftop. Do you think you'll be able to see and hear little Sally Hellscreamer, as Alice calls her?"

Hemlock nodded. "I should, and you might be able to as well."

Morgan cocked an eyebrow and pointed at himself.

Hemlock grinned at him, "We need to make you into a bit of bait. To do that, what you're going to do may make you more in tune with some things from the Sidhe."

Morgan winced, "How exactly are we going to make me into bait for a nightmare?"

"You just have to think broadcast some negative waves," Hemlock croaked. She tapped the side of Morgan's head, "And we're going to amplify those waves by loading you up on a shit ton of DMT from the Druggist!"

# NIGHTMARES
# BY NIGHT

L ater that evening, Hemlock led Morgan out to the roof of the old red brick Victorian townhouse. They were both a bit out of breath, having climbed through most of the staircases in the home. The roof had a railing around it and a set of patio furniture, two wicker couches with thick cushions and a matching wicker chair. The light of Boston bathed over the Back Bay rooftop, leaving little need for the strands of lights along the rail.

"This has always been up here?" Asked Morgan.

"Yep," Hemlock said, "Most of the house has been furnished throughout four generations of Connals. Built in 1890 by my great-great grandfather. The rooftop and a study were furnished by my dad. This was the last thing he added to the house before he died."

"Do you come up here often then?" Morgan stood at a railing looking out over Boston and further out Boston Harbor to the north-east. "The views are wonderful and it's so quiet, I'd be out here anytime it wasn't raining or snowing."

Hemlock sat silently on one of the wicker sofas. She stared down at her hands and feet. Morgan turned from the railing to her. She smiled softly and chuckled. "You would expect I'd be out here all the time, it is a breathtaking view of the city. But I can barely bring myself to come up here most days." There was a leaden weight to her voice through her normal dry, hoarseness.

"Because of your dad?"

She nodded. "If it wasn't the most convenient place without some ad hoc breaking and entering, I'd have even gone to any other rooftop in Boston tonight. But, here we are, close to midnight and soon to get to work."

She pulled a blue knit stocking cap from her pocket after a moment's contemplation and put it on. "Do you need a hat out here? It might get a bit cold tonight."

"Sure," answered Morgan, "if you have a spare."

She reached into her coat pocket again, thinking for a moment before pulling another stocking cap from her pocket. She handed it to Morgan, who put it on without looking at the color or pattern. It was bright green with a pattern of pink snowflakes knit around it.

She laughed at the hat on Morgan. "What?" Asked Morgan.

Hemlock pointed to the hat. Morgan took it off briefly to see the hideous color and pattern. He cocked an eyebrow at the hat and glanced back to Hemlock.

"I went through a phase after I was first handed my sentence for banishment. I didn't want anything to do with my dad or his world, I hated being bounced from my other world so easily. I couldn't leave though, the banishment held me at the time with my father. So, I found other odd ways to rebel. When he would take me on stakeouts and cases, instead of paying attention or trying to learn anything useful, I taught myself to crochet. I made that hat. My old man, he saw through it all. He said he loved that hat, and would wear it out whenever he picked me up from school."

Morgan turned the hat over a few times in his hands. He held it out to give back to Hemlock, "I can always run down and grab the one in my luggage."

Hemlock closed her eyes and shook her head. "Nah, it's perfect for you tonight. With that hat on, I won't have any problems with finding you if we end up somewhere else. It's like a beacon for me anywhere. Besides, I need to stop grieving for dad sometime. If I'd have gotten over some of these things, even just a week ago, the last guy would still be alive."

Morgan sat down on the wicker couch opposite Hemlock. "What happened a week ago?"

Hemlock fished in her pocket for a few moments and brought out a small box. She sat it on the cushion next to her. "Burns, you ever wonder about the consorts, interns, whatever you want to call them that came between my dad's death and you showing up on my doorstep?"

Burns shook his head, "I hadn't given it too much thought, other than you said they ended up dead. I guess I should learn from their mistakes though."

"Yeah," Hemlock croaked, "Pretty accurate way to look at it." She turned over the small box in her hands, running her thumb along its edges. "Thing is, they were all Sidhe. In a way, the whole consort role had ended up being an internship role for them too. Problem was that they were so damned pretentious, they didn't think they were in any real danger in this realm."

Morgan leaned back on the couch and looked up at the night sky. "So, how did the one bite it last week?"

"Well," Hemlock said, "We wrapped up the first case with Davinpor being my new consort. A cheating spouse case. I like to celebrate the end of a case with a drink under the stars."

"Up here?"

She shook her head. "No, if I had, Davinpor would probably still be alive. We were having a couple of glasses of whiskey on the little roof down above the stoop. The cheating spouse came to the house, he wasn't happy that we put in our report with his wife, and he was looking at a sudden divorce."

Burns snapped his head up, "The guy killed your intern?"

Hemlock winced, she held out a hand and wobbled it. "Kind of, though he was a wizard, he brought a pistol and was shooting at us, but the bullets wouldn't have done much to Davinpor. It was the fall that got him."

139

Morgan turned his head down towards where the stoop would be if he could see through the house. "Bullets wouldn't have hurt your fairy friend, but a fall off a roof ten feet from the ground did?"

Hemlock nodded, tight-lipped and sighed. "Yeah, the wizard threw a bottle at him. Caught him off guard and nailed him. Davinpor fell off the roof and impaled himself on that wrought iron fence in the shrubs. Cold steel is incredibly deadly to the Sidhe."

Morgan squirmed uncomfortably, rubbing his chest. "I'd think that would be mostly fatal to anyone. Although," he trailed off.

"Hmmm?" Hemlock asked.

"Oh, if you fell right," Morgan got up and walked to the ledge of the roof. He peered over to the lower roof on the stoop. "If a person fell just right, they would end up with missing most of their major organs, possibly only skewer a gall bladder. Certainly something you could survive, though not easily walk away from."

Hemlock strolled over to the roof's edge. She leaned on the ledge on her arms, crossing a leg behind the other. Together they stared off the building into the night over the Boston skies.

"It's a beautiful city," said Morgan.

"You haven't been out of the Midwest much, Burns?" Hemlock spoke quietly in her smokey rasp of a voice.

Morgan sneered and bobbed his head. "Not much, really. Couple of short vacations with dad and visits to a few places, but all tourist kind of spots."

"Orlando?"

He nodded. "Yeah, dad stuck to safe places like that, but looking out at this city, it speaks volumes to a person, doesn't it Hemlock?"

She nodded along as well. "I'm sure you feel a belonging to

wherever you were from back in Indiana. But for folks out here, the city offers something different. Most people could look out there, and they see a bunch of buildings and an overpopulated stinking mass of people. But, do you know what I see?"

"A beautiful city?" Morgan hazarded.

Hemlock shook her head. "No, it is a beautiful city. It's also a stinking city, a sweating city, a great many things. There's the old, and all the history. Buildings and monuments that have been here since before there was a country to say it belonged to. There's all the new buildings and industry. Among all that, there's the magic."

Morgan turned, leaning one elbow on the ledge. Hemlock kept looking out over the city.

"Tomorrow, you'll get to know more of the magical community of the city. We've got to go to that accursed party I promised Dierdre we would attend. You may start to get a better understanding of how much it all fits together. The old and the new, the magical and the industrial. You may think this city has stood and thrives by the constant work and toil of man. Partly true. Underneath that veneer though, you have the covens and the Sidhe. The Sidhe have been here longer than you can imagine. The covens play right into the whole scheme of it just as much. With both giving each other power, and the trade-offs of them all, it all balances and the city thrives from it. Boston almost has its own heartbeat. Like breath coming off the bay and drawn in by the South End, Back Bay, the North Side, Jamaica Plains, and all the other neighborhoods of this city. Do you see what I'm getting at Burns?"

She turned away from the city, looking up into his eyes. "Burns, do you understand what this means to us tonight?"

Morgan sighed and turned back to the city and the roof's edge. "This business with the nightmares and the drugs has pushed that balance, hasn't it?"

Hemlock nodded. "Most times, there are light meddling

habits between a practitioner here and there and the organized crime like Bobbi Cotter. We've got a missing link somewhere here, and it's got to be somehow, somebody linked well with the covens. Whoever this kid is with the nightmares, they have to be only one part, but there is something more at play. If we want to keep this city in balance, we've got to find the nightmares and track this kid back to the hideout."

"As you said earlier," Morgan said calmly, "We do this by getting me messed up on some drugs?"

"Not just some drugs," Hemlock rasped. She dug into her pocket, she pulled out three small vials and a vaping pen. "Some very specific drugs, and a bit of guidance."

Morgan picked up one of the small vials, holding it up against the lights cast off downtown Boston. The fluid inside was thick, radiating a tone between red and golden brown. It sloughed from side to side in a viscous ebb and flow.

"And these are vials of DMT from the druggist?" Morgan asked.

"Yep, enough to make you a beacon of spiritual activity in the night. If the nightmare were a hipster, your brain would become the avocado toast and a can of Pabst Blue Ribbon."

Hemlock plucked the vial of liquid out of Morgan's trembling fingers. She walked back over to the wicker couches. She unscrewed the cap from the vial and screwed it into place in the vaping pen. Morgan shuffled to sit next to her. She handed him the vape pen, and he held it gently in two fingers like a child pretending to hold a ball point pen as a cigarette.

"I'm not scared of a little drug trip or even a nasty drug trip," Morgan said, rolling the pen in his fingertips. "What I'm afraid of is how to stop it and how to cut this spiritual broadcast once we catch the nightmare's attention."

"Don't trust me, Burns?"

Morgan grimaced. "When you chum the waters, you bring sharks. The sharks that come end up eating the chum and want more food. You're whipping them into a frenzy, and I'm the chum. How do we stop the blood in the water?"

Hemlock dug through her coat pocket once more, pulling out a roll of heavy duty aluminum foil. She tore off a long sheet of it and began folding. When she sat back, Hemlock had a triangle of thick foil in her hands and popped it apart in the middle. She held it lightly in her finger tips and placed it gingerly on Morgan's head as though she was coronating a monarch.

Burns frowned and stared Hemlock in her smiling eyes. "You've got to be fucking kidding me? A tinfoil hat?"

"Trust me," Hemlock said, her grin growing wider. "Bit of shielding and it'll make your brain drop the signal worse than the WiFi at a coffee shop."

Morgan curled a lip and looked between Hemlock and the tin foil hat. "Is it too late to negotiate hazard pay and overtime?"

Hemlock gave him a sly wink. "Don't worry too much, Lenny said this is good for what we are looking to do tonight."

"Let's say me getting high as a kite and being an emotional lightning rod gets their attention."

"It will," cut in Hemlock.

"If it does," Morgan cut back, "What then? You shut the signal, and they lose interest, but you're left with me tripping balls, and they can easily fly off. How do we chase them if I'm too looped to walk straight?"

Hemlock dug into her jacket pocket again, this time pulling out a handgun. She brandished it, pointing the barrel to the sky and her finger sitting off the trigger.

"It's a little girl, Hemlock, you can't just shoot her!"

She let the gun slip around her grip to point down at the rooftop. "First off, we don't know how little this girl is, we only have hearsay through my mother from someone that maybe saw a little girl from over a hundred yards. Second, I'm not going to shoot her, it's for the nightmare! Third," she lifted the gun,

143

pointing it at the brick edge near the rooftop and fired. The gun made a soft pop and something hissed through the air, Morgan caught the light sound of a small piece of metal chinking off a brick. "This isn't a real handgun, Burns. It's only an air powered pellet gun."

"Shoot the horse, not the horseman?" Burns asked pointing gingerly to the gun.

Hemlock nodded. "Remember, nightmares are still corporeal, even if they have to will it strongly. I doubt it will feel it much, but I've got a drop of your blood sealed into each of these pellets."

"My blood?" interrupted Morgan, "Why my blood, and how did you get it?"

"I can't go leaving my blood around everywhere, people would use it. Your blood is more dispensable, and we can still use it with a tracking spell to hunt it down if we lose her."

"But how did you get a vial of my blood?"

Hemlock wagged a finger at him, "Spoilers. Now can we get a move on with our plan?"

Morgan stared down at the vape pen, it was a strange contraption of a glass vial of liquid screwed into a plastic stick. He had seen them before and knew roughly how they work, press the button and it activates a little heater to vaporize some liquid into a breathable mist. Inhale and wait for the uptake to hit the brain.

"I read a Rolling Stone article about hallucinogens once," he said. "They detailed some stuff about DMT. It was primarily about some shaman tea from the rainforest called Ayahuasca. Sounded hardcore. People had a varying degree of what they saw, but some common things were like melting trees and clockwork elves, crazy shit like that."

Hemlock nodded, her smile melting. "Look, I get it, it's a bit nerve wracking. I'll be able to see these things, but we need to bait them in to begin with. Normally, I'd try to get Lenny up here and pay him off to be the little beacon of sunshine that he is. Unfortunately, I have the feeling that I won't be able to get him up here for a while. So, I need you to take the hit on this one, literally."

She stared at the vape pen Morgan was rolling in his fingers and raised her eyebrows as if to say, "Anytime now will work."

Hemlock could feel the unease welling up in Morgan's face, and the color draining down his neck.

She sighed. "We've been through this at Lenny's. It's not that bad. It's not even Ayahuasca bad. He said it'll taste bad, but the hit shouldn't be bad. The whole trip shouldn't last more than twenty minutes, half an hour tops. He said Ayahuasca is a whole day kind of trip, like hours long, and a lot harder than this. That stuff you'll be on full out-of-body experience, with this," she pointed to the vape pen, "you should be mobile still. Just in case."

Morgan nodded, "Yeah, in case we need to chase a kid riding a nightmare half-way across Boston while I'm high as shit. You sure know how to make a guy's night, boss."

He took a deep breath. "Ah, fuck it, not getting any younger."

Lifting the vape pen to his mouth, he pressed the button for a few seconds. Morgan inhaled a long pull from the device. He tried to hold in the deep breath, but almost instantly started coughing and choking to exhale the vapor.

"Holy fuckballs, Hemlock. That tastes horrible. It's like sucking on an electrical fire."

"That bad?" She asked.

He nodded, bending over coughing more. "Yeah, it's like breathing in a tire fire and burning motor oil. I thought they started making vape shit taste like strawberries or bananas now, not this shit?"

Hemlock shook her head. "Nah, they make flavors for regular tobacco and weed. Some of these more, uh, exotic drugs don't get the flavor enhancers."

"Well, it's a fantastic incentive to stay the fuck off them." Morgan managed to get his coughing under control, he sat back on the wicker couch. He tried taking a few shorter puffs of the vape pen. Gradually, he began to hold in the vapor a bit longer each time, wrinkling his nose and grimacing with each hit of the acrid flavor. "I wonder how much I've got to take before I ugh."

Morgan trailed off and lay back staring at the sky.

"I think it's starting to sink in, Burns," Hemlock croaked. "Whatcha seeing?"

"Ugh, the sky, the sky. Yeah, it just split and peeled open. Like, if you took a lasagna and cut into it, then peeled a layer off the top of the noodles. The sky noodles peeled apart for me. You should see this, Sarge."

Hemlock nodded, "Sarge? Yeah, Burns, I think you're sufficiently fucked up. We need to do some broadcasting, so I need you to focus for me, can you do that?"

Morgan turned his face to her, the rest of his body limply following, so he laid turned towards her. He nodded slightly.

"I need you to think of the saddest moment of your life. Really focus on it for me. You don't have to tell me what that was, think about it in your mind and feel like you are back at that moment. Relive it as starkly as you can."

He nodded. "OK, it's that night I found out I never knew my mom."

Hemlock cocked an eyebrow. "I thought you knew your mother? She had the diabetes, right? Again, you don't have to talk about it."

Morgan rolled his eyes. "Nah, I found out. An aunt got drunk one night and spilled the beans, after the woman I thought was my mom had died. My dad told me later, my biological mother hadn't been in the picture. She dropped me with my dad after I was born and just gone. I guess it was a one time fling for them, and boom there I was. Dad was already seeing this other woman though, and she just took it all up, like her own personal mantel. She and dad got married, and they put all the paperwork together to have her listed as my mother."

"How old were you?"

A few tears gathered at the corners of Morgan's eyes and began to trail down through the stubble on his cheeks. "I was about eleven, she had been dead for about six months or so when that bomb got dropped. That felt amazing," Morgan moaned sarcastically, "First mom's dead, then boom, hey son, she was never your mom anyway."

Hemlock raised her hand to wipe a tear from his cheek, but Morgan grabbed her arm, right at the wrist, stopping her. He stared directly into her eyes, his pupils dilated widely. Then he shifted his gaze and Morgan was staring through the back of her head.

Almost at a whisper, he said, "Hey sarge, does this neighborhood always have a little girl riding side-saddle on a dark horse forty feet above the rooftops? You might need to call the HOA about that."

Hemlock's eyes went wide, she turned quickly to see the form Morgan had described gliding through the air with the horse trotting. "That's our cue," she said, "We need them to come in closer, but you shouldn't be here."

She grabbed Morgan by his hand and tried to pull him up from the couch. He didn't budge. She tried again, still with no luck. Hemlock turned to see the child closing in from a block away. "Aw, fuck it," she said, and picked up the pellet gun. She shot him in the ass and Morgan jumped up.

"Hey! Sarge! I think your couch has bees or wasps. You need to call somebody about that, couch wasps are no laughing matter."

"Great Burns," Hemlock rasped, getting him up and moving towards the stairwell door.

She looked over her shoulder and felt a need to rush him along, the beast and the girl were not far and starting to descend in a loop around the building. Hemlock shoved him into the stairwell, sat Morgan down on a step, and slammed the tinfoil hat on his head. "Don't move."

Morgan stared up at the edge of the tinfoil hat that jutted into his periphery. "No problem, Sarge. I'm going to talk to the silver monkey. Hey, this guy's on my head, that's crazy."

Hemlock left him on the step chatting with his new silver monkey and edged closer to the rooftop door slightly ajar. She put her ear to the opening, hoping to hear some indication that the nightmare had landed.

Unable to hear anything outside, Hemlock shifted the gun to her left hand and fumbled around in her pocket once again. She pulled a small extendable mirror out. Hemlock had randomly found it at an auto parts store, it was like a little circular dental mirror, but sat on a telescoping rod. Slowly, she extended the rod and edged the mirror outside the cracked door, trying to peer out.

In the tiny mirror, Hemlock caught a glimpse of them. The girl was thin and wan and appeared as though she couldn't be more than nine or ten. Even at that age, she looked like she could be malnourished. The nightmare seemed to match her paleness and gaunt appearance. Though it took on the form of a full-size white gray horse, it's ribs and sunken sallow skin were clearly visible from the tiny mirror. The pair hovered in a circle close to the rooftop, but not landing.

Hemlock stared back down at Morgan. He seemed to be complementing the silver monkey on his head for being well-behaved and not pooping on anything. She stashed the mirror back in her pocket and held the gun tightly in the grip of both hands. Hemlock took a deep breath, readying herself. She may not have that much stopping power in this little pellet gun, but she knew she had the element of surprise. Hemlock also thought, not ever interacting with a nightmare in person before, she had no idea if it would scare the beast or make it charge her.

She nudged the door open with her foot, and caught a soft tune on the air. It didn't seem like singing in a classic sense of the definition. Hemlock recalled something similar with Gregorian monks chanting, but it was more melodic in a sharp tone. The haunting harmony on the night air kept the nightmare the little girl rode calm as it galloped softly a few feet from landing on the roof.

They were closer to the edge and turned away, surveying the sky for their prey that had disappeared. Hemlock slid from the stairwell door into the shadows beside the exit. She lifted the pellet gun, steadying it with both hands. She took another deep breath, and fired until the air cartridge hissed empty. The gentle pop and hisses in the night weren't enough to spook either mare or rider at first, when they looked around confused. When two pellets hit square and lodged in the right rear flank of the night-mare, it registered plenty of shock. It reared up, nearly throwing the young rider form its back and galloped straight up and out over the Boston sky.

# HIGH ON THE TRAIL

Hemlock threw open the door to the stairs, holding the gun with the barrel pointed towards the sky. "Morgan!"

Morgan stopped licking the wall, tongue still splayed out mid-stroke, and his eyes darted up to Hemlock's silhouette in the doorway.

"Burns," Hemlock said in disgust, "What on Earth are you doing?"

"I'm wricking da waww," he tried to say, not removing his tongue from the textured wallpaper.

"Please put that away and tell me why you are licking the wall."

Morgan's eyes bounced back and forth between the wall and Hemlock. He slowly pulled away from the wall, easing his tongue back into his mouth in an exaggerated motion with his right hand. "I got bored with talking to the hat and the wall asked me to lick it. But, not in like a sick way like a," he winked conspiratorially, "Like a dirty wall would ask."

He turned his head back to the wall and gave it a gentle petting as though it were a small kitten. "Because, y'know this wall, Sarge. And this isn't a dirty wall."

Hemlock pointed the gun at Morgan. "You can lick the wall more later. Get up, we have to chase little Sally Hellscreamer and the nightmare. They're on the move."

"I dunno Sarge, this seems important right now. This wall really wanted me to be thorough."

Putting the gun back into the coat pocket, Hemlock hustled

down a couple of steps and grabbed Morgan's elbow with her free hand. "Come on, Burns. I shot you once, don't think I won't do it again."

Morgan staggered to his feet and followed her down the stairways, through the house, and out the front door onto the sidewalk of Braddock Park. He stared into the night sky above him as Hemlock was rustling around in her pockets again. "Pretty night, strange though. It wasn't this cloudy earlier?"

"Hmm?" Asked Hemlock still fishing for something in her jacket pocket. "Morgan, I'm trying to find something, so we can track them based on your blood after I shot that thing in the ass with it."

"No, just saying," said Morgan, hazily and pointing up to the sky, "The clouds. It wasn't cloudy earlier, now there's these strange ones up there."

Hemlock gave a quick peek skyward. She kept hunting through her pocket, but kept her gaze up. "What the hell are you going on about, Burns? The night sky is clear."

Morgan turned his head and started to walk, and spin a bit in place. "No, right there, it's just one cloud. It's like a streak in the sky. Kind of like what you see trailing from a plane across the sky, but it's got a color to it, a bright bluish green color. Bit hard to see in the night, and it stops right on your roof." He turned again in place, still tracing the sky with his finger. "It continues out that away though, over the city center, then it doubles back south or southwest."

Hemlock stopped rummaging in her pockets and stared more at the sky above them. There was nothing but stars and darkness, not a cloud to be seen. She turned back to Morgan, who was smiling at the tip of his finger as he brought it down to poke the tip of his nose and laugh. "There are no clouds I can see, but you can see them?"

"It's only the one line of a cloud in the sky, Sarge," Morgan said.

Hemlock's eyes widened, she walked over to Morgan and grabbed his shoulders. "Burns," she rasped, "That's not a cloud! You beautiful tripping bastard, I shot the damn thing in the ass and it's bleeding! The nightmare is losing bits of its corporeal essence and leaving a trial you can see while you're high!"

Morgan tilted his head. "Is that good Sarge?"

She nodded, "Yes, it's great. Can you follow the trail? Lead the way and I'll follow."

Hemlock kept a hand on Morgan's elbow, as he began walking her down sidewalks, weaving across streets and slipping down alleyways.

Morgan almost walked into a light post, but Hemlock tugged at his elbow at the last moment. He stared ahead at the black metal pole and stood still.

Hemlock nudged his elbow, "Burns, we're in a bit of a rush here, can we keep moving?"

Morgan hushed her and nodded at the light pole. "Yes, thank you, I'll let her know." He turned to Hemlock and wrapped an arm around the light post. "Sarge, this is Dmitri. He wants you to know that things aren't the same with your mother, but that it's OK. Ben Franklin will be unclogging the toilet, so you can take a bath with the pudding before the mast head falls."

Hemlock furrowed her brow and nodded. "Dmitri gave you all of that, did he? Just now?"

A smile turned up on one side of Morgan's face, but it curled up the left side to his eye while the right stayed flat, with only his left eye widening with the smile. "Dmitri is very wise."

"Ah," said Hemlock. "Morgan, I think we've been relying on your direction a bit much for now. I believe we're on the right track, but maybe I should confirm it."

Morgan pursed his lips. "Definitely Sarge. It's like Professor Milner always said in Writing for News classes, 'If your mother says she loves you, get two sources to verify.'"

"Right, just take a break," Hemlock said, and pulled a marker, paper, and a small vial from her coat pocket. She knelt to sketch some symbols and circles on the paper, while Morgan paced back and forth.

He stopped next to her. "Hey, Sarge, do you have a pair of scissors?"

Not paying attention to anything but the spell she was drawing out, Hemlock dug in her labyrinthian coat pocket. She pulled out a pair of short scissors with silver blades and black finger grips. She handed them to him absentmindedly.

As she finished sketching, Hemlock's ears pricked to a silent clipping and swooshing. She tilted her head up to see Morgan making cuts in the air around a blue United States Postal drop box. Morgan was patting at the metal surface with one hand, the other holding the scissors to glide and cut at invisible threads along the surface.

"What in the hell are you doing now, Burns?"

Morgan shook, like he was awakened from a deep dream. He looked around, then saw Hemlock. "I think I was having a dream that I had to give this mailbox a haircut. Or at the very least, it wanted me to style its hair."

"Are we done or do you need to give it a shampoo and rinse first?"

Morgan glanced back between Hemlock and the mailbox. He pocketed the scissors. "It was a bizarrely realistic dream, Hemlock. I don't know how we got out here, but the last thing I remember from the dream was this mailbox said his name was Chuck. Chuck was covered in long purple hair. He wanted me to cut or style it for him while he told me about his plans to retire to take up deep sea fishing in the Gulf of Mexico off the Alabama coast line."

He staggered a bit and rubbed at his forehead. Morgan opened his mouth a few times, sliding his tongue in and out over his top teeth. "Did I eat something weird? Or does DMT give you awful cottonmouth?"

Hemlock stood, capping her marker and sliding it back into her jacket pocket. She picked up the piece of paper and vial before walking to Morgan. She took her scissors back, sliding them too back into her pocket.

"Burns, I don't know if DMT gives you cottonmouth, but that could always have been because you were licking the wallpaper in the stairwell to my rooftop."

Morgan froze in place, he scraped his tongue a few more times, eyes slit and a deep frown of disgust. "Gross, and you just let me lick the walls?"

Hemlock sighed. "No, I was shooting a nightmare in the ass with a pellet coated in your blood. You see, so we can track the thing back home. When I put you in the stairwell, you were having a nice conversation with your tinfoil hat I'd made you."

Morgan reached up and patted his head, there was no tinfoil hat any longer.

"I think you lost it a few blocks ago, but don't feel bad. Even if you were still broadcasting your negative emotions, our nightmare stopped caring the moment I shot it."

Morgan nodded, still frowning. "You think you spooked it?"

"Yeah," said Hemlock looking around to get her bearings. "I think when the kid got it back under control she was scared of something like that happening unexpectedly and headed home. At least, I hope we're following her home. We'll find out soon."

Morgan looked over at what Hemlock was holding, she had the piece of paper balanced in one hand with the small vial of blood laying on top. "What's this? Trying to track my blood?"

"Yep, once I activate this, the vial will move around the spell circle to indicate which way we should go and how close we are to the target. As we close in, the vial will go closer to the center."

"Won't it be a problem that I've got most of my blood right here?" Morgan waved his hands over his body. "I might be skewing your spell work here."

Hemlock picked up the vial and shook it lightly. It made a gentle rattling noise. She held it still up to the street light. Morgan could make out a small metal pellet amid the blood.

"It's not just on the blood, Morgan. So, unless your bloodstream is riddled with pellets like these, we should be fine. Now hold this for a moment."

Morgan held out his hands, Hemlock laid the paper and vial across his hands. She reached into her pocket once more pulling out a small pocket knife. Hemlock unfolded the blade. She closed her eyes, concentrating and clearing her thoughts. Opening her eyes, she pierced the skin near the tip of her finger and squeezed out a tiny drop of blood on the center of the circles and spell symbols.

As Hemlock was closing the knife and putting it away, the vial began sliding around on the paper. It settled eventually to pointing them that they should head south. Hemlock took the paper back from Morgan and began to lead them through the darkened midnight streets of Boston.

They meandered through the winding roads around Dudley Square. Motion sensing lights on houses flicked on and off as they walked down residential blocks. Morgan and Hemlock kept popping on and off main roads following their blood-laden compass through the gloom. Every so often, a set of blinds would flick a few slats down as a nosy inhabitant peered out to see what had set off their or a neighbor's porch lights.

Morgan followed as Hemlock began to lead them down Warren street, and they crossed back into the Roxbury neighborhood. Morgan nudged Hemlock and pointed to the vial, it was slowly coming to rest towards the center of the circle.

"It can't be a coincidence that we're getting close to these things, and we aren't too far from the Stevens house, right?"

Hemlock shook her head. "No, I don't think so. I think it may confirm what we'd been thinking about the elder Mr. Stevens being the first victim. If so, then it makes sense they would have started close to home and moved further away as they got comfortable."

Turning down Georgia street, Hemlock and Morgan stalked watching the vial on the paper as they crept along. They watched as the vial slid to the center of the page and began to spin. Hemlock put the paper and vial away, and they looked up.

They were in a suburban neighborhood, all around them were neat old Victorian and Georgian style homes, trim manicured lawns. The house they were in front of stood out on the block. It was a massive old Victorian. The wood siding had a few sections missing, and other parts had badly faded or chipping paint. An upper window on the second floor was cracked, and another window had an old air conditioner hanging crooked. The yard was yellow and brown with patches of tall crabgrass and dandelions. Old mail and newspapers cluttered in a pile by the front door on the porch.

"Hmm," whispered Hemlock, "This place has seen some better days."

"Or some nightmares recently," replied Morgan.

The house was dark, except for two lit windows they found as the detective and the intern snuck around the untrimmed hedge surrounding the home. Thin Venetian blinds covered the windows and silhouettes walked around inside behind them.

Morgan nudged Hemlock and whispered, "Is there any way we can get closer to hear what they are saying? Like do you have some invisibility cloak or spell to hear inside?"

Hemlock mocked thinking for a moment, tapping her chin. She whispered back, "Sure, I have invisibility potion for just this kind of occasion, let me grab you a vial."

"Really?"

She slapped him upside the back of his head and shook her head. "Of course I don't randomly have something like that available. It takes a long time to brew and the shelf life is worse than a ripe avocado."

"Any ideas then?" He asked, and Hemlock shushed him. A taller silhouette in the window was flailing its arms and even from outside the hedgerow, Morgan and Hemlock could discern shouting.

Suddenly the taller figure stormed off and a side door on the house swung open. Morgan stooped more than Hemlock to hide his bulkier self behind the patchy shrubs. Through the thickets, they could spy the pale girl coming from the home. Behind her was another form, but it wasn't familiar. The figure looked like a squat man with skin that coiled in rolls. It was hairless, and hard to determine an age. It could have been a fat kid, or an old man. One thing was clear though, the nightmare was walking with a limp in its right leg.

The girl stepped barefoot into the yard and stared up at the pale moonlight shining down. Her sharp features were made more acute in the dim light. The little girl's sunken facial features appeared nearly skeletal from the shadows cast by her own brow and cheek bones. Her hair wasn't blonde either, it was long and had tangles, but it seemed to be completely white. The loose dress she wore was also once white, but had some stains on it and ended in tatters at her shins.

Morgan took his cell phone from his jacket pocket. He clicked it on and made sure he had all the sounds turned off, pulled up the camera app, and checked the flash setting. He snapped a few quick images of the yard and the girl leading the strange little creature. Morgan flicked the setting over to video and let it start recording what she was doing.

The little being nudged the girl, and she came back from staring at the moon. Morgan had to look over the screen on his camera. In the screen, it appeared that the white balance shifted. As though little Sally Hellscreamer was glowing or reflecting more light from the moon than should have been possible.

She strolled across the yard, absently holding the hand of the limping creature of the night. They approached a garage, made mostly of cinder block and cement. It had been painted at one time in an attempt to match the antique yellow white of the house. Now it had large sections of paint chipped to reveal the bare gray block underneath.

When she opened the door, a dozen more squat little flesh mound figures crowded into the space. She began to chant her listing haunting melody again. The little figures stopped jumping around excitedly and filed neatly ahead of her, clearing the space needed for her to go into the garage. When she shut the door, the sounds of her song hung mutely in the crisp Autumn winds.

Hemlock and Morgan waited. Morgan had clicked off the video recording on his phone, but kept the screen active and the camera app open. After about fifteen minutes, the gentle wail of a song faded as the light inside the garage clicked off. Darkness flooded the little crack under the doorway instead.

They sat and waited in the darkness at the back hedge line of the house for over another half hour. Finally, Hemlock nudged Morgan and nodded back towards the street. They snuck back around the house towards Georgia street. She held a single finger to her lip and pointed north. Morgan understood, nodded and began walking with her back up the blocks.

Morgan flipped through the photos on his phone as they walked back. "This is odd, take a look at this Hemlock. The girl is in the photos, but the nightmares don't show."

Hemlock nodded, "Yeah, should be in that little book. Nightmares are weird like that. They don't photograph, but the strange thing is that most mortals can't see them when they look right at them, but they can see them with mirrors."

When they had made it a few blocks away, Hemlock asked, "Did that seem strange to you?"

Morgan chuckled. "Malnourished child that looks more ghost than girl bunking down in a garage with creepy flesh critters? Creepy critters that I'm guessing are a bunch of night-mares? What's odd about that?"

"That's what I thought too," Hemlock rasped. "We'll have to hit the police station and Griff tomorrow, see if we can run down some more information about who lives here. I'd guess at least the person yelling at her in the house was a parent, but I'm not sure why they make her sleep out in the garage with the night-mares. Is she that abused that she's not allowed in the house with them?"

Morgan shrugged. "Maybe she can control them, but the parents can't, so she sleeps with them out in the garage to keep them in line?"

Hemlock grimaced, a frown turning one side of her face down. "It's more questions that need answers." She dug in her coat pocket again, pulling out another fresh stick of chalk. "A couple of them, we should be able to get an answer or two about still tonight. Ready to go chat with mom again?"

"Why not? It's only about one in the morning and I've been tripping balls part of the night," Morgan said sarcastically. Hemlock had already begun drawing the teleportation spell circles on a section of sidewalk. "Might as well have another fun family reunion with the Shadow Court Queen and her spooky riders of the storm."

"Riders of Danann," Hemlock corrected him. She stood and spit on the circle, willing it to life. Morgan put his phone away into his pocket, and they both hopped through the portal.

# THE CHARITABLE QUEEN FAND

**M**organ and Hemlock hopped out of the portal together. Morgan took in his new surroundings. Loud rock music with a heavy driving bass line drifted through the walls. They weren't outside. They found themselves in a dim room with a single fluorescent light glowing a soft neon green on one side of the room. The fluorescent bulbs flickered lightly as he tried to adjust his sight to the change of lighting and space. The odor of urine and stale beer mixed with vomit overwhelmed Morgan, and he staggered backward from the center of the room. About the same time he caught sight of a toilet in one corner of the room, he felt something splash as he stepped back. His heel sank with the splash, and he tripped. He was only able to catch himself by planting his other foot firmly in whatever was the source of the water.

He looked down and Morgan realized that the sudden drop was a trough urinal running along the wall. The splash had been a standing mixture of urine and stale beer, with some odd bits of food and cigarette butts floating. Morgan groaned and stepped out of the urinal trough, shaking the liquids off each boot and jean leg. "Well, good thing I did the waterproofing before I hopped the flight out to Boston. Where are we now Hemlock?" To himself, he muttered, "Why don't I start asking that shit before I just hop blindly into a portal with you?"

Hemlock stepped to a sink under the flickering fluorescent light. The mirror above the sink was dirty and covered in graffiti. She checked her hair and teeth. "We're at the Stinkin' Ship. Well, we're in the men's bathroom of the Stinkin' Ship."

"Are you saying Stinking or Sinking Ship?"

"Stinkin'. No G, Burns, it's a biker bar. Out in an area of South Boston closer to shore. Well, I say biker bar, but it's a draw between the dock workers and the bikers. A lot of them do both, so it's a blurry line."

"We're visiting your mom though?" Morgan asked. "Here?"

"When you think about it, Queen Fand is running her own biker gang with the Riders of Danann. She allows half of them a human form to imbibe and party on alternating weeks. She brings them here, and they celebrate what they like to call, quote, Thirsty Thursday."

Morgan nodded. Hemlock opened the restroom door, a leather clad rider passed down the hallway in front of them, but stopped as the door swung open to block his path. With no helmet on, his bleached white skull grinned at them, though it had no choice in the matter. Small dots of orange light shone from deep in the dark eye sockets. Someone had put a sticker of the face of a kitten on the skull's forehead. The rider was carrying a grapefruit and a watermelon.

Hemlock ran forward with her arms open and exclaimed, "Bob! You old son of a bitch!"

Morgan craned his head to see around Hemlock. Bob dropped the produce, letting the watermelon crack on the floor and the grapefruit rolled towards Morgan. He picked up the grapefruit while Bob and Hemlock embraced.

Hemlock turned around, still arm in arm with Bob and pointed at him, "Bob, mom had been telling stories about you to Burns here. Where are my manners? Bob, this is Morgan Burns, my new consort slash intern. Burns this is Bob!" She pointed wildly at the rider with her free hand.

Morgan jostled the grapefruit and leaned forward to shake Bob's hand. "Glad to meet you, heard a lot from the Queen about you, I'll bet your ears were burning." He chuckled and extended his hand but Bob stared at it. Eventually, Morgan pulled it back awkwardly.

Bob took the grapefruit from Morgan's hand, picked up his watermelon and pushed past the restroom door.

Hemlock slapped Morgan in the chest with the back of her hand. "Ears are burning? Morgan C. Burns, really?" She said in hushed horror.

Morgan raised an eyebrow, then his eyes widened. "Oh, are they sensitive about the whole skull thing and not having faces and whatnot?"

Hemlock nodded, "It's bad enough to get mistaken for Ghost Rider everywhere you go, but having people throw jokes at them like that is low."

"So, I shouldn't ask them how they drink beer?"

She shook her head, "No Burns, do not ask them anything like that unless you want to be willing to try it tomorrow." Hemlock scoffed with an upturned lip, shaking her head. She turned away from him and walked out of the men's room. Morgan followed closely behind her.

They came out of the hallway into a what seemed like the inside of an old ship converted to a bar. The walls felt like rough-hewn wooden planks. All the booths and the bar though had smooth carved wood, the seats of the stools had lost their finish. Worn down by decades of butts sliding on and off. The bar was filled with chatter coming from every direction, and almost all the patrons were more leather clad bikers. Bleached skulls smiling from everybody, regardless of how happy they were.

Behind the bar was one of the few non-skeletal beings in the whole place. Queen Fand herself stood behind the bar, her short red hair staying perfectly in place while she made drinks and passed them around for her riders. She wore a lean white tank top, her pale skin and toned arms bare for a night of work.

Morgan leaned close to Hemlock and whispered, "The Queen slings her own drinks?"

162

Hemlock shrugged. "The relationship between our family and the Riders of Danann is sacred. Even if they did get the power they asked for the price they are paying in death, we are still grateful for all the services they provide us. We learned long ago that loyalty and honor aren't things easily bought and paid for once. So being a servant to those that serve us helps to maintain that relationship. I myself, when not banished, serve the Riders on nights like this as well."

Hemlock found a single stool at the end of the bar and sat down. Morgan stood by her, leaning at the end of the bar and trying not to be in the way of the opening for any other waitresses that would pop past on a regular basis.

Queen Fand noticed them as she set two margaritas and three more open beer bottles on the bar. She nodded her thanks to the riders that took them to head back to a booth. Fand strolled down the to them. "Not your night to be here, but can I get you kids a drink?"

Hemlock flashed a half smile at her. "I wouldn't want us to intrude on the Rider's night out. We mainly came here to ask you a couple of questions."

Fand leaned forward on the counter. She reached out and ran her thin delicate fingers through Hemlock's razor shock pixie cut hair, trailing a finger along the curved top of an ear. She sighed sadly. "You found the kid and the nightmares, didn't you?"

Hemlock nodded, Morgan turned away, feeling he had intruded on a private scene.

"I'm good for a few minutes break," said the Queen. She flipped a tumbler on the bar top and drained a long pour into the glass. As she set the glass down in front of Hemlock, Fand also grabbed a bottle of beer from a cooler below the counter. She set the bottle down in front of Morgan. She rested her thumb nail under the edge of the bottle cap, "You like stouts right?"

When Morgan nodded, Fand's thumb flashed and the bottle cap flicked off the bottle with such force the cap flew and embedded itself in a wood post behind Morgan. He looked back and forth between Fand and the beer. Morgan carefully took the bottle from Fand. He tilted it towards her and said, "Uh, cool, thanks," before taking a long drink from the bottle. He nodded his approval instantly.

Fand rested her elbows on the bar. "So, what have you two crazy kids been up to?"

Hemlock huffed a long breath out. "Well, since we saw you last night, we found out that the new drugs showing up around town are definitely distilled memories, and they can compel a person to act out a version of that memory."

Fand raised an eyebrow, "How did you confirm that?"

"Remember Lenny?" She asked. Her mom nodded. "Well, we got Lenny to take a big dose of it while we were coming to see you. He said the trip was the clearest he'd ever had. Lenny saw through the eyes of a guy that was killing someone over having a song called Titties and Beer by Frank Zappa stuck in his head."

When Hemlock said the name of the song, the riders broke out in a raucous chorus, "Titties 'n' Beer, Titties 'n' Beer, Titties 'n' Beer, Titties 'n' Beer."

Hemlock rolled her eyes. "Anyway, we went to talk to the grandson that got arrested for at least one of the murders this morning. He confirmed, and gave us an almost identical account, down to eating the victim's tongue. Only difference for him was the song, Brittany Spears' Hit Me Baby One More Time."

The Riders all called out once again in unison, "Hit Me Baby, One More Time," then laughed loudly.

Morgan and Hemlock both chuckled at the chorus. "From there we decided to hunt down the source, that kid and the nightmares, which sounded like a reasonable connection. Especially given the time of the first victims and when you noticed them starting to disappear. So we talked to Alice."

Fand's eyes went wide, "You went to Alice? Again?"

Hemlock shrugged, "Yeah, so?"

"Alice is psychotic!" Fand threw her hands up. "She's fun for kicks, but even I think she's crazy! Why did you go to Alice again? For Gaia's sake, if you needed a knowledgeable resource on anything, you should have come for Bob!"

Fand pointed through the crowd, Hemlock and Morgan turned. Bob was using a hunting knife to carve pieces out of his watermelon. He had cut the grapefruit in half and was affixing the halves into parts of the watermelon. He pulled a glove off, revealing a skeletal hand. Bob shoved his hand up the watermelon and began using the fruits as a makeshift ventriloquist dummy. "Knock knock," Bob made the fruit dummy speak.

"Who's there?" asked the crowd.

"Pine cone."

"Pine cone who?" parroted the crowd

They both turned back to Fand who was chuckling. "Yeah, always a hilarious joke." She studied their straight faces, "Jeez, tough crowd. Continue, what did Alice tell you?"

"She gave us a rough idea of how to find little Sally Hellscreamer and the nightmares," Morgan continued.

"Who's Sally Hellscreamer?" Fand asked interrupting.

"The kid, Alice called her that because of the strange singing she does to control the nightmares." Fand nodded, Hemlock continued. "Basically, she flies above the city on one of the nightmares and is attracted to strong brutal emotion. So we got some DMT vape from Lenny. Burns here got pretty fucked up on it and thought a lot about how he doesn't know his biological mom. Next thing we know, we were a beacon for them, and they popped up in a snap."

Fand turned to Morgan, "Oh that must have been horrible to find out. Did you ever find your real mom?"

Morgan had been mid-sip on his beer and choked on the sudden redirection. He coughed and sputtered, shaking his head no.

"We ended up following her back to her home and spying

on her. She fought with someone in the house for a while, then went out to a garage. It looked like all the nightmares were out in the garage, and she appeared to be sleeping with them out there. Not in the house. So we have no idea what to make of that. But, also she was creepy."

"Creepier than sleeping in a garage of nightmares and riding them across the Boston night sky?" Fand asked.

"Yeah, it's hard to describe. She appeared starved, and pale. Not too lively." Hemlock nudged Morgan, "Burns, show her the pictures, maybe that'll help."

Morgan pulled up the photos on his phone and handed it to Fand. She started swiping and scanning through the pictures. "Best I can describe her as was death warmed over," added Morgan.

Fand kept swiping through the photos, then flashed the same mischievous grin Hemlock had perfected. "Morgan, you really should delete your dick pics," she said with a wink.

Morgan fumbled for the phone, trying to turn it quickly so Hemlock couldn't see, "What? I thought I did delete those?" He saw it was a picture of the house number of Sally's home. "Oh, I see. Screwing with me." He put the phone away and scowled.

Hemlock and Fand both laughed as Morgan reddened and blushed.

"Look," Fand said getting serious again, "There's a reason she looks like death warmed over, that kid is dead."

Morgan raised an eyebrow, Hemlock sighed. "I'm sorry," Morgan said setting his beer back down, "How is that possible? I thought I just heard you say the girl is dead?"

Fand nodded. Hemlock glanced up at the ceiling and cursed, her hands flat on the bar. "She's a frickin' banshee isn't she?" Hemlock slapped her palm on the bar, "That's why she can sing like that and how she can control the nightmares."

"What?" asked Morgan bluntly.

"It's probably even in that damned little book Yamata gave you. Check the index for banshees and you'll see." Hemlock picked up the glass and finally took a drink of the whiskey her mom had poured her.

Morgan rifled through his jacket pocket and pulled out his copy of Nightmares In a Nutshell. The deranged horse smiling on the cover felt like it made more sense now that he had seen one in person. He flipped to the index, "Let's see, banshees, page 43. Uh, yeah, says 'Few things are known to influence or control a nightmare. The one thing guaranteed to keep a nightmare under command is the wail of the banshee."

Fand gave a nod with duck-face lips as if to say, "Told you so."

"The kid is just dead? She looked so real and normal, not like the ghosts I went trapping with dad," Hemlock said.

Her mom spread her hands out palms up. "What can I say, Hemlock? Appearance is part of what makes the banshee different. They can pass for almost completely normal, it's what helps them get close enough to sing the warning to others about to die. Anymore, as pasty as some people get, it would be very hard to discern a banshee from just another pale hipster."

Morgan took another sip and set his beer down. "How does a person become a banshee though? I mean, what's the difference between a person dying and becoming a ghost versus becoming a banshee?" He asked.

Hemlock sighed. "Usually, it can come down to age and type of death. If the person is young enough and the death is brutal enough, you'll get a banshee. The older the person is, as long as the death isn't natural or is sudden and brutal, then you're more likely to get a ghost. It's not an exact science though, no one's worked out thresholds or cut off points."

Fand scrunched up her face, "Well, your great uncle Zenmo made an attempt at determining those thresholds."

"I don't recall you ever mentioning that I had a great uncle Zenmo. What happened?"

Fand puffed out her cheeks and blew out a deep breath. "You guys good with your drinks? Need a refill?"

"Mom," Hemlock stopped her with a touch of her hand. "What happened with Zenmo?"

The Queen slumped her shoulders. "Your grandfather beheaded him at dinner."

Morgan and Hemlock's jaws dropped.

"What?" Fand said upon seeing their shock. "With the trail of corpses he was leaving behind, it was a danger to our kind. It's one thing to kill when threatened, even for sport, but in the name of that kind of science. Well, it did not go over well with the family. Your grandmother was pissed."

"Gee," Hemlock said, "I can't imagine why. I mean you're just having a nice dinner party. Everybody's having a wonderful time, then Wham," she chopped the bar with her hand, "One of the guests is beheaded at the dining table. I can't see what pissed her off so bad."

Fand waved a hand dismissively, "Nah, she wasn't pissed that someone got killed in the house, that happened all the time. She was angry that they had done it before she served dessert. Your grandma had worked so hard on a mixed berry pie, and she just wanted Zenmo's opinion on the pie, but your grandfather couldn't wait. Your grandfather said something about if he had pie before killing Zenmo, he'd be too full to swing the ax properly and wouldn't have done the job right."

"OK," Hemlock stood and tossed back the rest of her drink. "I think Morgan and I should cut out of here before you decide to tell us more fun family stories, and you need to get back to the Riders."

"Where you two headed next?" Fand asked as she poured another beer for a thirsty Rider.

"We got an address," Hemlock said turning to the door, "Now we need some names. We'll get some sleep and meet up with our guy at the police station in the morning to see if we can get any leads on the kid. Maybe he knows she died, what the parents are into and all that."

Fand passed the drink to the rider and hopped over the bar. She leaned in close to Hemlock and Morgan, pulling them in close. "If you two keep on this, you are going to find out some more uncomfortable facts."

"Like what?" Whispered Hemlock.

"Like that whatever that kid died of, her parents likely did it to her. The fact that she can be controlled is dangerous. Those parents must understand to control a banshee you have to have their body or at least bones to hold them in thrall."

They mulled that thought momentarily. "So, what are you suggesting?" asked Morgan.

"Those parents and whoever they are working with are pissing off a lot of people. They're pissing off your mobsters by taking on the drug trade, they're pissing off the magical community by bringing some heat on them. When it all comes tumbling down, something horrible will be the end of it all. I'd hate for you two to get involved further, but there is something I want."

Hemlock rolled her eyes. "You want the kid?"

Morgan grimaced, "That's horrible!"

Fand shushed them and pulled them in tighter. "Yes, we've been wanting to get a banshee in the Riders for centuries, but this may be the best place for her. This kid seems to have already been dealt a raw deal. If this comes to a head like I expect, some witch, wizard or warlock will figure out the banshee. They will destroy the body and then that kid is automatically destroyed for eternity. I can offer her a fair deal. A hundred years of service in exchange for a second chance at life."

Morgan cocked an eyebrow, "You can do that?"

Hemlock gave a short nod, "Yes, as Queen, she can, but I think the price can be shorter considering it's a banshee, right mother? We can say, twenty-five years?"

"A quarter?" Fand scoffed. "I was going to tack on that I shorten your banishment, but if you're willing to stay put for the whole sentence, I can take that deal."

"And expenses," added Hemlock swiftly.

"Of course, I always pay my debts," Fand grinned and released them.

# COLD CALL AND
# COFFEE

**D**etective Sergeant Griffith started his morning how he always did at the station. He had one last cigarette by the car and stubbed it out when it was down to a filter, tossing it in the standing ashtray near the front door. He said hello to the uniformed officer at the front desk, dropped his lunch in the fridge and grabbed his coffee.

Most days he got his favorite cup, a cup his children had painted for him one Father's Day years ago. Sometimes Leon would grab that mug, but he hadn't done that since Griff suggested he could load blanks in Leon's gun without him noticing. He'd even done it when they were on range training once to prove how easy that would be.

Griff grabbed the "Wurld's Bestest Daddy" mug from the cabinet. He chuckled at the thought of Leon's face when he realized that Griff was pissed about him taking the mug. He poured the coffee black and grabbed a handful of sugar packets, popping a little plastic stir stick in his mouth to chew. He walked back through the precinct to where he normally sat among all the other desks.

The Detective Sergeant sat the coffee down and punched the button to boot his computer up. He pinched two packets of sweetener and flipped them back and forth, shaking the grains to the other end. Griff tore the paper open. As he looked down to pour the sugar into the coffee, he realized it wasn't a black cup of coffee staring up at him anymore. It was the faces of Hemlock Connal and her new intern.

Griff jumped, startled by the sudden faces in his coffee, the sugar granules flew all over the lap of his gray slacks. "Goddamn it, Connie, what the fuck?"

"Hey Griff, got a few questions for you, buddy," Hemlock said smiling up from the cup of coffee.

"How are you in my coffee? You realize I need this coffee to deal with Kowalski's shit, right?"

"Well," Hemlock said, "We needed to ask a few questions and it seemed easier to cast a spell to have a little chat instead of coming all the way down there. We get to skip signing in with the desk person, having to see Kowalski too, et cetera."

"Easier to cast a little spell?" Griff asked in mock disdain. "You realize I'm now in a station house having a conversation with a friggin' cup of coffee?"

"Oh, you're the only one that can see or hear us," replied Hemlock. "No worries about that part."

Griff nodded. "One second." He fished around in a desk drawer briefly, then slid on a single-ear Bluetooth headset. "OK, now at least I don't look like some sort of psychopath talking to myself here."

"Great, Morgan's got an address here, we need some information about the people that live there."

"Do I look like Google?" Griff asked the coffee, his nostrils flaring angrily.

Morgan leaned forward in the cup. "Sergeant, we could get the names from Google, but we needed to see if there were any active investigations. Could you tell us about anything on that front or any suspicious reports?"

"You know, Connie, your dad never called me on a cup of coffee, he always came down here or used a fancy device called a telephone. How is it ever easier to call me through coffee than it to use a phone? I know they give you fits, but doesn't your intern have a phone?"

"I'm sorry Griff, I didn't have a direct number for you and you're the only one I trust with these questions right now."

"I'll do it this one time, but don't you ever show up in my coffee again." Griff took a deep breath. "I can't even begin to tell you how disturbing this is to me. What's the address?"

Morgan rattled off the address he'd taken a picture of the night before. Griff punched keys and waited on his screen to refresh.

"Home is owned by David and Tiffany Maersk, purchase about four years ago, previous known address somewhere in Cincinnati. Says they have one child, a daughter named Sally."

Griff peered over to the cup, Hemlock and Morgan were staring at each other in shock. "There may be some interference, did you say the daughter's name was Sally?"

The detective nodded hearing Morgan's chuckling, "Yeah, why's that funny?"

Morgan caught his breath, "Nothing," Morgan said. "Before we had names, we'd nicknamed her Sally Hellscreamer. Bit ironic, is all. Is there anything else?"

"Looks like they are the focus of some watches from narcotics. The house is listed as a possible supplier for something, but it's not listed. Maybe something newer that isn't in the system yet." Griff clicked through some more screens. "I got some surveillance photos here. What's your interest in these folks?"

"We think they may be the ones supplying the pills you found at the residence of that serial killer suspect and at the scene of the cheerleader drug hit. At this point, we're more interested in the kid though. Does narcotics flag them for anything with child protective services?"

Griff tapped a pen on the desk while clicking around the files. "Mm, it depends. If surveillance thinks the kid could be in real danger, they'll flag CPS for a visit, but a lot of times, they worry that'll spook the target. So, they'll wait, then go with CPS on a visit to raid the house. In this case, CPS was flagged for a home visit a few years ago for possible domestic abuse."

"Got any notes on that?" Morgan asked.

"A teacher had some concerns and reported the family. CPS home check turned up nothing, they never say who reported it, but I guess the parents figured it out anyway. Says here they pulled Sally from Boston Public Schools to homeschool not too long after that."

"Anything else about the kid after that?" Hemlock asked. "Any other domestic calls, well visits, hospitalizations, open murder investigations, anything like that?"

"Nope," replied Griff. "No violent crimes reported, murder investigations or anything else. I've got some photos pulled up from the narcotics' surveillance. Sounds like the mother is a bit strung out, dad might have an anger issue, and that kid needs to get some serious time out in the sun."

"The kid shows up in pictures?" Hemlock called up through the coffee.

"Yeah, spooky looking thing," Griff said scanning through the photos. "She definitely could use a sandwich or five. And stop playing with imaginary friends in the yard all the time."

Hemlock muttered to Morgan, "The nightmares didn't show up on the cameras for narcotics too."

"What's that?" Griff asked.

"Nothing," Hemlock replied swiftly, "Just something between Burns and I."

"Sergeant," Morgan popped in, "Is there anything else odd in the photos from narcotics' surveillance? An extra person or anything strange?"

"Define Strange," Griff said.

"Odd or out of what you'd think to see in some semi-suburban home," said Morgan.

"There is another figure in some pictures, but they don't seem to have any shots of him coming or going. Just shadows and shapes of him behind blinds and curtains. Tall guy, a lot of hair, but nothing else I can tell about him."

"Pony tail?" Morgan asked through the coffee.

"Yeah, and here's another odd thing. Some pictures our mystery guest appears in, the surveillance got photos of other parts of the house at the same time. The front porch photo with the same time stamp something shows up and it's not there before or after big hair guy."

Hemlock leaned forward, her nose showing in most of the cup. "Can you see what's on the porch?"

"It's a bit grainy when I zoom in, but it appears to be a guitar case with something like pan pipes laying on top of it."

Together, Morgan and Hemlock said, "Fucking Jayne."

"Jayne? Who's Jayne?" asked Griff.

Leon strolled by with his own coffee at that moment, leaning over Griff's shoulder.

"Hey Sarge, whatcha looking at there? Maybe I can focus it up."

Morgan and Hemlock watched as Kowalski leaned over and tapped a few keys, then said, "Oops".

"Oops Leon? You delete an entire open investigation file from the server and spill coffee all over my damn computer and all you can say is 'Oops'? Get the hell out of here!"

They saw Leon shuffle off embarrassed.

"Griff," Hemlock said into the coffee, "Did Kowalski just delete everything?"

"Yeah, asshole deleted the whole case file from the main server and fried my computer too. IT is going to give me so much shit about this," Griff said fuming.

Morgan leaned forward. "But you're sure you saw a guitar case and pan pipes?"

Griff shrugged, "As weird as it sounds, that's what it looked like. Does that mean something?"

"Gives us a lead, but I wish we had a picture to back it up," said Hemlock. "We'll let you get back to your day, thanks again Griff."

"Yeah, next time use the damn phone," he replied. "I like to actually drink my coffee, and I'm not drinking this after seeing you two floating around in it."

The liquid rippled out and became a plain surface of black coffee once more. Griff cursed under his breath.

# BOY? GIRL? DEMON?

In a walkway between Numbers Four and Five Tileston Street, cobblestones began to shimmer and shift into a swirling circle. From the swirling portal, Hemlock hopped lightly and took a few steps forward, stopping in front of a wrought iron fence. She wore the same trim black leather jacket with magic enchanted pockets, a faded yellow BeeGees T-shirt, and a pair of acid washed jeans with neon green Converse Chucks.

Morgan hopped out of the portal behind her wearing a blue button up shirt with a light plaid pattern tucked into khaki pants, and a dark gray sports coat. He exited the portal and attempted the same move as Hemlock. Unfortunately, he had been turned around and was also wearing his heavier steel-toed boots. Instead of taking a few steps forward down the alley, he took a step directly into the brick wall of Number Four Tileston.

Hemlock smiled softly, swiping a hand across her forehead to flatten out the part of her pixie cut. She grabbed hold of the wrought iron gate before her and swung it open. "It's so refreshing Burns," she growled.

Morgan stumbled over to her, dabbing at his nose, and checking for blood. "What's that, boss? Running into brick walls? Because that's what happened to me, and I can assure you, it wasn't refreshing."

"No, sorry Burns," Hemlock continued. "Being able to touch any metal. Fringe benefit you could say of the temporary banishment. Having most of my Sidhe nature stripped, I can touch cold steel and wrought iron. Normally, just opening that gate would've left me with some nasty burns. Skin would blister right up when I'd touch it." She chuckled.

"Yes sounds lovely, are we in the right place?" Morgan asked.

Just as he said that a red Honda pulled up, it had a Lyft and an Uber symbol on the dash and the rear windshield. A woman stepped on the curb, she wore a red skirt and a white blouse with red high heels that matched her lipstick. She carried a Hermes handbag over one shoulder and a gift bag in her other hand that erupted with pink and blue tissue paper. She frowned immediately upon seeing Hemlock.

Hemlock smiled at the woman, "Amanda! How are you?" She asked with so much energy that Morgan stumbled back in shock. "I thought you lived two blocks away! Did they have to run you out of another neighborhood or couldn't bear to walk among us riffraff of Boston?"

"Hello Hemlock," Amanda grumbled, "Deirdre said you would be coming, I thought she was joking."

"Now, why on this side of the Sidhe would I miss a party like this?"

She scowled and kicked shut the car door with her heel. "Well, there were some of us that believed maybe your banishment would be over by now and you weren't going to be on this side of the Sidhe."

Hemlock tsked. "Oh, Mandie!" She sighed and smiled wider. "Now you wouldn't expect someone as big of a stickler for the rules as Queen Fand let me off early, would you?"

Amanda rolled her eyes. "No, but I would expect her to at least have you kept well enough for her daughter to not be hopping portals to get around Boston." She scoffed, "Hemlock, between possibly being seen and stumbling around dirty alleyways." Amanda pointed to Morgan standing behind Hemlock. "You've even managed to drag along some poor man that stumbled into your portal and did you even bring a gift for the happy couple?"

"Mandie, Mandie, Mandie," Hemlock rasped, walking forward she clapped a hand on Amanda's shoulder and turned to point at Morgan with her free hand. "This isn't some random stranger. This stranger happens to be Mr. Morgan Burns, my intern for most of this week now."

Hemlock turned back to face Amanda, "And I didn't forget a gift, it's right here." Hemlock started fishing into her pocket, reaching further back until her arm as past her elbow into the pocket, and she was bent over sideways. Finally, she wrenched her arm free and a small package came with it. It had soft edges, no sharp crisp lines of a box, and it was wrapped in comics news print. She waived it irritably in Amanda's face.

Amanda rolled her eyes again and sighed. "Whatever Hemlock, I guess I'll see you up there. Try not to ruin this one."

Hemlock waited as Amanda walked on ahead. She turned to Morgan, "That's just the kind of fun we're heading into." Hemlock pointed up to the rooftop of Number 5. "Up there you'll find perfectly civilized witches and wizards from covens all over the greater Boston area."

"Not Amanda there, though?" Morgan asked. "I take it there's some history?"

Hemlock crossed her arms and settled back onto her heels. "Most of the covens are squared with who I am, my history and what I can do. But a lot of the North Enders, Deedee excluded, are stuck up rich bitches and assholes. The fuckwits think my banishment should have been permanent and stripped me of all magical ability, human, fae or otherwise."

Morgan nodded. "And the gift?" He pointed to the small wrapped package.

She turned the package over in her hands, "Oh, simple but useful thing. It's an infinity towel. I spellbound the comics page around it, the towel will turn blue if they announce it's a boy, green for a girl."

"Not pink?"

Hemlock squinted at him appraisingly. "There's a gross assumption Burns."

Morgan frowned. "What exactly is an infinity towel?" He asked.

"Wonderful thing," she nodded to the building and they started walking. "It is a towel that no matter what you use it on, will not get wet. It will keep drying. Fantastic tool for parents of young children, they are always spilling drinks or barfing on things."

"That does sound useful," Morgan agreed.

"Yes, but the damned things are dry clean only." Hemlock opened a doorway and they climbed stairs, following signs in the hallways and stairwells that led them to the roof of the building.

On the roof, Morgan and Hemlock found they were nearly the last guests to arrive. The terraced rooftop overlooked Paul Revere Mall, with a new view of the statue of Paul through the tree line along the parkway. Hemlock set her gift on a long table at one side of the roof with other gifts wrapped in varying shades of pastel and brightly colored tissue paper.

Another side of the roof had another long table with finger foods and drinks. Morgan made a line for the table while Hemlock was dropping her gift off. He picked up a plate and started to load up with miniature club sandwiches, cut fruit and cheese cubes.

He had skipped the deviled eggs and was grabbing some cutlery when a familiar voice surprised him. "They aren't really from the devil y'know, they are safe."

Morgan turned with a smile. "Deirdre, now I am glad Hemlock and I came today." Her curly black hair rained down over her shoulders, but her fervent green eyes held a relaxed gaze on him. She wore a black dress that clung to her willowy frame, with a skirt that feathered out towards her knees. The sleeves only went past her elbows, and thin white belt matched her white collar.

"You do look quite remarkable today," Morgan said, "I'm glad to see you out of a lab coat and not slicing into anyone."

Deirdre's lips curled in a slight grin. "Mr. Burns was it?"

"Morgan, please. I don't think I'm quite old enough to be Mr. Burns to anyone," he replied.

"Well, Mr. Burns," she said with a slight chuckle, "It looks like you're awfully hungry today."

Morgan tipped the plate slightly, almost losing a strawberry. "Been a bit busy with this case. Hemlock and I have been running all over the city, hard to get a bite to eat or a wink of sleep these days."

"For Oberon's sake," Hemlock's gritty, sandpaper roughened voice caught them both off guard, "She's flirting with you Burns. She meant how you were staring at her, not how much food you have on your plate."

Burns did lose another strawberry when he jumped at the sound of Hemlock's voice. He still attempted to stammer on, "Well, yes, sorry, but Deirdre, you do look quite stunning today."

She smiled, Hemlock groaned. "I'll apologize for my intern, Deedee." Hemlock grabbed a plate herself. "He's not wrong, and I've probably been running the playful banter out of him lately, we have been quite busy."

"Yes," Deirdre agreed, smoothing her skirt before picking a few deviled eggs for herself. "I think you two have been keeping my office busy too. I heard from Detective Sergeant Griffith that you two called in that guy they picked up for the serial killings. We've been busy processing all the DNA evidence from that house."

Hemlock ate a whole deviled egg in one bite, and tried to talk through swallowing the rest of it. "It's not over yet." She swallowed the rest down, trying not to spray any. "I think we're closing in on the source, but honestly, I'd expect your office to keep getting more victims to process until all of this stuff is off the streets."

Deirdre sighed, "I was afraid of that." She picked through the plate, "Still, I am glad you two took time to come today, it's good for you to interact with the covens more."

Morgan swallowed hard and coughed into his hand. "So, you're in the North End coven, then?" He asked Deirdre.

She began to nod and answer, when Hemlock cut in, chewing a piece of celery. "Deedee's about the only one in the North Enders worth a shit."

Deirdre tilted her head to Hemlock and gave her a strained smile. "Now Hemlock, Julia and Eduardo aren't that bad, and they're the happy couple we're here to celebrate with today." She nodded across the roof. Julia was a short long-haired blonde in a frilly blouse, stretchy slacks, and looked as though she was sporting a basketball under her shirt. She was paying attention to a conversation, but her brow was furrowed. She was biting at a fingernail, switching to another nail as Morgan watched. Julia stood next to a man wearing jeans and an untucked collared button up shirt the shade of fresh salmon with his sleeves rolled up. He wore sunglasses on his stubbly and dark skinned face, with his black short hair slicked back.

"To think she came out here a few short years ago, she grew into the coven and fell in love with Eduardo" Deirdre said.

Hemlock nodded, "Yep, fresh in town on a massive inheritance from her recently deceased parents and a healthy trust fund to keep her in a certain lifestyle. That kind of thing doesn't hurt."

"Well," Morgan said turning back to them, "I'm sure they're quite a lovely couple, however that works."

"What do you mean by that, 'However that works'?" Deirdre asked with a narrowed gaze from her penetrating green eyes.

"Oh, I simply figured," Morgan stumbled through his words, "Maybe they pledged to serve the same dark lord or something or rather."

Deirdre grimaced her lip curled.

"I mean," Morgan continued, "Does each coven serve a different dark lord each. Like the little difference between Wesleyan and Baptists? Or does each coven member pick their own patron dark lord?" He began to trail off.

Hemlock laughed and almost choked on a small block of cheese. She coughed, "Excuse me, I have to get some alcohol. Burns, please keep digging that hole. We'll see China soon." She strode off, smelling out an open bar.

Deirdre put her plate down and stepped in close to Morgan. She pushed a sharp, clear manicured fingernail into his chest. "Not all of us come into our power by dealings with dark lords and demons, I'll have you know, Mr. Burns. Some of us come to it through hard work, honoring the right spirits and maintaining an order on our own."

Morgan backed away a step from the poking nail, but leaned back in close. He whispered, "So you didn't trade your souls to the lord of the flies or anything?"

She chuckled and smiled, shaking her head. "Hemlock Connal has filled your head with some very cruel ideas, Mr. Burns, I mean Morgan." She grinned widely and Morgan floated closer. "No, I didn't trade my soul to anyone. I may owe Fand a favor or two, but nothing near a service term as a Rider."

Morgan nodded, then turned back to the party. "So, what happens next? How does the magical community reveal if the child is to be a little witch or wizard?"

"Amanda has something planned," Deirdre replied. She softened again and became more conversational. "These gender reveal parties keep getting stranger and stranger, even in the magical community. We aren't immune to hype as you might expect."

Morgan nodded. "Most of these sorts of parties I had heard, about pop a balloon or cut a cake and it shows blue or pink. There was one I went to that involved a burnout though."

"A burnout?" Deirdre asked, tilting her head. "What happened there?"

He chuckled. "They had it on a country road and had a car with tires coated in some material that would blow blue or pink smoke. It went well enough at first, the blue smoke started billowing as the driver gunned the engine higher and higher."

She cocked an eyebrow. "I feel there's a but to this story," she said with a grin.

"Oh, there is." Morgan laughed. "The country road was basically a tarred blacktop and whatever they coated the tires with heated up much more than they expected. The driver kept the burnout going longer than he should. People started cheering at first when they saw flames shooting up from the wheels, until he stopped the car and jumped out running. The flames kept going, hit the gas tank, and blew up the car."

Deirdre's eyes widened and her jaw dropped. "Crap," she said chuckling, "Was everyone OK?"

"Oh yeah," he nodded, "Just a blown up car, and some crop damage. It was in mid fall in Indiana. The field corn had dried out, but they hadn't harvested yet. The field nearby went up like an abandoned church on a Thursday night."

She stopped chuckling, "Did that happen a lot?"

Morgan curled his lip, "Mm, well, you'd have to grown up in Clinton County to understand."

Hemlock walked back up holding a tumbler glass with whiskey. "What'd I miss," she croaked, taking a sip.

"Funny," Deirdre said, "I thought they were only serving beer and wine at the bar."

"They were," Hemlock said with a wink and tip of her glass. "Our new friend is here, Burns, by the way."

Hemlock pointed with the glass in her hand towards the opposite corner of the roof. Deirdre and Morgan turned. Through the crowd of mingled witches and wizards, Jayne sat on the corner wall in jeans and a tan short-sleeved polo shirt. His Birkenstock clad feet swayed back and forth, and his grungy looking dreadlocks sat stiffly against the wind and refused to budge.

"Jayne?" asked Deirdre. "What's Jayne got to do with anything? He's a moron."

From the edge of the roof near Paul Revere Mall, a ringing tink tink tink brought a hush over the crowd of chattering magical practitioners. Amanda had slipped her high heels off to stand on a chair, she was clanging a spoon against an empty wine glass.

"I want to thank you all for coming as we celebrate this joyous occasion in the lives of our friends," she nodded to the couple, "Julia and Eduardo. Today we will help them figure out if we will be welcoming a new baby witch or a little bouncing wizard. To do that, over the statue of my glorious and mystic ancestor, Paul Revere, the leaders of the great covens have cast a spell. The clouds will show us the child in utero."

As Amanda continued her prepared remarks, Morgan stepped back to between Deirdre and Hemlock. He leaned in to whisper to them both, "Why does she keep rambling on about Paul Revere?"

Deirdre whispered back, "He was actually a gifted alchemist. Alchemy was part of what made him a good silversmith. He tried to stay under the radar that way, but Paul got thrown into history by force with the revolution."

Hemlock nodded and sloshed her drink around. "That whole midnight ride, Burns?"

"Of course, one if by land and two if by sea."

"Well," Hemlock continued, "The leaders of the revolution didn't trust an encoded message even by lights. Revere summoned a pair of minor demons to watch from the Old North Church, and they would signal to him in a light only he could see."

"Ah," said Morgan.

"Something the matter, Mr Burns?" asked Dierdre turning back to him.

"Nothing," he said, "Just finding out that one of the pivotal

185

figures in the American Revolution was famous for alchemy and demonology. It's a bit skewing to my history is all."

"Hemlock!" Deirdre whispered and kicked her ankle. "You haven't been giving him the updated history lessons?"

"Ow, dammit Deedee," she replied hopping away. "We haven't had time. I'll give him a book tonight if we survive."

Deirdre scoffed, and Amanda was still continuing her speech. People were starting to get bored, a few checking watches.

Hemlock covered her mouth and shouted in a badly impersonated high-pitched voice, "Get on with it, show us the kid!"

Amanda scowled from her makeshift podium as more random members of the crowd shared similar sentiment.

"Alright," she called out rolling her eyes, "Without further ado, let us see the child. Archmages of the covens please come forth."

Seven other witches and wizards stepped towards the same rooftop edge near Amanda. Julia stepped into their circle and the Archmages all held hands around her. They began to chant and raise their arms high. As they did so, the clouds began to roll in from the bay and surrounding areas. Mist and cloud formed and roiled into a large mass over Paul Revere Mall.

Morgan cleared his throat. "Won't a lot of other people across Boston wonder why there are clouds forming into what seems like the world's largest three-dimensional ultrasound?" asked Morgan.

Deirdre replied, "The non-magical people tend to explain a lot of what they see from us away. Conveniently enough, their brains don't have the capacity to accept things outside of nature as they understand it. So they say it was a coincidental cloud formation, or don't even bother to acknowledge it at all. Frankly, it's a minor miracle that you are able to accept and see what you have witnessed."

"Well," Morgan said, "My interview with Hemlock did include

a blood test with a yokai trapped in an old Curious George doll. Oh, and a brownie cleaning bird poop off hemlock's shoulder."

Deirdre raised an eyebrow and nodded. "Still, there's something curious about you Mr. Burns. Your brain holds some surprising elasticity to it."

They watched the clouds forming shapes and smoothing into curves. Soon, they could see the little bumps of eyelids shut, a round button of a nose, little fingers balled up into fists. The image rendered itself together in the clouds, stretching downward and moving as the baby shifted and kicked in its mother's womb.

Amanda called out to the other Archmages, "Just a moment more everyone!"

"Has anyone thought out the optics on this?" Hemlock asked Deirdre and pointing with her tumbler glass at the clouds. "I mean, the fact that we're about to all be seeing like the biggest little pecker in the sky?"

Morgan started to reply, "How can you be sure, it's going to be a," he trailed off as the clouds shifted once more showing a penis on the massive baby shaped in the sky. The crowd cheered, and the Archmages changed their chanting, which shifted the color of the cloud cover to a light blue shade.

"It's a boy!" Called out Amanda, already late as the crowd was approaching to congratulate Julia and Eduardo. "The clouds will keep it up for a bit longer as the spell begins to weaken!" Her excitement in the announcement tapered down as she realized no one was paying attention anymore.

Morgan walked forward, still staring at the celestial ultrasound playing out in the cloud banks above Paul Revere Mall.

A voice from the back of the roof called out, "Hemlock!"

Hemlock and Deirdre turned to the voice, Jorge Andario was limping across the roof in his EMT uniform. His lip was bloody with a split straight down the middle of it.

"Jorge," Deirdre said, squinting through the crowd to see his injuries. She started to examine his face closer as he approached, "What happened to you? Who did this?"

He didn't pay any attention to Deirdre, "Hemlock, you didn't call Bobbi Cotter with an update. She went by your place and couldn't find you. She found me instead, they seem to be getting impatient."

"Shit," said Hemlock, "Here drink this, it'll help." She handed him the tumbler of whiskey. He drank it down in one gulp and started coughing.

Jorge's eyes opened as big as saucers. "Dammit, Hemlock, that was straight bourbon!"

"Well, yeah, whiskey actually," Hemlock replied.

"I thought it was something to make me feel better."

She shrugged, "I dunno, a good single malt always helps me out. But you mean Bobbi's boys did this to you?"

"In all honesty, I tripped on a fire hydrant on my way up here," said Jorge.

"What?" Deirdre asked.

Jorge sighed. "Yeah, Bobbi and one of her boys drove me over here to come get Hemlock for an update just because I mentioned she might be at this party. I got out of the car and started to come up here. I got distracted by the giant baby wang in the sky and tripped over a friggin' fire hydrant, cracked my shin right on it. Then I fell right into a concrete step and split my lip open on that."

Hemlock and Deirdre leaned back away from Jorge saying, "Ah," together.

"So, Bobbi Cotter is sitting in a car downstairs waiting for me now?" Hemlock asked.

Jorge nodded.

"Fuuuck, I hate dealing with them." Hemlock said. "Hey Deedee, if I don't come back in ten minutes, get Burns somewhere safe and have him lie low, not the house either."

"Why do you deal with gangsters if you don't like them?" She asked.

Hemlock started to walk away and said with a wave, "I've got to pay the bills somehow."

"Should we be worried?" Deirdre asked.

Jorge shook his head, "Nah. Hemlock knows how to handle herself. Besides, unless she has the whole thing solved yet, there's only a slim chance Cotter would hurt her before Hemlock gets her results. Bobbi likes to know she can pick up a phone and get an answer. When she gets frustrated, Bobbi tends to be a bit more hands on."

Morgan was still gawking at the baby, which had now turned around. He squinted into the cloud banks and turned back to the crowd. Only seeing Deirdre with Jorge, he shouted across the crowded rooftop, "Hey Deirdre, is it normal for the babies of a witch and a wizard to have a tail?"

A sudden hush fell over the whole crowd, Deirdre's eyes grew wide, as the assembled mass of the magical community ran towards the roof's edge. There, plain as day, was the backside of the prenatal infant. It was sitting peacefully above the tree lines of Paul Revere Mall with a tail whipping back and forth, as playful as a cat.

Eduardo could be heard shouting now, "Jules, why the fuck does my baby have a tail? You gonna tell me that tails run in your family? A bunch of Mormons straight out of Salt Lake City? Hell no, and it certainly doesn't run in my family."

Morgan took this moment to back away from the clusters of people that had come to the roof edge. He made his way back through the onlookers to find Deirdre and Jorge. "Have I caused a bit of a scene? I guess this isn't normal?"

Jorge and Deirdre both shook their heads together.

Deirdre said, "A little nub from an extra vertebra or two could be considered normal, like a little deformity or a mutation. But, remember, there's nothing too great, aside from training, pacts

189

or deals that really set a normal person apart from your normal witch or wizard."

She nodded up to the tail whipping through the clouds. "To get a dagger-tipped prehensile tail like that can only mean one thing. That one of the parents has a direct blood line with a demon or devil from one of the dimensions. And your pool of candidates for that role are extremely slim in the Boston Metropolitan area."

Morgan inhaled abruptly, "Oh, Jayne!" He started looking around frantically. "Where's Hemlock? We've got to find her."

"She went down to chat with Bobbi Cotter about your case," said Jorge.

The happy couple was arguing louder, and had seemingly come to the same conclusion as Morgan. Eduardo's voice came over the crowd, "Where's that fucker Jayne? I want to cut off more than the tail on that asshole!"

Heads bobbed around in the crowd, and cluster by cluster, each group realized that Jayne was missing too. Jorge, Deirdre, and Morgan headed towards an edge overlooking the street where Bobbi had been parked.

"The car's gone," Jorge said. "Bobbi's got Hemlock." Jorge rounded on Morgan. "How much have you guys figured out?"

"Pretty much all of it," Morgan said. "We were coming here in hopes to confront Jayne about some stuff after the party. It appears that idea went up in," he pointed out to the dissipating clouds, "Well, you know."

"I think you better tell us what all of it entails, Morgan," said Deirdre.

Morgan sighed and proceeded to tell them about the drugs. What they were causing people to do, how they had talked to Fand about missing nightmares, and how they managed to lure a nightmare being ridden by a child. He left out his various proclivities he had experienced under the influence of DMT. Morgan finally told them how they had tracked the kid back. How they referenced it with the police, found the evidence pointing to Jayne, and where the drugs were all likely being produced.

When he was finished, Deirdre frowned. "So, there's a home in Boston with a banshee and a crap ton of wild nightmares being held by some asshole parents?"

"Yes," Morgan replied.

"Bobbi Cotter could torture this information out of Hemlock and send a bunch of gun toting Irish mafiosos there any time tonight?"

Morgan winced, "I suppose so."

"And you also just caused a mass panic that spooked Jayne bad. He'll probably go there to pick up a batch to sell while he's on the run leaving the city, so he won't be killed by everyone at this party."

"This is starting to sound bad," Morgan nodded.

Jorge shrugged, "Can't get much worse. Once Eduardo realizes he's got Jayne's blood on tap from Julia and that kid, it won't take them long to get a tracking spell going. What do you think are the odds that a whole group of the Archmages of the covens will descend on that house full of nightmares and a banshee at the same time as the Irish mob?"

Morgan blew out a long breath. "Knowing how our luck is going, pretty damn good odds."

Deirdre rolled her eyes. "Hemlock wanted me to get you somewhere safe. What do you think?"

"I think," said Morgan shutting his eyes, "I think I need Bob."

# WHAT ABOUT BOB?

**M**organ, Deirdre, and Jorge snuck away. Everyone else at the party was trying to either diffuse the arguments between Julia and Eduardo or find Jayne. The trio crept down the building and exited to the street.

Deirdre and Jorge tried to keep up while Morgan was walking up the block. He kept poking his head down alleys and looking around corners.

"What are we looking for?" Asked Deirdre.

"That depends," replied Morgan, still peeking around corners.

"Can you make one of those teleportation portals like Hemlock always makes me jump through to get places?" He turned to look at her and Jorge. Morgan nodded to Jorge "Or you, can you do it?"

Deirdre and Jorge turned to each other, then both back to Morgan and shrugged. Deirdre grimaced. "A teleport spell for a normal human practitioner is usually very dangerous, you either have to be very precise or have been to the location before. Hemlock still has some of her fae nature to fall back on when it comes to spells and magic, so she can easily fudge it a bit and still not end up stuck in the middle of a fire hydrant."

Morgan nodded and started walking again.

Deirdre slapped Jorge on the chest and tried to keep up again. "Where are we going then?"

"Jorge got here in Bobbi Cotter's car. You got a car, Deirdre?"

"No, I took an Uber over."

"Here," said Morgan, and walked through a side entrance to

a multilevel parking garage. He led them up to the second level and walked up the ramp peering around the corners and back over his shoulder. Morgan stopped in front of a dark green 1970 El Camino SS with a pair of black stripes running up the middle of the hood. He grinned at the car, "Oh, this is what I'm looking for. Jorge, be a lookout for us, make sure nobody's coming." He turned to Deirdre, "How about unlocking something? Got any magic that can unlock a door?"

Deirdre smirked, "Opening a lock is easy, but it won't start the ignition." She walked over to the driver's door. She whispered a short incantation and the locks popped open.

"I don't think I can help you guys steal a car," said Jorge. "Where are we even going?"

Morgan sneered at Jorge. "You can ride around Boston with the Irish mob but you can't help me steal a car to get us out to Fellsway in time to ask Fand for something?"

Jorge's eyebrows shot up, and he shook his head, "Uh uh, no, I can't go see Queen Fand. She blames me for a few things with one of her Riders. I can't go, intern, I can't do that."

"My name is Morgan, Jorge, and it's fine, only room for three anyway, and we'll need space for Hemlock." He pointed up the aisle of cars, "Now go stand watch up there and let us know if anyone's coming."

Morgan watched him for a moment, making sure Jorge wouldn't run off. He turned back to Deirdre and opened the driver's side door. Morgan pulled the cable to pop the hood, then went around to the front of the car.

He reached into an inside pocket of his sports coat and pulled out a long cord. "What's the plan?" asked Deirdre. "You actually know how to hot wire one of these things?"

Morgan smiled and held up the cable for her to see, it was a simple stereo auxiliary cable. "Here's the fun thing, Chevrolet allowed a lot of us to do our own magic. I had a buddy with one of these in high school." He released the latch and raised the hood.

"Oh, but Dan didn't have one like this." He whistled, "Wow, we really got a lucky strike here."

Deirdre crossed her arms, "What's that all mean?"

He peered around the engine, then put one end of the aux cable on the positive terminal for the battery. "What I mean is Chevy made only so many of the SS models like this one. Should be the same though." Morgan grunted, stretching the cable and reaching around the engine block. "See, Dan lost the keys and didn't want to rekey the ignition, it was cheaper for us to jump the car every time, you simply need a little jolt to the starter." Just as he said it, Morgan must have reached the right spot. The starter cranked, the ignition turned over, and the engine roared to life.

Morgan shut the hood, and shooed Deirdre into the passenger seat from the drivers side. He slid in next to her and kicked on the radio.

"So, this model of car is special because it's easy to hot wire?"

Morgan shifted into first and started to edge the car down the parking garage ramps. "Nah," he replied, "All Chevys from the seventies were like that. This car is unique because only so many El Caminos were made with a seven point four liter V8 engine that can get us over four hundred fifty horsepower."

He leaned out the window and waved to Jorge. Morgan shouted a number to him, "It's my phone number. I want you to go back up to that party and call or text me if they get on the move to hunt down Jayne. You got all that?" Jorge nodded, taking out a pen from his pocket to write the number on his hand.

Morgan gunned the engine, charging a parking garage exit. They burst through to the street, leaving splinters where a wood arm had been on an automated pay station. He cranked the wheel hard to the left, drifting across the lane and squealing tires, Deirdre braced herself against the door.

"Here's the thing," Morgan said, "We've got about 15 minutes til dusk and I don't really know the roads here too well yet. I need you to tell me how to get out to Fellsway Bridge over the Mystic."

Deirdre was panting, "Yeah, I think I know the way out there. Uh, hang a left on Hanover, then left on Commercial, follow that to a right on Washington. That'll turn into different roads, keep straight on the roundabouts and it will take you right there."

Morgan slammed the car around the corner to Hanover, almost causing an accident with a tiny Ford Fiesta that honked with a menacing "Meep meep". He largely ignored traffic signals, though found himself somehow hitting green lights the whole way. It wasn't until Washington dumped into Rutherford, that Morgan realized Deirdre held her eyes shut and was chanting.

"We're not going to die," he said. "I'm a very good driver."

"I'm not nervous," Deirdre replied, "I'm using a luck incantation to keep other things out of our way, please don't break my concentration."

Morgan was sure not to break her train of thought again after that, as he nearly slammed into an ice cream delivery truck at the highway ninety-nine roundabout. He popped the clutch, gunned the engine and dropped back into gear to drift around half the roundabout, pulling back out on Mystic Avenue at speed.

He slid the car to a stop at the small park off the Fellsway bridge where he and Hemlock met Fand a couple of nights before. Throwing open the door, Morgan could see the sun peeking from below the horizon, dusk was falling over the Mystic River.

As the last spray of sunset filtered over the horizon, motorcycle engines revved to life over the bridge. Morgan began hammering the horn. It made a loud, "Awooga awooga" noise, like the sound made in an old cartoon when a stunned wolf's eyes pop out of his head. Morgan and Deirdre looked at each other, "Horn is definitely not original equipment," Morgan said between honks.

The strategy paid off though. As the bikers came over the hill Fand and her riders turned towards the El Camino and came to a thundering stop around Morgan and Deirdre. Tonight it was Queen Fand in green riding gear surrounded by four riders instead of two, all in matching black leathers. They all dismounted, the four closed into a line behind Fand.

Queen Fand pulled the helmet from her head, tossing her head to one side to flip a bit of hair off her forehead. She glanced between Deirdre and Morgan, then peered into the car. "Where's Hemlock?"

"That's why we stopped you out here, Queen Fand," said Morgan. "Hemlock was taken somewhere while we were at a gender reveal party today looking for someone."

Fand's expression soured, "You were hunting someone at a gender reveal party? And Hemlock got captured," she danced a finger along an imaginary subtitle line, "At a glorified baby shower?"

"It's a long story," Morgan said rubbing his forehead. "We did find the guy at the party, but he got away during some confusion I caused because I noticed the baby sported a tail. At the same time, Hemlock got picked up by an Irish mobster client. This whole thing has ended up a long mess from where we started a few days ago."

Fand crossed her arms and shifted her hips. She sighed, "I'm not sure what you expect me to do about any of this. Hemlock is still in her banishment period, I can't intercede on her behalf."

"Yes, your majesty," Morgan said twisting his hands. "We know," he looked across at Deirdre, staying completely silent in Fand's presence. "I know you can't get involved, but," he took a deep breath and nodded to the riders, "What about Bob?"

Fand squinted and wrinkled her nose. She turned to peer over her shoulder at the accompanying Riders of Danann. She looked back and forth between Deirdre and Morgan. "I don't take this request lightly, but I can smell the rubber peeled from those tires." She nodded to the El Camino. "I'm guessing you stole the car to get to me in time to make this request?"

Morgan nodded.

"Hmm," she purred. "Deedee here is in my debt for a few things, but I think I'll need to take tribute in another manner."

"Bob can't decide to honor the favor of Hemlock without your leave?"

Fand chuckled and raised a hand to her mouth, nibbling at a slender finger nail. "No. Bob is a Rider, in service to me, and not to a banished subject, princess or no." She pointed the same long finger Morgan. "You however, could request his help for the night. If the price is right to you, he will help you from dusk until dawn to find my daughter, secure her release and help you with any other tasks necessary."

Morgan glared over the roof of the car at Deirdre. She gave him a slight nod. He turned back to Fand. "What is your price, Queen Fand?"

"A night's favor," she said flatly.

"I am no knight, though," replied Morgan.

Fand closed her eyes and sighed. "No, you will do me a favor, when I need it in the future, as a full night's service to me. That is my price."

Morgan furrowed his eyebrows, "A night? That doesn't sound so bad. Can I put a contingency on that? Like, um, no, uh sexy stuff, OK? I mean, you look good and all, but I don't think I want to get involved in that way with you, no offense."

Fand dropped her arm from where she was chewing her nail again. She looked at him with disdain, lip curled. "Morgan Burns, while I appreciate your chastity, I have more than enough con-cubines awaiting me wherever I may travel. So, no, I won't be plucking your innocence. Just work for me for a night. That may be finding something, driving," she nodded at the car, "Or any other task I might find."

Morgan shifted his jaw and nodded uneasily. "And Bob won't kill me either?"

The Queen flashed a wicked grin, the same Cheshire grin Morgan became accustomed to seeing on Hemlock. "Favor to me trumps Bob's murderous desires. Do we have a deal, Mr. Burns?"

He blew a long breath through puffed out cheeks. "Yeah, alright. A night's favor from me in exchange for Bob's help tonight. Do we shake on it or what?"

Thunder cracked, Morgan felt a hand on his shoulder and almost jumped out of his own skin. The four Riders still stood in a line behind Queen Fand. Another identically dressed Rider appeared behind Morgan, complete with dark visored black helmet.

"The pact is sealed, Morgan Burns. You should use Bob wisely," Fand said turning around. She slung her helmet back over her pixie cut. Her four Riders followed her in all mounting their motorcycles and riding off in loud engine revs.

Morgan turned to Deirdre. He pivoted his head to peer at Bob. He nodded towards Bob at Deirdre, who shrugged. Morgan pursed his lips and turned face Bob and leaned against the car.

"So, Bob, um, what we need to do first is find Hemlock. She's being held by Bobbi Cotter, I think. Would you have any ideas on how to do that?"

Bob unfolded his arms and stepped forward. He pointed a finger at the radio. The radio tuned loudly, running through stations and static. When it stopped, a deep growl of a voice came through the speakers, "Give me your arm." He held out his gloved hand.

Morgan stared at the hand in silent trepidation. Bob gripped his wrist tightly. He brought his other hand over to rest on Morgan's outstretched forearm. A razor sharp talon burst through his glove, and, with a quick flick of his wrist, a one-inch cut appeared in Morgan's arm through his shirt and jacket. Blood welled and flowed from the wound, soaking through the clothes, and Bob scooped it like a soup.

He flipped the visor of his helmet up. The clawed finger went into the visor bloody, but came out clean. The radio crackled again, "Get in the car, I'll hop in the back and give directions."

Morgan and Deirdre slid onto the bench seat of the El Camino. Bob jumped into the cargo bed back end without a sound. If it wasn't for the slight dip in the shocks, Morgan might not have known anyone had climbed into the El Camino's bed.

"How does Bob know where Hemlock is by your blood?" Deirdre asked nervously.

"Um," Morgan started to reply, he glanced at the radio. "Oh, she had a pellet gun, she soaked the pellets in my blood."

Morgan shifted into first and began to turn the car around, he glanced over and saw Deirdre's pursed lips.

"When we were trying to track the nightmares, she soaked the pellets in my blood and shot the nightmare with it. We did this exact same thing, used my blood to track back to the nightmares. Fand must have told that to Bob, or he overheard us tell Fand last night."

A hand thumped the roof. "Right, Queen Fand. Sorry," Morgan reiterated to the radio." He looked over at Deirdre, "That must be it though, he's doing the same thing. Just wish he didn't cut so deep." Morgan turned his arm back over and realized his arm wasn't bleeding, there wasn't even a stain on his jacket or any cut in the material either.

Deirdre shrugged. "Fae magic can be insanely strong, I think this won't be the first thing Bob does tonight to surprise us."

"Let's hope so," Morgan said.

Bob's voice came on the radio and started barking short instructions. Morgan followed them as best as he could, sometimes having to turn suddenly and drift or swerve to take the right direction.

The directions eventually led them to a strip mall in South Boston. Most of the shops were closed down, but there were still lights on and vehicles parked nearby an appliance repair shop at the end of the strip.

Deirdre's eyes widened. "I think this is it, there's a new black Lincoln Continental down there. That's what Bobbi Cotter drives."

Morgan nodded. "What's the plan, Bob?" He asked the radio.

Static crackled on the radio, then it spoke clearly. "Go to the edge of the parking lot. Drive as fast as you can straight at the front window of the shop. Slam on your brakes as you pass the last car."

Deirdre gawked at the radio, "This is madness, he'll be killed."

Morgan grinned a broad smile in the dim lighting of the parking lot. He said chuckling, "Not if he's already dead."

He turned the car and headed back to the furthest point of the parking lot. Bob knocked the roof twice. Morgan jammed the accelerator to the floor and didn't let up through shifting gears. He'd made it to third gear and over fifty miles per hour when they reached the last car.

Morgan popped the clutch, threw the car into neutral, and slammed the brakes all at once. The tires locked and squealed angrily. The El Camino barely stopped at the curb, but not Bob. Bob flew cleanly, like a massive dark bullet, over the hood of the car and through the shop window.

Following the immediate crash, everything went silent. Morgan and Deirdre stared anxiously at the broken window. The lights went out in the building. Gunfire erupted. The cracking sounds breaking the night quiet like a whip and giving brief spasms of light in the windows from the muzzle flashes. The gaps between gunfire became filled with screams and cries of agony.

A bright flame filled the store front, and a person ran through the window Bob crashed through. The ball of fire followed the man, and he lit up instantly, engulfed in an inferno that killed him in a painful moment of horror and scorching torture. The flaming man fell before the car, knocking his head open on the corner of the El Camino's hood.

Morgan pursed his lips, he and Deirdre glanced sheepishly at each other. "I'm sure that will buff out," Morgan said with a grim nod.

They turned back to the store front. There in the doorway, amidst the fury of wreckage behind him, stood Bob, Hemlock over his shoulder in a fireman's carry. Deirdre and Morgan leapt from the car and came to meet Bob on the sidewalk of the strip mall.

Hemlock was covered in soot and blood. Her eye was bruised and purple, her lips both split and bloodied. Her breathing was shallow and weak.

"She needs a hospital," Deirdre said checking her pulse. "She's not going to live much longer in this state."

Bob pushed them both back. He pulled something from his pocket in a balled up fist. Opening Hemlock's mouth, he shoved something in and shut it again. Bob flipped open his visor. Green vapor curled through the cool night air and fell over Hemlock, settling gently over her before being inhaled in a deep breath.

Hemlock sat up suddenly, eyes wide as saucers. She coughed violently and spit out a large clot of blood. "Shit, that hurt," she said looking around. She reached a hand out and Bob helped her stand. "Thanks, Bob. Always a pleasure."

He gave her a thumbs up and hopped back in the bed of the El Camino.

Deirdre started looking Hemlock over, checking injuries again.

"I'm fine, Deedee." Hemlock swatted her away. "How'd you guys find me?"

"Bob," Morgan said. "I may have traded a small favor to your mom to get the use of Bob for the night. He took some of my blood and used it to find you from that pellet gun you still have loaded with my blood."

"Oh," she said nodding and casting a dark gaze to Bob standing in the El Camino's cargo bed. "Where'd you get the car?" Hemlock rasped in her normal tone.

"I stole it from a parking garage," Morgan said.

Hemlock cocked an eyebrow at Morgan, "You're full of resourcefulness and surprises tonight."

"You like it?" He asked.

"It looks like a mullet on wheels," she replied. "What happened at the party?"

Deirdre sucked in a deep breath, "Yeah, you missed some excitement. About the time you left was when Morgan pointed out that the celestial ultrasound featured a tail. They quickly realized it was likely Jayne's kid, and he split before they could grab him."

"But it won't be long before they use the kid still in Julia to track Jayne down and," Morgan nodded back to the car.

"Yeah," Hemlock nodded, "And he's probably raiding his suppliers before skipping town. Which means a shit load of wizards and witches wiping out everything in that house, including our banshee and all the nightmares."

"Yep, so we should hit the road?"

Hemlock hesitated, "It would be faster to teleport, but I should get my strength back and you do have this lovely piece of American craftsmanship." She gestured at the car.

A short tinkling chime came from Morgan's pocket. He pulled his phone out and frowned at the screen. "We've got to get going, Jorge just texted me. They've got a bead on Jayne. The North Enders and a few of the other covens are on their way already."

Hemlock nodded, "Better drive fast then." She turned at the doorway to Bob. "We might have some incoming that would make our job harder tonight, Bob. If you see anything in the skies, shoot it down."

Bob reached behind him and swung back a shotgun.

Morgan pointed and said in a worried tone, "Where'd that come from?"

"He's being a show off again, he always loves that Benelli," Hemlock said. She pointed up at Bob, "Non-lethal with them Bob, I've still got to work with these people."

Static fed back on the car radio once more. Bob came over the speakers, "Just rock salt tonight."

"Great choice," she said.

"By the way," Morgan said hopping into the El Camino, "What did Bob shove in your mouth?"

"My teeth," Hemlock said sliding onto the bench between Morgan and Deirdre.

As they sped away into the night, Bobbi Cotter hobbled out of the trashed store, screaming, "You dirty fuckers!"

# THIS HOUSE IS
# NOT A HOME

**M**organ slid the car with a screeching skid onto Dorchester street, barreling southbound. He kept the El Camino moving as much as possible, only slowing down occasionally for traffic. In the dark skies overhead, a whooping cry called out.

Hemlock tried peering out through the windshield and Deirdre leaned her head through the passenger window. "It's the Ringers from The Neck," Deirdre yelled over the roar of the engine.

"Who are they?" Asked Morgan.

"A bunch of fancy assholes that think they're so amazing because the pretentious jerks fly everywhere on broomsticks." Hemlock shook her head, "I hate these guys. Bob, see if you can shoot them down," Hemlock said to the radio.

The roof thumped twice. Bob fired the Benelli, five successive shots that went off like a cannon echoing through the street. A body thumped into the road as Morgan sped past it. Two more brooms crashed and tangled with each other before smashing into a window above a liquor store.

Another broomstick rider came down nearly in front of the El Camino, slowing to a spinning stop. Morgan swerved, gunning the engine again to barely miss the downed wizard.

Morgan had to slam on the brakes a block later to avoid plowing through a pair of cars stopped at a light. A car pulled up next to his passenger side. Deirdre glanced over. She turned her back to the car and whispered to Hemlock and Morgan, "The red To-yota sedan that pulled up has three witches from the Cambridge Coven."

Morgan and Hemlock leaned forward to peer over. Three women in black sat crammed tightly together in the back of the Toyota. They leaned back. "Why'd they take an Uber?" asked Morgan.

Hemlock sneered, "I guess they aren't fans of the Massachu-setts Bay Transportation Authority." She knocked on the win-dow, "Bob, shoot out the tires on the red Toyota." Bob loaded a regular buckshot round in the shotgun.

The light changed, Bob leaned over the edge of the cargo bay. He gave a quick two fingered salute to the Uber driver, then leaned the Benelli over the side. He fired one round into the front driver's side tire, leaving them stranded on a flat while Morgan peeled out and sped away.

Morgan parked the car a block away from the house on Geor-gia Street. They shuffled out, leaving the car running.

"Deirdre, I want you to stay with the car in case we need it again," Hemlock said. "Bob, I need you to run interference with anyone that tries to come at this place. Remember, no deaths if possible." She pointed to Morgan, "Burns and I will sneak in through the back, see if we can grab Jayne and the kid and get out. Everyone clear?"

Bob gave a slight nod, Morgan and Deirdre both did the same. "Great, let's try not to die Morgan."

They walked up the block, Hemlock and Morgan turning to head up an alley. Bob left them, strolling up the street while he pushed more shells of rock salt loaded ammo into the twelve gauge.

Hemlock and Morgan reached the back of the house. Hem-lock hopped over the short chain link fence, Morgan following her. "Think they're already starting to prep an attack out front?" Morgan asked.

He was instantly answered by shouting from the other side of the home, then the quick firing of the Benelli cracking through the noise.

"Guess so," Hemlock replied. "Come on, let's try to head in the back."

The garage in the back of the house was dark and padlocked. "Fat lot of good that will do," Hemlock said pointing to the lock. "If they wanted to they could tear down the wall. Hell, they could melt through the wall without having to worry about the constraints of modern physics and masonry."

"Think Jayne is actually here?" asked Morgan as they approached the back door.

"The covens wouldn't be trying to meet here if he wasn't," said Hemlock in a whispered rasp. "Shh, listen."

Through the thin backdoor window panes, the soft muted tones of arguing floated in the quiet of the night. "Sounds like two men," Hemlock said.

"Give me the money and any of the current stash you've got distilled. I've got to leave town tonight," yelled one voice.

"Jayne," lipped Hemlock. Morgan nodded

"We don't have anymore distilled. The last of it was at the Santiago's house on Dorchester, and that all got picked up by the cops when he got killed," replied a second voice.

"Fine, where's the kid?" asked Jayne. "I'll just take her instead and start up a new operation, the beasts will follow her anyway."

"Oh no you won't," replied the other voice. "Between Tiffany going all strung out on Meth and the other shit that kid put me through, I'm not giving her up now that she's making me money."

Something made a sharp click behind the door and Jayne said, "I'm not asking your permission. She's coming with me."

"You think I'm afraid of you and that little," said the other voice before being drowned out with a gurgle and cough.

Footsteps receded into another part of the house. Hemlock turned the handle and opened the door. The scene was grisly, a man lay on the floor wearing grease-stained jeans and an old ripped flannel shirt. He had a scraggly and patchy beard. He was covered in his own blood. He slumped on a mismatched chair in a dining set that was part seventies chrome table and chairs, with some decrepit wood chairs. His breathing was shallow, and blood still pumped in a steady but slowing stream from his neck.

Hemlock crept forward. She stepped around carefully, avoiding a puddle of blood on the dirty linoleum. The man's eyes tracked her and Morgan as they entered the kitchen. She knelt close to the dying man, "Are you David Maersk?"

The man's eyes went wide, and he tried to suck in a deep breath. His mouth opened and closed, like a fish gasping for water. Each time, more blood pumped through the gash in his neck.

"It's fine, David," Hemlock said, she pushed back on his shoulders to ease him back to sitting. "Look, I'm going to be blunt. You are going to die, there is nothing we can do to fix what Jayne did to you. Your wife, Tiffany is probably dead by now too. It's not too late for Sally though. You know what she is, and I can help her, but I need her bones. Tell me where they are."

David shuddered again and rolled his eyes.

"Mr. Maersk," Morgan came close to whisper, "If you don't tell us, Jayne will find them first, and then he'll have killed you and taken everything from you." Morgan shook his head and stared straight into David's dilating pupils. "You don't want to give him everything, do you? Let us help Sally."

With another groaning breath and choking sputter David raised his left arm. He pointed to the kitchen sink and dropped his arm. His eyes rolled back and the blood stopped sputtering from his neck.

Hemlock and Morgan both turned to glance around the kitchen. The dishes were piled up all over counter tops and on the stove. The cabinets were all made of old light colored wood, some of their doors and drawers were falling off or half off hinges. Hemlock stood and went to a doorway. Peering down a hall, she whispered back to Morgan, "Check the sink."

Morgan shrugged, "Nobody would do this? Would they?"

Hemlock waived him on, mouthing, "Go, check."

Morgan knelt in front of the kitchen sink, he pulled open the dirty wood doors. Under the sink he found a lumpy, full burlap sack. He pulled the sack out, it knocked around as he withdrew it and peered inside. "Son of a bitch, he was keeping her bones under the kitchen sink," Morgan said softly.

Footsteps came thundering from down the hall. Morgan shoved the sack back under the sink and shut the doors quickly. As he stood, Jayne ran into the room.

"Ugh, you two," Jayne said in disgust. "Haven't you two done enough today?" He held the bloody switchblade out toward them.

"Jayne," Hemlock said, "I think you either need to run or give up now."

He laughed, "Why would I do that? Like you could do anything to me, you don't have any of your fae magic anymore. You're still banished Hemlock. And your little boy toy here can't do shit to me either."

Morgan stepped back, bumping right into the counter. He looked back into the sink, sitting right there was a meat cleaver.

"Look Jayne," Hemlock continued and drew his attention, "There's nothing else for you here. But the covens are either here or on their way, we ran across two of them while on our way. If that's not enough, one of the Riders is outside too."

"Like I'd believe that bullshit story," Jayne said shaking his head. As soon as the words left his mouth, Bob fired another four quick rounds from the Benelli.

Morgan took that moment to his advantage. He grabbed the

rusty cleaver from the sink and lunged at Jayne. He brought the cleaver down at the hand with the knife. Jayne tried to sidestep and parry the move, but wasn't quick enough. The cleaver came down and wedged with a sickening thud into his wrist.

Jayne screamed in pain and rage. He dropped the switch-blade, but kicked back. Morgan let go of the cleaver, and Jayne ran off through the house with the kitchen implement still lodged in his arm.

Hemlock and Morgan chased after him, thudding against a door just as he slammed it on them.

They stepped back, Hemlock blew out a huff of breath. She waved at the door, "Go on, kick this thing down."

"Can't," Morgan said pointing at the frame. "Hinges on our side."

"So?"

"You can't kick it down when you're on the side with the hinges," Morgan explained. "Besides, at that point, it's easier to pop the hinges and pull the door off the frame."

Hemlock flashed a smug smile, "Can you do that?"

"Got a pry bar?"

"You didn't bring one?" Hemlock asked.

Morgan held out his empty hands. "Gee when I got dressed to head to that gender reveal party, I should have stopped to say, 'I know what I'll need tonight, I'll need my good crowbar. I can't forget that."

"Good crowbar?" Asked Hemlock. "As opposed to what? Your bad crowbar? How many friggin' crowbars do you need?"

The floorboards began to vibrate. The bathroom beyond the door in front of them began to growl. Lights in the hallway dimmed and a red luminescence shone through the cracks beneath the door. The door rattled in its frame.

Suddenly it all stopped and the lights came back normally. The door swung open. The bathroom walls and floor were all the same shade of pink tile and the sink was cracked on its pedestal. The toilet looked like it was growing enough bacteria that some may get adventurous and make an evolutionary leap to walk out of the house to discover disinfectant.

Morgan and Hemlock stepped lightly into the bathroom, their shoes making a gentle splash in a thin layer of water that coated the floors. The tub was filled to the brim and had over-flown. The water was a hazy pink, slightly darker than the tile itself with a woman lying dead just under the water line. Morgan knelt to check her, but she and the water were already getting cold.

"I think we found the mom," Morgan said with a sigh. He turned to find Hemlock staring at a series of symbols scorched on the pink tile wall. He leaned close to sniff the smoke still waft-ing off them. Morgan crinkled his nose and blinked tears from his eyes. "What's that horrible odor?"

"Brimstone," Hemlock replied. "He was here, and we missed him. Jayne popped out into a demon dimension, could be with his dad or some other one that wants to use him."

"Think he killed Tiffany over there?" Morgan asked nodding to the body in the water.

Hemlock frowned and shook her head. "Nah, see the marks on her arms and the water. There's a syringe in there with her and the water isn't tinted enough for being bled to death. My guess is she overdosed and drowned, then Jayne managed to get enough blood from her to draw his escape portal."

A subtle whimpering and crying came from the doorway. Morgan and Hemlock turned to find Sally standing in the frame. Her pale translucent figure took harder round edges. Sally re-gained her color as tears ran down her face to freeze into ice crystals on her cheeks. They froze at the moment; the little girl sniffled and asked quietly , "Mommy? Mommy?"

She whimpered again and took a deep breath. Sally screamed, "Mommy!" The scream echoed and filled the house with a deafening screech that blew through octaves in waves. Every window in the house shattered in a rain of glass and shard blowing outward.

When Hemlock put a hand on the girl's shoulder, the scream stopped. She smiled with sadness in her eyes at Sally. "Kiddo, I know you've been through a lot, and a lot more tonight. I'm Hemlock and this is my friend Morgan. We tried to get here in time, but a bad man was faster, and he hurt your dad, maybe your mommy."

Sally sucked up a spectral trail of snot that had thawed above her lip. "I don't care about Daddy, he made me like this, but I still wanted my Mommy."

"Listen kiddo. We're sorry about that. Right now though, a bunch more people are on their way here and if they find you, they'll hurt you too. They'll end you permanently. Can Morgan and I help you?"

She looked up at them both and said, "Isn't Morgan a girl's name?"

Morgan rolled his eyes, Hemlock smiled with less sadness in her eyes. "It should be," she said. "Now, if you'll come with us, you can visit my Mommy, and she might be able to help you. Would you like that?"

She sniffled and nodded. Hemlock took Sally's hand. Together with Morgan, they went downstairs. Morgan fetched the burlap sack of bones while Hemlock sketched a teleportation spell on the linoleum. They all hopped through together as fire began to engulf the outside of the house amid the thunderous roars of Bob and his Benelli.

# AN UNCOMMON DELIVERY

Hemlock and Sally stepped out of the portal onto a patch of grass. Morgan flew through behind them, tripping over the edge and landing on his back looking up at the star strewn sky with the burlap sack of bones on his lap. He tilted his head to look around.

The night was quiet, except for the sounds of the Mystic river gently lapping at its banks and the highway whine of an intermittent car. "We had to come back to the Fellsway Bridge?" Morgan asked.

Hemlock shrugged, still holding Sally's hand, "It's just where we can easily find each other."

Motorcycle engines roared like lions through the night. Queen Fand and eight of the Riders of Danann pulled up to the grassy park. The riders dismounted, falling into a line behind the Queen. Approaching Sally and Hemlock, she removed her helmet and smiled warmly down at the child.

"You've given a lot of us quite a fright, young lady." Fand turned to Hemlock and said, "Why don't you and Morgan give us a few minutes here."

Hemlock nodded and tapped Morgan's shoulder. He got back to his feet, and they walked away a short distance.

"Should we leave?" Morgan asked.

"Not yet," Hemlock replied. "I want to be sure she holds to the twenty-five-year offer and I've got a small bone to pick with her about something else."

They stood against a tree together, watching Fand and Sally illuminated in the headlights of the motorcycles. After a few minutes of discussion, Sally fell to the ground sobbing. Fand knelt and embraced the young girl.

When they stood again, the Queen and the little girl walked hand in hand to Hemlock and Morgan, leaving the Riders behind.

Sally wiped the last remnants of icy tears from her cheeks. "Your mother has agreed to protect me and give me another chance at life." She stared down to her feet, "I have to give her time though."

Hemlock nodded, "I know, twenty-five years, right?"

"Yes," Queen Fand cut in, she held the girls shoulders. "But, we came to a reasonable compromise, five years alternating. Sally will provide five years of service, then be given five years of life. She will not age past twenty in that time. When her service is up, her life is her own to do with as she pleases."

Morgan cocked an eyebrow, "That's incredibly generous of you."

"It's nothing, really," Fand winked at him. She leaned down to Sally's ear. "Why don't you call your pets and go join your brethren?"

Sally patted Fand's hand on her shoulder. She turned and walked to the middle of the little parkway. She sang out to the night sky, giving calls far and wide. Winds rushed from the south, and a pack of wild horses galloped down from the skies. She patted them all on their muzzles. Sally mounted the largest nightmare, petting its mane fondly. She sang out once again, and the rest of the nightmares herded together, galloping out over the Mystic River. They didn't bother running across the Fellsway Bridge, but went straight over the water, disappearing over the horizon. Sally turned her nightmare and trotted back over to be greeted as the newest Rider of Danann.

Queen Fand turned back to Hemlock and Morgan. "Thank

you both for bringing her to me and returning the nightmares to their rightful place. I'll look forward to your night of service, Morgan Burns."

Hemlock cleared her throat.

"Yes, dear?" Fand asked.

"When were you going to tell us, mom?"

"Tell you what dear?"

"Don't make me be the one to tell him, mother," Hemlock said in her hoarse voice. "Let him at least hear it from your lips."

"I have no idea what you're talking about," Fand was stopped short. In one smooth flick of her wrist, Hemlock threw a dagger she had palmed. The dagger whistled soaring through the night air before landing with a wet thud into Morgan's heart.

Morgan's eyes bounced in confusion back and forth between Fand and Hemlock. He clutched at the knife stuck in his chest and tried to suck in air, but couldn't keep any in. His eyes were wide in terror as he sank to his knees and fell over in a final moan.

Fand sighed, her eyes on Hemlock filled with rage. Her nostrils flared and she closed her eyes. "You realize, it won't kill him, right? It will be extremely painful, but it won't kill him."

Hemlock's lip curled and she scoffed. "He's got a knife in his heart mom, Morgan Burns, your son, is dead. The only one in pain right now is you."

Morgan's eyes shot back open, and he drew in a long croaking breath. He stood in shock and coughed out blood. Morgan pulled the dagger from his heart and dropped it to the ground. Blood briefly sputtered from the wound before it closed up.

Morgan staggered backward, falling back on the ground. He caught his breath and looked between mother and daughter again. In unison, Hemlock and Morgan asked the same question, "How?"

Queen Fand chuckled and clapped, jumping spiritedly up

and down. "It worked, it worked, it worked." She danced around and kept laughing.

She settled down and stood close to her children. "Morgan, I'm sorry to only now tell you, but, yes, I am your mother. I left you with your father to be raised in secret as a human. You two were born very close together, my sweet little darlings."

Fand curled her fingers on their chests. "You are practically twins, just from different fathers. It happens in the Sidhe. Before you went back to your father though, Morgan, I cast a spell on you both. It was old magic, a blood binding. Neither can die while the other survives. As long as one of you is alive, the other won't die."

Hemlock yelled, "You set it all up!"

Fand shrugged.

"The bird was you, wasn't it mom?"

The Queen nodded.

Morgan gasped, "The internship listing was a ploy? My friend I was supposed to stay with, you had him arrested?"

Fand nodded again, flashing a wide grin.

"My father's death?" asked Morgan.

She frowned, "Tragic, but I'm afraid that was inevitable. Your dad never took care of himself. I may have had him popped a bit early, but that aneurysm was due within a month."

Hemlock and Morgan stared at each other, dumbfounded. "Oh, and Hemlock, you get a freebie tonight, but for every time you kill your brother I'll tack another year on your banishment."

Nearby, an engine roared, breaking the sudden silence in the night. The El Camino jumped the curb and came to a lurching stop in front of them. Deirdre hopped out the passenger side, running over to Hemlock and Morgan, Bob got out from the drivers side.

Dawn broke over the east, and with first light Fand put her helmet back on and walked off to her Riders. Sally began to gallop ahead while the Riders revved their engines and fell into a convoy with Fand in the middle.

Bob began to walk down the hill to the Mystic River. Before he hit the water, lightning struck, and he disappeared mid-stride.

Deirdre turned to Morgan and poked at the stain and slash in Morgan's shirt. "Were you stabbed in the chest?"

"Yeah," he chuckled nervously and itched his forehead. "Hemlock kind of killed me."

"What?" Deirdre turned to Hemlock wide-eyed.

Hemlock shrugged and smirked, "He got better."

Deirdre turned back to Morgan, and he flashed her a nervous smile.

"Hey sis, does this mean I'm not an intern anymore and like a full partner?" Morgan asked.

Hemlock pursed her lips, "Don't make me stab you again, Burns."

"You don't want another year added on, do you?"

"I can stab you without killing you," Hemlock said.

They kept arguing like siblings all the way home in their new stolen El Camino.

# AFTERWORD

I hope you have enjoyed reading "Another Dead Intern" as much as I enjoyed writing it. I've currently planned it to be a series with new installments written as I can find time. There are a number of stories and adventures I have planned for the characters you met in this novel.

If you did enjoy this or any of my future novels, do me the favor of leaving a rating and a review on Amazon, Good Reads or anywhere really. Ask any author and they will tell you that little blurb of enthusiasm you have for their book means as much or more than the royalties they may see from the sales.

Be sure to follow me on social media as well if you want to know when I release the next set of adventures of Hemlock, Morgan, and yes, Bob too.

# ABOUT THE AUTHOR

## Joel Spriggs

I hope you have enjoyed reading "Another Dead Intern" as much as I enjoyed writing it. I've currently planned it to be a series with new installments written as I can find time. There are a number of stories and adventures I have planned for the characters you met in this novel. If you did enjoy this or any of my future novels, do me the favor  of leaving a rating and a review on Amazon, Good Reads or anywhere really. Ask any author and they will tell you that little blurb of enthusiasm you have for their book means as much or more than the royalties they may see from the sales. Be sure to follow me on social media as well if you want to know when I release the next set of adventures of Hemlock, Morgan, and yes, Bob too.

# BOOKS BY THIS AUTHOR

## Over A God's Dead Body

"It's an offbeat comedy in the vein of American Gods"

In the same style of humor as Douglas Adams and Terry Pratchett, you'll find the Norse gods and characters hilarious. If you are looking for a humorous adult version of the Magnus Chase series, you'll be laughing at how Esmy and Jake deal with Loki.

Esmy is frustrated by a lack of pockets on women's pants. Living with her librarian brother Jake in a small Indiana town and working at a private college, Esmy feels like she is is stuck in a rut.

Meeting Loki ignites their lives like a powder-keg. This simple, seemingly innocuous encounter leads Esmy and Jake to discover the campus's mysterious depths, involving sasquatches, vampires, and much more with the supernatural, magical and paranormal.

In a crudely comedic high-stakes game of maneuvering, Loki's freedom and Esmy's survival come down to a fight over a God's dead body.

## Little Drummer Boy

A darkly humorous paranormal Christmas short!

Boston's strangest private investigator, Hemlock Connal, is back! Along with her longest surviving intern, Morgan Burns. When a demonic drummer boy walks down their road leading a small team of zombies, the detective duo take a much needed break from a boring financial case.

As they follow the horned drummer from Boston to the middle of nowhere, they find the zombie squad has more secrets than just marching through the night. Hemlock and Morgan get led through a dark journey of black market organ theft, drug sorting undead, all leading up to meeting the big man himself.

Confronted with the ultimate arbiter of the holiday season, will Hemlock and Morgan survive the test of naughty or nice? Find out, in Little Drummer Boy!

## The Bear Was Not There

What began as a routine task of finding a treasured stuffed koala for his daughter, quickly turned into an adventure for one father. Along with a talking pet cat, he must follow the koala's trail to encounter werewolves, pixies, aliens, and more to achieve his original goal: getting his children to sleep.

If you enjoy wild adventure, poorly drawn post-it notes, sci-fi, and fantasy all blended together, then you'll love this fantastical journey.

Buy The Bear Was Not There to start the madcap wondrous adventure today!

## The Hitchhiker's Guide To Coding

Are you looking to change careers? Ever think of software development?

Software Developers are in high demand and can earn a high income. Believe it or not, these jobs also don't require a college degree. Many people are able to become self-taught software engineers and developers everyday.

Learn how to take those steps with this guide. With this short book, you can learn how to take the first steps. It will teach you strategies for how to choose a language to learn, how and where to learn a programming language. The Hitchhiker's Guide to Coding will also help you understand how to gain some experience as a new coder. You can discover strategies for finding and applying to jobs and finally, what to expect when on the job. All of this is brought to you by an author with over 16 years of experience in software engineering.

Download your copy today and embark on your journey to an exciting career in programming!

## The Headless Floridaman

A Floridian trailer park meets the Legend of Sleepy Hollow in this hilarious horror novella

Five tweakers in a Florida trailer park think they've committed the perfect crime: kill a drug dealer. They feel pretty good after dumping the body and splitting the loot. The killer crew isn't as cocky a couple weeks later as the headless drug dealer hunts them down one by one. Will they be able to escape or can they rely on help from a plumber to combat the resurrected menace?

Pick up a copy of The Headless FloridaMan to find out!